HOYDEN

(a boisterous girl)

Tony Dickenson

Published by New Generation Publishing in 2023

Copyright © Tony Dickenson 2022

First Edition

The author asserts the moral right under the Copyright, Designs and Patents Act 1988 to be identified as the author of this work.

All Rights reserved. No part of this publication may be reproduced, stored in a retrieval system or transmitted, in any form or by any means without the prior consent of the author, nor be otherwise circulated in any form of binding or cover other than that in which it is published and without a similar condition being imposed on the subsequent purchaser.

Paperback ISBN: 978-1-80369-552-5
Hardback ISBN: 978-1-80369-553-2

www.newgeneration-publishing.com

New Generation Publishing

For
Csenge, Herbie, Jan, Leslie, Mya, Niamh, Sara,
Svetlana
Ella, Hannah
&
Gina

"It was shown that on leaving school, about the most of which is expected of a young lady, is that she will go home and "do little pretty things to wear" – nothing more. This is all wrong; a woman should have every honourable motive to exertion which is enjoyed by a man, to the full extent of her capacities and endowments. The case is too plain for argument. Nature has given woman the same powers, and subjected her to the same earth, breathes the same air, subsists on the same food, physical, moral, mental and spiritual. She has, therefore, an equal right with man, in all efforts to maintain a perfect existence."

Frederick Douglass' Paper 25, 1853

1

Colin had breakfast ready for her when she came down. Kettle boiled, kiwi and yoghurt on the kitchen table, two slices of sourdough in the toaster.

"Morning," he said, glancing up as Stella lumbered in.

"Morning," she whispered, opening the fridge.

She pulled out the jam and dropped into a chair at the kitchen table.

"Why on earth do they put these on so tight?" she said, suddenly seething, straining to twist the lid.

"Here, let me do it," Colin offered, cautiously, his arm stretching towards her.

"I can do it!" she snapped, momentarily exasperated.

She ran hot water over the jar, wiped the lid dry, twisted it, and the seal popped open.

During breakfast they scrolled through their phones, Colin skimming *The Telegraph*, Stella checking emails and her agenda for the day. Documents at the office to sign. Meeting with a barrister at two. Another rape case.

She sighed.

"What is it love?" Colin asked, hesitantly. "Another?"

She drew in a long, slow breath.

"A twelve-year-old. Foster father. How the hell do these animals get through child protection safeguards?"

"Is she OK?"

"I'll find out later."

Until Colin came along, Stella had little interest in men. What drew her to him were qualities rarely seen in men. Gentle ways, considerate manner, patience.

He knew when to be near and, most importantly, when to be absent. He rarely disappointed.

As Head of Admissions at University College London, in addition to overseeing student welfare, he liaised with outside organisations, private companies and other universities. He also closely monitored the careers of successful alumni, frequently inviting them to talk to students about what had shaped their careers.

"Do you have much on today?" Stella asked.

"As a matter of fact I do," Colin replied. "A very busy week - Freshers' week. Giving *the* talk. Have fun, study hard, stay safe. The usual health and safety advice students ignore. Some, poor things, especially girls, you should see their faces, away from home for the first time. The apprehension. The innocence."

"Why only girls?" Stella replied briskly. "Are boys immune to feelings?"

"You know why," Colin replied, in a similarly frosty tone. "Because girls pay attention. They listen. Boys, well most, don't. Not to me, to no one. They just want to mess around, or be in the pub, or play computer games. Stella - you know this."

She did. Little had changed since her schooldays at a state comprehensive just outside Birmingham where, each day, a handful of boys averse to any form of guidance, traipsed into classrooms solely to wind teachers up, relentlessly chipping away the confidence of new teachers, especially young women.

Happy to see the back of school, Stella moved south, to study law at University College London. One of the first universities to open its doors to women in the middle of the 19th century, still today, it produces more female lawyers than anywhere else in the country, and has a reputation for shaping girls into strong and confident young women.

The few close friends Stella made there quietly assumed she was gay, mainly because whenever they spoke about men, she fervently insisted they couldn't be trusted. But she wasn't gay. In fact, she had a secret crush on the quiet, studious, young man who worked in the university library. He aroused in her a certain curiosity, and she often found herself looking up from her books to seek him out. She liked the smooth skin of his clean-shaven face. And his hands. In the hope he might talk to her, she sometimes checked out books she didn't need. On days he wasn't there, she missed his impeccable courtesy, his timid ways, the way he looked up at her and whispered *thanks*.

After university, Stella joined Thomas & Taylor as a junior solicitor. A London law firm representing women, most of its cases dealt with domestic abuse, rape, occasionally murder, barbaric acts that served only to reinforce her distrust of men.

However, in her second year at the firm she received an email from UCL Admissions inviting her to talk to girls about how the university had helped launch her career. Many of her colleagues, also graduates of UCL, frequently participated in university events, but Stella had reservations.

The wording of the invitation troubled her. Why, she wondered, should her perceived wisdom be of value only to girls? And was it really in the best interest of a new generation of women to glibly remind them that they required protection from men? A hundred and seventy years of educating women, why had her alma mater reverted to form?

Over lunch the following day, Cynthia, professor emeritus and friend, informed Stella of a "shake up" in admissions.

"New personnel, complete clear out, most likely the reason for the thoughtless language in the email. Give the talk," she advised. "And while you're at it, have a word with the new admissions team. About language, especially when reaching out to professional women."

Stella decided to accept the invitation, but on condition. As a good deal of what she had to say focused on the behaviour of young men, she made it clear that they needed to be in attendance.

Within minutes of tapping the send button, Head of Admissions, a Mr. C. Wilson, delighted with her confirmation, assured her that all first-year students would attend.

On the day of the talk, she arrived on campus early and wandered those parts of the university that summoned happy memories. In the library, she sat again at her favourite desk, thinking of the countless hours she had spent researching, analysing cases, studying judgements. Then, lingering in a haze of solitary, sentimental reflection, quite unexpectedly, she thought again of the young librarian who checked out her books. And she smiled.

She made her way to the Admission's office, and as she entered, stopped suddenly when she saw, just moments ago in her thoughts, the young man from the library.

"Ms. Shaw," he said, offering Stella his hand. "Colin Wilson."

"Stella, please," she replied, the skin on her neck suddenly warm.

"I run admissions. I doubt you remember me, I used to work in the library. I wondered if it might be you."

"Hello Colin," she responded, her hand lingering in his. "I see you've moved up in the world."

"Yes, you could say that. Lot busier these days, that's for certain," he replied, smiling. "Looks like you've not done so badly yourself. Thomas & Taylor. Very impressive."

"Just about pays the bills," she said, and they laughed.

He invited Stella into his office and offered humble apology for his oversight in asking her to address only girls, adding light-heartedly that "lessons had been learnt." One of many in a series of discussions by professional ex-graduates from all walks of life, her talk required little formality. A few improvised words, perhaps the importance of key skills, building a portfolio potential employers might be interested in, a few questions at the end.

In his office after the talk, Colin praised Stella's natural manner in addressing the students. They chatted for half an hour or so, and as she got up to leave, he suggested they meet for coffee sometime, and gave her his card.

Stella often walked through Lincoln's Inn Fields on her way to the office. Resting on a bench in the shade of a Silver Maple tree, she thought of the young librarian. Colin. Head of Admissions. She smiled. This most pleasant chance encounter, though only fleeting, had confirmed how she had always imagined him. His timid, green eyes lacked the hard, cold glare she noted in most men. And for what was in fact only a poorly-worded email, she had certainly judged him too harshly. A peculiar tug shivered through her. She wondered, hoped, that perhaps, he might feel it too.

A week later she called him. She had a lunch date with a friend near the university. Was he, perhaps, free for coffee afterwards? Nervously, she waited thirty minutes, drew in a deep breath, and called again. Her friend had just cancelled. Could he join her for lunch?

***

In their favourite restaurant, Luigi's, she accepted his proposal a year later. After a small wedding, they settled quickly into a new home in Islington. Their lives slowly merged, Colin soon good friends with Celia and Sara, Managing Partners of Thomas & Taylor, and Stella providing practice interview sessions for law students at UCL.

Keen to learn more about matters affecting women's lives, Colin regularly accompanied Stella to events exploring feminist perspectives. Chiming perfectly with cases Thomas & Taylor tackled daily, issues ranged from childcare to governmental strategy and, most pleasingly, Stella liked the way he enthusiastically wanted to discuss salient points of each event with her afterwards. In fact, everything about him pleased her. How he listened. The delicacy of his words. She *knew* he really cared for her. The reason she shared with him details of the most traumatic experience of her childhood, when she was just fourteen.

She was with her best friend, Emma. On their way home from the cinema one evening, as always, they stopped at the local chip shop. Sitting on the wall outside, chips in hand, a car suddenly screeched to a halt, its tyres thumping heavily against the kerb. Drunk, laughing, three young men leapt out.

"'ello lovelies, give us a chip," one spluttered, grabbing Emma's arm, trying to snatch her chips.

Stella stepped in, trying to pull him off. But then, suddenly, they were surrounded.

"Wanna go for a ride girls?" another said, slugging down a mouthful of beer.

Stella turned, tapped the chip shop window and mouthed to the girl inside to "call the police." One of the men suddenly had her by the arm, pulling her towards the car. But she resisted, squirming from her coat and running, thinking Emma just behind her. But then she heard that scream. She stopped, turned, and saw Emma bundled into the backseat of the car.

In woodland thirty miles away, police found Emma's naked body the following morning. It took weeks to track down the killers and months for the trial to begin.

During pre-trial proceedings, police interviewed Stella many times. Though terrified to see again the beasts who had killed her best friend, she insisted on giving evidence. Recounting the horrific events of that night proved a harrowing, tearful ordeal, but what she most remembered about the trial, not the callous brutes smirking across the courtroom at her, but those outside the court each day, girlfriends and family members protesting these men's innocence, despite irrefutable evidence including confessions and DNA.

Ms. Hart, the school counsellor, dealt mainly with minor adolescent spats and truancy. After a moving memorial service for Emma at school, she met with Stella and her parents and they set up weekly meetings. In the first meeting Stella broke down, confessing how she felt personally responsible for Emma's death, that she shouldn't have run, but stayed, somehow helped her. Ms. Hart instantly accepted she lacked adequate expertise to help Stella, advising her parents to seek professional help.

On the advice of the family doctor, her mother made an appointment to see a Dr. Lutz, a child psychologist specialising in trauma. However, Stella flatly refused to see him, making it clear that under no circumstances would she discuss details of that night with any man. Dr. Lutz recommended a colleague, a young woman, and Stella's mother begged her to meet with her, promising that if the first session proved unhelpful, she wouldn't make her return.

***

Stella liked Dr. Bergeron immediately. Her gentle manner, her smile, her kindness. In early sessions they spoke only of general, everyday matters. Family life, school, things that interested her. But nothing of that night. No mention of Emma. That would never happen. To anyone. Ever.

Stella soon looked forward to the meetings, and much sooner than expected, in the fifth session, a breakthrough came when she suddenly burst into tears. Pulling up a chair next to her, Dr. Bergeron held her hand.

"I miss her," Stella stuttered. "Why did they do that to her?"

"Stella. Listen to me very carefully," Dr. Bergeron began, suddenly very serious. "What happened to Emma that night had *nothing*, absolutely *nothing*, to do with you. It had *nothing* to do with Emma. You couldn't have done more than what you did, alerting the girl in the chip shop. That's all you could have done. Those men are responsible for what they did. Only them."

"But I ran. I left her alone. With them. And look what happened. They killed her. Why did they have to, have to, kill her? Why?" she sobbed.

"Stella, listen," Dr. Bergeron repeated. "Listen carefully to what I'm saying. You are *not* to blame. These were, *are* depraved men. Monsters. The like of which should all be locked up. But their actions, what they did that night, taking Emma like they did, will *never* be your fault. Never. We can't undo what happened, and memories of that night will linger, but you *must* keep telling yourself, find a way to accept, believe, that this is *not* of your doing. Those men are responsible. *Them*. By blaming yourself - you give *them* power. You cannot allow that to happen. You cannot let them have anything of you. No part of you

Stella. Nothing. Certainly not your happiness."

Dr. Bergeron handed Stella a tissue.

"It's going to take time for you to see a future not scarred by that night. But, but, in some way Stella, and again, I want you to think about this, what these beasts did to Emma started with them, and stops with them. I repeat. *Them*. Only *them*. And, and, I know, this is difficult, it probably feels impossible right now, but when we talk about that night, we do so with the truth. And the truth is that you bear *no* responsibility for what those monsters did. You're young, your feelings are still so raw, but you have a long life ahead of you Stella. I know it may sound strange now, but together, we'll try and get your life back on track. You cannot let the vile actions of these vile men dictate how you feel about yourself. Or, let them take from you your happiness.

"As I say, it may sound and feel too impossible right now. But try to think of ways in which, in which, somehow, you might, in some small way, draw strength from that most horrendous night. Perhaps, think about what Emma might wish for you now. About the possibility of a future *not* defined by that night."

Incremental, purposeful, delicate, Dr. Bergeron's methodology allowed Stella to unravel her thoughts and feelings. Soon, she was able to find the words to talk not only about what happened that night, but of the good times she shared with Emma. And slowly, she learnt to smile again.

Dr. Bergeron chose a very special day, Stella's sixteenth birthday, to move on to the next stage of her treatment.

"Happy birthday Stella! Sixteen-years old!" she said, on her feet and clapping when Stella came into her office.

On Dr. Bergeron's desk, a pretty, glazed cupcake, iced into its swirling crown a large S. Reaching into the bottom drawer of her desk, she pulled out another, biting into it, the cream smudging her cheek, making Stella laugh.

As they ate the cakes, they discussed plans for birthday celebrations and fast-approaching GCSE exams.

"Dr. Bergeron, have you ever heard of a woman called Boudicca?" Stella asked, curiously, excited about an upcoming History project.

Wiping cream for her lips, Dr. Bergeron's face lit up. Smiling, she placed the half-eaten cupcake on a napkin and stood up. Rounding the desk, she leant on the wall behind Stella, next to a painting hanging there. Stella noted the look of awe in her eyes as she admired the magnificent warrior woman on rearing horse, tawny, long hair falling about her hips. Around her neck, a heavy, golden necklace, and in tenacious grip, a sword, a fierce and steely glare making her intent crystal clear. It was time for war. Surrender: impossible. Submission: never.

"Do you know who this is?" she asked.

Intrigued, Stella shook her head.

"Stella. This is Boudicca," Dr. Bergeron continued. "Look at her, just look. A valiant Celtic queen. Queen Boudicca. Not about to take any shit from the Romans, she stood up to their ferocious legions, to their wicked colonialist aggression, and led her army, Iceni tribesmen, into the final and most brutal of all British uprisings. I look at this incredible woman first thing each day. At her power, her control, her determination. Every morning she speaks to me. Tells me, reminds me, that I, me, you, all women, we possess her qualities. Like her, we're responsible for our own destinies. What do you think? Of her?"

"That's her? Boudicca?" Stella asked.

"Yes, well, no doubt something like this. We don't really know *that* much about her. But, for me, this *is* Boudicca. Powerful, loyal, unwilling to bow down, not for anyone. Certainly not the Romans. Just *look* at her Stella. Look how steady, determined she is. Sometimes when I'm low, or pissed off, I sit here and look up at her. She gives me strength. She steadies me."

"What does that say?" Stella asked, looking at words in a frame below the painting.

"It's so long ago, we don't have a whole lot of reliable evidence from that period," Dr. Bergeron replied. "But the Romans did keep records, and these are the words of Tacitus, a famous Roman historian, certainly alive at around the same time as Boudicca. In response to Romans raping and slaughtering women, including her daughters, he recorded these words, Boudicca's words, before going into battle, words which, like this painting, inspire me. Come, come here and read."

Stella stood up and drew in a deep breath.

"It is as one of the people that I am avenging lost freedom, my scourged body, and the outraged chastity

of my daughters. Roman lust has gone too far. But heaven is on the side of righteous vengeance. In this battle you must conquer or die. This is a woman's resolve; as for men, they may live and be slaves."

Dr. Bergeron smiled.

"Stella, as women, we've always helped and relied on each other. I always seek guidance, strength, direction, from other women. And though we rarely hear of how women have been instrumental in building empires, or of how, in moments of extreme adversity, the courage they have shown, we have always been there. Enduring, persisting, surviving. Lots of brilliant women doing amazing things. Quietly, we have played our part. And so it's these women's stories I want to read. It's their examples I want to follow. We just have to dig a bit deeper to find them. Like the story of Boudicca. Whether or not she existed, when I look at this painting, this, for me, *is* her. Woman. Leader. Succumbing to nothing, to no one, especially not cantankerous old men," she said, laughing, slipping back into her seat, her eyes back on the cupcake. "Did your teacher mention any other women?"

"There was one," Stella replied, trying to recall the woman's name. "Oh, I've forgotten her name. No, wait, Emily Pank…"

"Emmeline Pankhurst!" Dr. Bergeron exclaimed. "Kudos to your teacher! I must meet her. It is a her?"

Stella nodded.

"Along with Boudicca, Pankhurst is my all-time heroine," she continued, noting Stella's excitement. "She was *some* woman Stella. Did your teacher mention why she was famous? Anything about a group of women, a movement she belonged to?"

"The suffragettes?"

"That's right. Denied the vote, these furious women rose up, and like Boudicca, leading from the front, Pankhurst gave stirring speeches up and down the country, encouraging women to join the movement, imploring them to act, take to the streets, protest, demand the vote, demand their basic human rights. By bringing women together, she formed the Suffragette movement, a group of no-nonsense, brave women, standing up for injustices all women faced. I was about your age when I first learnt about Pankhurst and other suffragettes. What most impressed me then, and still does, was their determination to improve the lives of *all* women. They knew that to achieve their aims, words would never be enough. They needed to act, and they did, taking direct action, even breaking the law. They refused to submit. Many went to prison. And, I suspect, like Boudicca, they were thinking long term. Thinking of the lives of women and girls to follow, future generations, like you and me."

Dr. Bergeron paused to take in air.

"Stella. We - you, me, we are a new generation of women, successors to women like Boudicca and Pankhurst. I remind myself of this every day, first thing, before I do anything. Like I said, I look up at that painting, at her, Boudicca, and think of what she was prepared to do, prepared to sacrifice, for me, for all the other women I'm sure she inspired. Pankhurst, Mary Wollstonecraft, Millicent Fawcett, now, incidentally, with a long-overdue statue in Parliament Square. And relatively more recently, women like Maya Angelou, Rosa Parks, Angela Davis. And so many others. They blazed a trail for *us* Stella. And now it's our turn. We must do our bit ..."

She suddenly stopped.

"What's the matter? " Stella asked.

"Stella, will you listen to me going on! Way too heavy for a birthday celebration. Tell me more about your birthday plans."

"No, no, Dr. Bergeron, please, continue," Stella implored. "You said, we must do our bit. Tell me how. Tell me more about Pankhurst, and Boudicca. And those other women. Who were they?" she asked, turning in her seat and looking up at the painting.

While Dr. Bergeron would never be able to erase the harrowing memory of three beasts intruding in this young girl's life, what she could do was provide her with armour she'd need as a woman. For the next couple of years, until Stella began university, their discussions explored the world into which all girls are born, obstacles they face, and injustices they continue to endure, and not only in far-flung, mediaeval theocracies, but here at home.

Central to many of their discussions, the origins of men's hostility to women and the important role politics played in improving women's lives. And of laws, made by men purely to favour their fortunes. Laws that repeatedly, actively, side-lined women resulting in limited opportunities, lives of drudgery and, very often, lives of unimaginable violence.

In her final year at school, just before Easter, Stella

rushed into Dr. Bergeron's office, her face glowing. In her hand, an envelope. Inside, an unconditional offer to study Law at University College London. Instrumental in guiding Stella towards this university, she smiled, thinking this the perfect institution to nurture the slow and feisty defiance she'd seen flourish in her young charge. She just hoped she'd done enough to stoke in her the courage that long ago had once stirred in Queen Boudicca and Emmeline Pankhurst.

2

Celia Thomas' god-fearing parents required little in return for providing their only daughter with an idyllic childhood. Only that she love Jesus and do well in school. But raising a young, black girl in Atlanta, Georgia, in the mid-1960s, a hotbed of explosive unrest and civic turmoil, they required help. For this they regularly called on the Lord Jesus Christ and Saviour to safely guide her, as did Celia herself, hollering her own jubilant "hallelujahs" in church on Sunday mornings.

However, as curious adolescence crept in, with it came doubt, and Celia had questions that required answers. About the world, the Lord, the rationale behind his mysterious workings, and the hysteria around that golden ticket of eternal salvation. This dwindling interest in the divine troubled her parents greatly, and when she developed a meaningless passion for softball, they were convinced that such erratic, futile diversions from the path of righteousness could only have disastrous consequences.

But they needn't have worried. As much as Celia loved softball, her curiosity for learning knew no limits, and remaining top of her class, as captain of the team, she led her high school to state championships in both junior and senior years. In fact, during those final years of high school, provoked by her love of reading, especially the novels of Alice Walker, Celia kept secret a desire she had shared with no-one.

Charting the life of a young black woman who falls in love amid civil unrest, Walker's novel, *Meridian*, had inspired in Celia a desire to be a writer. To achieve such lofty ambition, she required the tools, and with college on the horizon, she had singled out Spelman College to deliver them. Sister school to Atlanta's Morehouse College, the prestigious black men's university and proud alma mater of Martin Luther King, Walker had studied at Spelman. Just the thought of walking in the same corridors, sitting in the same classrooms as her heroine, made Celia giddy.

But she also had another, more immediate reason for choosing Spelman.

Celia had never found boys even remotely interesting. She suspected other girls might feel the same, like the two girls on the softball team who admitted to being more than just good friends. Dropped from the team, then removed from school, Celia had no wish to follow them. She just had to be patient, bide her time, be careful, confident that among the huge student body at Spelman, there would be other girls like her.

Celia graduated first in her class. On graduation day, her proud parents looked on as she delivered a rousing valedictory speech urging her classmates to always follow their dreams. A few days later, she moved one step closer to following her own when an acceptance letter from Spelman arrived.

She moved into dorms a week before classes began. On her first morning on campus, as she waited at the checkout in the university bookstore, a glossy magazine on the rack next to the chewing gum caught her eye. On its cover, two young women, college students, about her age, smiling. She flicked through the pages, stopping abruptly when she saw FICTION CONTEST WINNERS emblazoned across the top of a page.

The magazine ran a monthly competition for aspiring young female writers. Both curious and excited to assess the winning entries, she bought a copy and hurried to her room.

Though the winning stories certainly had merit, a couple of short stories she had written over the summer were better, and so she sent them off for the following month's competition.

Reporting on issues affecting women both at home and abroad, Gloria Steinem - feminist, journalist, and social activist - had co-founded the magazine she called *Ms*. The feature article that month looked back on the success of a rally in Washington just a year before when over 100,000 women had gathered in the nation's capital demanding changes in Equal Rights legislation.

Many of these women called themselves *feminists*, the first time Celia had seen the word. Discovering that many of the protesters proudly identified as young, black and gay, a trickle of fevered excitement shivered through her, an excitement which quickly bloomed into exhilaration as she realised that not only had she found her tribe, but that somewhere outside the stifling, cloying world of an angry, deeply-divided south, there existed a wonderful, freer-thinking world. And in that world were girls just like her. Falling back into her pillow, she smiled, and in a silent yet thrilling ceremony that followed, she declared herself part of this women's collective, a solemn yet defining moment in her young life, one in which the loneliness she once thought might be with her forever, silently slipped away.

Two weeks later *Ms* provided yet another surprise. From its gleaming offices in New York City, a letter arrived seeking permission to publish one of her stories.

Three weeks later, alone in her room, the following month's edition trembled in her hands. She drew in a deep breath as she opened it, slowly turning one page at a time, a momentary paralysis overwhelming her when she suddenly saw her name. Staring blankly at the page, she thought of the thousands, perhaps millions of women reading a story she had written. This most profound *moment*, this first legitimate step in becoming a writer sent a sudden surge sweeping through her, making her heart race and sending gentle tears of joy trickling down her cheeks.

Keen to meet more like-minded women, Celia called the Atlanta chapter of the regional support group listed in the back of the magazine. A week later, in the backyard of the home of Cheryl and her partner, Alison, she met a dozen or so women gathered below the shade of a dogwood tree. For the next couple of hours, Celia sat in revered silence, observing, listening to these attractive, intelligent women speaking so passionately about their own and the lives of other women.

On the agenda that day, another gathering in the nation's capital in just over a month. The National

March on Washington for Gay and Lesbian Rights. Much discussion centred around the assassination of Harvey Milk the year before, and a woman in Florida, Anita Bryant, an anti-gay activist who had successfully repealed a gay-rights ordinance in Dade County. Over 600 miles away, mid-semester, Celia dismissed any possibility of joining them on the march, and at the end of the meeting confessed to Cheryl that for most of the discussion, she had felt a little *lost*.

"You're a freshman?" Cheryl asked.

Celia nodded.

"Wait here," she said, disappearing into another room, returning moments later with a list of books. "Here, check out some of these. Required reading for every aspiring feminist."

In the university library the following afternoon, Celia looked at the list. From a glowing review in *Ms*, she recognised the first title, Germaine Greer's *Female Eunuch*, the reviewer describing it a "commanding account that would shift perspectives on how women viewed the world." She returned to her room with the library's only copy.

Immediately gripped by Greer's passion, in wonderfully blunt, unambiguous language, she unapologetically pointed a very damning finger at feminists' principle adversary. Men. Since ancient times, they have regarded women as inferior. Restricting all aspects of their lives, they have been methodical in their subjugation, caricaturing them in fanciful stories, revisions of old myths, legends, fairy tales, depicting them as frivolous, helpless creatures, always in a state of absolute hopelessness - lost, bewildered, distressed, either weeping or sleeping, all in the hope of being rescued by any available superman.

Portraying women as subordinates and objects of pity in fairy tales, these wicked deceptions evolved into perceived *truths*. Proliferated for thousands of years by nomadic traders criss-crossing the globe, varying versions of these tales all retained a common thread. Women, by nature, were unfortunate, pitiful, with little to offer. And there was little to be done to help them. Because this is how God made them.

With the invention of the printing press in the 15th century, ideas about women as imperfect gained traction. Throughout Europe, printing presses thumped out the Bible, the perfect propaganda tool to bolster lies disguised as *truth*.

Genesis establishes in its first story that Eve, the first woman, was the lesser of God's first two humans. Helpless, so easily tricked, (for just eating an apple) she condemned us all to lives of derision and misery. The original poster girl for all human weakness, she alone brought about all of human suffering.

Many would argue that the invention of the printing press was a great leap forward for man. For men, this was certainly the case. However, for women it was bad news, this new technology enabling men to compound their servitude, making it easier to manipulate laws to sustain and solidify control by printing off and easily distributing deeply-rooted edicts that instructed women on how to behave, how to mother, even what to do with their bodies - ideas that still, today, continue to pervade even the most liberal, free-thinking of modern societies.

In *The Second Sex*, the next book Celia read, Simone de Beauvoir made it clear that men would never cede their indisputable rights to unworthy wives, sisters, mothers, daughters. To put a halt to this systemic lunacy, she argued that it was down to women to shape their own perceptions of womanhood, and only when they united, stepped up, made demands for change, by any means necessary, might they free themselves of servitude.

At the next group meeting, Celia excitedly detailed what she understood about Greer's and de Beauvoir's arguments, provoking a most invigorating debate. At the end of the meeting, before leaving, in a moment of unexpected fervour, she informed Alison and Cheryl that she would join them on the march in Washington.

A month later, Cheryl, Alison and Celia were stomping their way along Fourth Street, just behind the Salsa Sisters, the oldest black lesbian organisation in the United States leading the march. Nestled within this exalted bastion of female solidarity, arm in arm, they edged their way up the National Mall, along Pennsylvania Avenue towards the White House, slowing to a stop at the Washington Monument to listen to rousing speeches.

Over that magical weekend, Celia attended many talks and debates. Central to the endless, heart-wrenching accounts of women's personal struggles, sacrifices, and the seemingly insurmountable obstacles obstructing their pursuit of equality, was a simple, shared desire. To live lives with integrity and dignity. On the long drive home to Atlanta, she reflected on their stories, on their sacrifices, and promised herself that no matter the challenge, these were the values that would now guide her through life, a pledge put to the test sooner than she had expected.

Celia had told her parents that she had spent the previous weekend with friends, camping in the north Georgia Mountains. The following weekend, on her next visit, she handed her laundry bag to her mother and rushed off to see friends, returning an hour later to an eerily quiet house. The only sound, whispers in the living room.

Sitting side by side on the couch, neither her father nor mother looked up when Celia entered. Her mother glanced nervously across the room towards the table, at the source of their discontent.

Next to neatly-folded jeans, a badge from the march her mother had found tucked deep into a back pocket. Doing her best to disguise the terror flooding through her, casually, Celia picked it up and looked at it, momentarily struck by the irony of the silhouette, the Statue of Liberty, that most famous iconic symbol of liberty, embroidered in its centre, the words curled around the border exposing her betrayal.

NATIONAL GAY RIGHTS MARCH
WASHINGTON D.C. OCTOBER 14, 1979

In the centre of the badge, a message from Harvey Milk. Assassinated just a year before, it offered only fleeting inspiration.

RIGHTS ARE NOT WON ON PAPER. THEY ARE WON ONLY BY THOSE WHO MAKE THEIR VOICES HEARD

HARVEY MILK

Sitting next to her stony-faced father, Celia looked at her mother. Small, lonely, head bowed, hands clasped together.

"Such a lifestyle is a sin," he said.

Looking up, his cold, piercing gaze demanded an explanation.

"God made me like this," Celia responded, provocatively, leaning against the wall, arms folded.

Tugging his wife's sleeve, he got to his feet.

"You must give up this detestation. You must change. I cannot support this, this, way of life. You have one week to change your ways, renounce this aversion, and return to the righteous path from which you have strayed. If not, well, you will be on your own."

He strode out of the room, her mother, silently, obediently, shuffling out behind him.

Celia thought of her pledge. Of the sacrifices so many women had made. To submit now, bow down at this first hurdle, to her father - or other men, she wouldn't be able to live with herself.

***

She stayed with Cheryl and Alison for a month, passing the time reading, writing, thinking about what she might do with her life. She often thought of her mother. By the standards of most black women of her generation she had led a comfortable life, her only real servitude - to an uncompromising husband. But had she ever felt truly free? Had she ever experienced *real* joy?

Occasionally they spoke by phone. Awkward, difficult conversations, always ending with her mother reminding Celia of her father's dictate. One morning, out of sorts, again she was thinking of her mother. Of *wasted* years in lonely subservience, not only to white people, but to an imperious husband who rarely talked to her. Thinking of how lonely she must have been, she read again what Greer had written about loneliness, that "it is never more cruel than when it is felt in close propinquity with someone who has ceased to communicate."

As she reflected on these words, the most absurd idea suddenly shivered through her. She ignored it, read on, Greer elaborating on the housewife's miserable and docile condition, each night, wide awake next to her husband, "listening to his breathing in bed, lonelier than any spinster in a rented room." And then, again, the idea suddenly returned, and for the remainder of the day, swilling, stirring, rattling through her, it refused to retreat. After a fitful night, Celia woke the following morning, feeling, believing even, that perhaps, the idea was not so absurd after all.

In a popular midtown drinking haunt that night, she sought Alison and Cheryl's advice.

"I have an idea. About what I want to do. It's a little crazy ..." Celia began.

Alison and Cheryl noted the glow in her face.

"I hope it involves ruling the world," Cheryl said, smiling. "Please, do tell."

"Close," she replied. "I have to leave."

Alison and Cheryl glanced at each other.

"You're welcome to stay. We have plenty of room," Alison assured her.

"Thank you. But I'm leaving Atlanta," she continued, taking a sip of beer.

"Where're you going? New York? San Fran?" Cheryl asked.

"England. I'm going to study there, attend classes by Greer. She's a college professor, in London."

"England?" they said, surprised. "Germaine Greer? In London? Really?" added Cheryl.

Enormous grins signalled their approval.

"Why not?" Celia replied. "What have I got to lose? I'm young, I have some money, college funds. It's risky, but perhaps it's time for some adventure. I want to try and do something different. I'll write. Let you know how it goes."

***

Unseasonably warm for late November, Celia dropped off her bag at a small hostel near Carnaby Street, just on the edges of Soho. In a small knapsack, a street map, her camera, and the latest edition of *Ms*. Purely by chance, in that month's edition, a four-page spread advising Americans visiting London recommended places of interest. Celia considered it a sign. She was doing the right thing.

Weaving her way through Soho's narrow streets onto Shaftesbury Avenue, she made her way to Piccadilly Circus to take photos of Eros, Greek god of love. Sitting among the hordes of young tourists on steps below the statue, she consulted *Ms.* for the next "must see" recommendation. A statue of the most famous Englishman ever. William Shakespeare. And "just minutes away" in Leicester Square.

Moments later, Celia was squinting up at England's most famous export. On a marble pedestal in a fountain flanked by strange-looking bulbous dolphins, he stood in majestic pose. On a scroll unfurling in his hand, words from *Twelfth Night*, Celia's favourite Shakespeare play, chimed perfectly with her new adventure.

THERE IS NO DARKNESS BUT IGNORANCE

With map in hand, she took Charing Cross Road to Trafalgar Square, made her way along Northumberland Avenue to the Embankment where she sat in a café just behind Charing Cross station drinking tea and watching boats drift by.

On her way back to the hostel, resting on a fountain wall in Trafalgar Square, she took photos of screaming children chasing terrified pigeons. Then, most delightfully, through the camera lens, she suddenly saw a group of girls arm in arm, laughing and skipping as they approached. Among them, a particularly pretty blond. Alluring eyes, short hair, beautiful smile. Just Celia's type. She lowered the camera and smiled at her as she passed, her eyes following them as they disappeared from the square. But no sooner had they gone, they suddenly reappeared, the blond breaking away from her friends, still smiling as she ambled back towards Celia.

"You're still here then?" she asked, leaning on the fountain beside her.

"Excuse me?" Celia replied.

"Well, it's just that I saw you as we walked by a minute ago. You American?"

"Yes, I am. I've just arrived. Taking in the sights."

"You alone then?"

"Yes."

"Me and my mates, we're going up the Charing Cross Road. For coffee. Come if you fancy it. Lots of cool bookshops on the way. Only if you fancy it, mind."

Celia hopped down off the fountain wall.

"I'm Celia," she said.

"Sara," the blond replied, holding onto her hand.

"Come on, let's go," she said, looking over at her friends, giggling. "Let's catch them up."

In a small lesbian-run cafe just off the Tottenham Court Road, Sara's friends bombarded the exotic American among them with questions. Not unlike their own Anglican rendering, Celia described the Bible Belt version of family rejection.

"So, you just packed up and left?" one girl asked. "Just as you started uni? That's quite brave of you. What are you going to do now then?"

"I thought I could study here, like Germaine Greer when she came to London," Celia responded.

Grinning, the girls looked at each other.

"Germaine, goddess of all wisdom," one joked. "Such a tragedy she's straight."

"Where are you staying?" Sara asked.

"In a hostel. Near to Soho."

"In a grotty hostel? No way! Come and stay with us," Sara insisted, nodding at Jenny, her flatmate. "We have a spare room."

"No really, I couldn't impose," Celia replied, momentarily disappointed that Sara and Jenny lived together.

"Don't be daft, no imposition. You simply must," Sara insisted, suddenly on her feet, taking Celia's hand.

By teatime, Celia had her own room above a pub in Clerkenwell. In the pub later that night, much to her delight, she learnt that Sara and Jenny, in their final year of law degrees, shared only a flat and not a bed. Outside in the street at last orders, a little drunk, she fell back against the wall and drew cold air deep into her lungs. Looking up at the stars, she smiled. She liked these girls. She liked London. But most of all, she liked Sara, suddenly at her side, grinning.

"Are you OK?" she asked.

"I'm great. Really great. Thank you so much," she replied, pulling her in and kissing her.

The following spring Jenny graduated and moved out. In the final term of her degree, Sara set about looking to land a pupillage while Celia worked cash-in-hand at the café near Tottenham Court Road. As graduation neared, Celia was growing increasingly anxious at the prospect of meeting Sara's father. As vicar of a small parish just outside Leeds, like hers, he had a fervent belief in the Lord and she feared he'd object to her being in his only daughter's life.

Waiting with Celia outside the Royal Festival Hall, the venue for the ceremony, Sara insisted she was worrying needlessly.

Standing beside him during the ceremony, Celia's concerns dissolved. As his clever daughter scaled the stage to collect her diploma, Celia handed him a tissue to stem his relentless tears of pride. Afterwards, on the terrace overlooking the Thames, he cried some more, proudly hugging and kissing Sara, and then, in a warm, tolerant, and quite unexpected tender act of love that brought tears to Celia's eyes, he pulled her into his embrace and declared an unwavering love for them *both*.

At dinner that evening, Sara's mother handed them plane tickets to Italy. A week later in Rome, blistering heat reminded Celia of sizzling Georgia summers. Naples lived up to all culinary expectations, on the menu for breakfast, lunch and dinner - pizza Napolitano. In Puglia, they stayed in a trullo, a traditional dry-stone hut with pointy corbelled roof, at night drinking local wine and looking up at the most beautiful starry skies.

On their return to London, early autumn had descended, the days drawing in. As Sara began her pupillage, she sensed in Celia a certain restlessness. One evening over dinner in a local restaurant, she asked what was troubling her.

"I just feel at a standstill," Celia confessed. "I'm nearly twenty years old and feel like I'm spinning in no particular direction. I need to be doing more with my life. Like you are. I want a life more like yours. I need direction, I want to progress. I want to go back to school. But I can't make changes to my life, your life, our lives, working illegally in a café."

As an American, Celia had no access to public services. She couldn't work, study, or visit a doctor. But Sara had already been thinking of their shared future, and made preliminary enquiries into their immigration quandary. Jeremy, a colleague in Chambers, understood their predicament perfectly. He too, had fallen for an American, Bill, an ocean away in San Francisco, and one day over lunch had *joked* that they might resolve immigration issues if he married Celia and Sara married Bill.

"The only thing I want is for you to be happy," Sara said, taking her hand. "Here, in London. I never want to lose you. I can ask Jeremy. I'm willing if you are. What do you think? Is this something you might consider?"

"YES, YES, YES!" Celia hollered, suddenly on her feet, arms in the air, applause rippling through the restaurant.

A month later, after two very low-key, very quick marriage ceremonies, the happy couples skipped through Soho, bouncing from pub to pub. Late into the evening, a little drunk, with a bright future now possible, a tearful Celia confessed to Sara that, like her, she had decided to study Law. She also told her of an ambitious project she'd been thinking about for some time. That together they open their own law practice.

"That, my beautiful wife, would be a dream," Sara

whispered, kissing her. "We'll make it happen. Together we'll be unstoppable."

"And, Sara Taylor," Celia said, coyly. "I've already thought of the firm's name."

"Me too, Celia Thomas," Sara replied, giggling. "Tell me yours first."

"I like the sound of …"

"Of?" Sara asked, laughing, nudging her. "Come on."

"I really like the sound of Thomas & Taylor."

"Me too," Sara whispered, and she kissed her again.

3

Stella's professors always referred to Thomas & Taylor in glowing terms. With the end of her degree in sight, when a Recruitment Evening flashed up on her phone inviting graduates and interested professionals to an Open Evening at its offices in central London, she decided to go.

With the firm's large central conference room in its Bloomsbury offices already packed, Stella nestled into a space at the back, the hum suddenly fading when two women entered. One, fifty-something, in light grey suit matching the colour of her hair, sat at a small desk beside a flat screen TV and flipped open a laptop. The other, in similar-style suit, perhaps a shade younger, skin glowing the colour of warm caramel, beautiful smile, surveyed the room.

"Well, thank you all for coming tonight," she began, in a delightful, American drawl, THOMAS & TAYLOR suddenly flashing up on the screen behind her. "I see some familiar faces among us this evening, so good to see you again, thank you so much for coming. And for you first timers, for showing an interest in the important work we do here at Thomas & Taylor, we welcome you. In whatever capacity you are here this evening, we do hope that Thomas & Taylor may be of service to you.

"So who are we? Introductions. My name is Celia Thomas. Beside me here, my partner, of the firm, and in life, Sara Taylor. We are the Managing Partners, and this evening we want to provide you with a summary overview of what we do. If you like, our *raison d'être*. But a little bit about our humble beginnings. As you can probably tell, I'm American, from Atlanta, and Sara is from Leeds. We're both law graduates of UCL, a university with which we maintain close ties. When we finished our law degrees and took up our first posts, as I'm sure many of you are well aware, we discovered the law was, and in many quarters still is, very much a boys' club. Working for other firms early in our careers, we witnessed first-hand the shocking, apathetic, substandard treatment women received then when dealing with the law, and continue to receive now. To put it bluntly, we had to do something. And so, since its inception, with women at the heart of everything we do, Thomas & Taylor makes every effort to address this imbalance. Our goal is simple. To improve all women's lives."

Applause rippled around the room. Stella felt her heart racing.

"The judiciary, at best, sees crimes against women as little more than a nuisance. Every day, abhorrent male violence against women and girls is routinely ignored, and so our aim is to change this. We provide outstanding legal services that best serve and protect women. By working closely with outside agencies and state institutions at every level, we monitor and challenge discrimination against women not only within the justice system, but further afield. Ultimately, our endgame is to eradicate all male violence against women and girls."

A slide suddenly appeared on the screen. Her partner, Sara, got to her feet and continued.

WHY WE EXIST

"Men have always failed women. And we know this will continue. But here at Thomas & Taylor we fight back, defending women in a more compassionate, holistic manner, providing them with the respect and courtesy they deserve. As Celia said, we monitor institutions - the courts, employers, schools - and what we continue to see, indeed what we continue to challenge, is simply astonishing. You will hear the word *challenge* a lot this evening, simply because this is an essential part of what we do and who we are. Women have been, and still are, short-changed, not only in the eyes of the law, but in all parts of society. We feel it is our duty to challenge what society casually overlooks, shrugs its shoulders at, ignores, and shine a light on all forms of institutional, structural oppression against women.

"Routinely side-lined, all of us are familiar with the most harrowing, despicable violent crime women habitually experience. When authorities turn a blind eye, women suffer. Many in silence. At Thomas & Taylor we have had enough, enough of the apathy that exists around issues so central to our lives. And it's not an improving picture, not by a long shot. In fact, worrying statistics reflect a clear inertia in the courts. Men who murder women receive ever lenient sentences, and we have the proof, the concrete data, available to everyone at the click of a button. And yet, what measures are taken by government and other institutions to address these concerns? None.

"Abuse and murder of women is an endemic,

global problem. We want to make a *real* difference in the lives of women and girls, and not only here in the UK, but wherever we can in the world. Just think of our Afghan sisters. And, more recently, fifty years after Roe v Wade, our American sisters, once more, their rights under attack, must take to the streets in protest to protect their own bodily autonomy. We support sister organisations throughout the world dealing with rogue governments far worse than our own. Alongside our legal work, Ana, our dedicated global outreach coordinator, monitors those governments which pose a threat to the lives of women and girls, and we do what we can to help them in their struggles."

"Here, on these premises, we have a first-class team of dedicated and hard-working solicitors," Celia continued. "Many are here this evening, but we're looking to expand. We're looking to recruit graduates passionate about helping women and ready to join a team with a clear focus - to stem the horrendous violence against women. We're looking for junior solicitors, graduates, who understand they will be dealing with the barbaric end of humanity. Rape, sexual abuse, young girls lured into pornography or prostitution. And, more recently, the increasing numbers of girls, some as young as eight, subjected to genital mutilation.

"Even in institutions you expect to be safe havens - prisons, mental health homes, immigration detentions - these are places where women are regularly subjected to violent sexual and physical abuse. I know there are women from the Met here tonight, thank you for coming. But no institution is immune from our scrutiny, including the police force. Until recently, even under the leadership of a woman, Cressida Dick, we found worrying levels of sexism at the heart of this institution. Thomas & Taylor will not be bystanders, we will always challenge pernicious discrimination."

When Celia brought the presentation to a close, an hour or so later, feverish applause shook the room.

"Are there any questions?" Sara asked.

Arms shot into the air, question on question from professional women, teachers, lawyers, doctors provoked rousing discussion, and when a young woman in the front row Stella recognised from lectures stood and asked for more detail about the firm's recruitment policy, she listened intently.

"We want to attract the best. Qualified graduates from the finest universities up and down the country," Celia responded, smiling. "I mentioned at the start of the presentation that we work closely with top universities. Indeed, as part of our outreach work, most of our solicitors regularly visit universities to give talks. Not only here in London, but in other parts of the country too. To attract the best, to get our name out there, we spread our net wide. Even as I look around the room now, I see a number of young women present, and to you, I say this. If what you have heard this evening appeals to you, if you feel what we do here matches your professional ambitions, then contact us. Who knows, perhaps right here, right now, there are future Thomas & Taylor solicitors among us."

Stella felt a shiver rush through her.

"Aside from academic qualifications however, ultimately, above everything else, what matters is a passion for the welfare of women and girls. But now, please, let me invite you all next door for drinks and nibbles. We'll be happy to answer any further questions there."

***

The following day Stella began a root and branch investigation of the firm. She browsed its website daily, and at least once a week called to enquire about upcoming events, talks, presentations, panel discussions in which the firm's solicitors were involved. In the days before these events, she studied their profiles, always arriving early, often first into the auditorium, taking a seat in the front row, and during the event scribbling furiously, word for word, notes which she then integrated into her assignments and lecture discussions.

Up most nights, well into the early hours, she laboured over her CV, editing draft after draft, seamlessly weaving into the cover letter anything to give her an edge. She had to strike the right tone, not appear overly desperate, yet make it clear how important it was for her to be part of the firm. On Christmas Eve, after a final edit, she drew in a long nervous breath, closed her eyes, and pressed the send key.

In mid-January, a letter from Thomas & Taylor dropped onto her mat. Immediately recognising the firm's crest in the top left-hand corner of the envelope made her suddenly very nervous. Inside, quite possibly, a rejection letter. She would wait, open it that evening, placed the letter on the kitchen table, and sat staring at it. But then, she changed her mind, ripped it open and squealed with delight as she read the summons - for her to appear at the firm's Bloomsbury offices the week after Easter.

In the intervening months, she worked tirelessly. She wanted to know everything about the firm, beginning with reviews of online opinion pieces by the firm's solicitors, most impressive those written by Celia and Sara. Printing them off, again she made detailed notes of key phrases and words, picking apart the subtext, looking for subtle, nuanced implications of the law. On the walls of her flat she pinned graphs and tables outlining ever-increasing trends in violence towards women. She watched YouTube documentaries and short films of scarcely-known women activists. In recorded mock interviews, she impressed friends with knowledge of both recent and historical statutes from the Equality and Human Rights Commission which she then played back to critique. And yet, despite such meticulous preparation, she worried that she had missed something, a loose end that would find her wanting in interview, waking one night in a cold sweat realising she had nothing to wear. Trudging in and out of shops along Oxford Street the following morning, she finally settled on a navy blue, two-piece suit and a cream-coloured blouse from Selfridges.

The day of the interview arrived. Stella walked back and forth past the solid Georgian door of the firm's offices a number of times before entering. Ana, the outreach coordinator and firm's receptionist, buzzed her in, greeting her with a warm smile and a lanyard. After a quick call to the partners, she led her along a narrow corridor to the central conference room.

Celia and Sara rose and shook Stella's hand.

After small-talk niceties, the interview began. Stella responded confidently to a series of standard questions taken directly from her application. University courses, work experience, placements, and, most importantly, why Thomas & Taylor? So well-rehearsed, she even found herself enjoying the experience, but an hour passed quickly, and with other candidates to see, Celia brought the interview to a close asking Stella if she had anything further to add. Or perhaps, some questions?

Suddenly lost in thought, Stella looked blankly across the table. Momentarily puzzled, Celia and Sara glanced at each other.

"Is something the matter?" Sara asked.

"No. No, sorry," Stella replied, drawing in a sudden, sharp breath. "I'd like to add a couple of more reasons why I think I'd be an asset to Thomas & Taylor. As I said earlier, I learnt about the work this firm does right here, in this room. Ms. Taylor, Ms. Thomas, everything you said at the Open Evening I attended convinced me I wanted to work under your guidance. Everything I have done since then has led me back to this room."

Stella shifted slightly in the seat. Closing her eyes, she drew in another long breath.

"You said a couple of reasons?" prompted Celia.

Stella opened her eyes.

"I was fourteen. With Emma, my best friend," she continued, pausing to clear her throat and take a drink of water. "We'd been to the cinema and, as always, we stopped for chips on the way home. We were attacked by three men. They took Emma, dragged her into their car, drove off and murdered her. This is something that happened in my life. Something I think you should know as you consider my suitability to work for you. The work you do here is important, and for this reason, you don't need a weak link. But please, be assured, I won't be that. You may question whether I am *over* what happened to me that night. Well, the truth is, I'm not sure. I'm not sure anyone could ever be *over* something like that. But what I do know is that what happened to me that night provides me with a purpose in life. This purpose is to improve the lives of women, an ambition I believe I can best achieve here at Thomas & Taylor. I can be an asset to this firm, but to be part of it, I want this event, this crime, something that happened to me as a girl, on record. You have to make a decision about my fitness to work here, and if you believe that what happened to me that night may hinder my ambitions to serve women, it's only fair you know of that episode in my life. So, I want you to know. However, I also want you to know that what happened that night now gives me strength, emboldens me. And yes, sometimes I think of that night. How can I not? But I have worked so hard, and I have chosen law, not as a way of *surviving* that awful night, but because I want to do right by women. And girls. That's what I strive to do. And I believe Thomas & Taylor can provide me with the opportunity to do this."

Their faces hard to read, Celia forced a smile.

"Thank you Stella," she said, getting to her feet. "Once we've interviewed the remainder of the candidates, we will be in touch. Within the next week."

Walking through Russell Square afterwards, Stella sighed as she replayed key moments of the interview in her mind. Why hadn't she used more citations? Especially in response to questions on the role of the Human Rights and Equality Commission. But why worry? At no point in the weeks leading up to the interview had she even considered talking about that night. Her confession had certainly undone a solid performance. Of the same opinion, she imagined Celia and Sara in conversation afterwards. She had confused a therapy session with a job interview, and such self-indulgent declarations, mad ramblings from a self-pitying, desperate and damaged woman, most inappropriate. Sheer madness. A serious flaw. Weakness. How could she have got it so wrong?

During research for the interview, Stella had read of a couple of impressive American women, sisters, Sarah and Angelina Grimke, stalwarts in the antislavery and women's rights movements in the 19th century. In a Bloomsbury bookshop, as an assistant tapped their surname into a database, Stella's phone suddenly rang. She normally rejected unlisted numbers, but on a whim, took the call.

It was Celia. But she had said a week. Calling so

soon after the interview meant only one thing. An act of mercy. A pre-emptive culling. A courtesy call. Polite elimination.

"Stella," Celia began. "We both thought your interview went well …"

Tears welling in her eyes, the phone trembling in her hand, Stella turned and walked away from the counter.

"And so I'm calling really more out of courtesy…" Celia continued, pausing to clear her throat.

An interminable interlude followed.

"Stella, this call is to extend our congratulations. Both Sara and I are united in our decision. We believe that you are an excellent fit for our firm. And so, it gives me great pleasure in welcoming you to Thomas & Taylor."

Stella released a stifled scream of delight. The assistant smiled and silently clapped.

"God. I don't know what to say," she stuttered. "Thank you. Thank you so very much. Oh my god. I can't believe it. My god!"

"Well done Stella. Excellent interview. Please call the receptionist who you met this morning. Her name's Ana. I think you've spoken to her a number of times by phone. Make an appointment to come in next week to discuss your training contract and other mundane matters. And again Stella. Welcome to Thomas & Taylor."

4

On Friday evenings the firm's solicitors usually met in a pub near to the offices. Here Stella heard stories of the *old days*, just a generation ago, of women struggling to enter the legal profession. For those women who managed to infiltrate the inner sanctum of this male preserve, few lasted long. Either unable or unwilling to tolerate *lads' talk*, many took up other occupations. But some, like Celia and Sara, refused to be bullied, persevering in the knowledge they were laying the groundwork for the next generation.

When Celia and Sara established Thomas & Taylor, many city firms made little effort to disguise their hostility, making it clear that they regarded them as annoying upstarts who had crossed a line. Simply put, they were not welcome. Much like a primary school playground, the words *dykes*, *radicals*, *feminists*, even *lezzies*, often a combination of these, were freely bandied around within legal circles. But they understood that hard-nosed, inept men feared bright and ambitious women, and though at times setbacks seemed insurmountable, bitter slurs and insults served only to give them even greater belief in themselves. As women, they understood patience and, above all, they understood the rules of the *long game*, and so they persevered, working tirelessly to make the firm a success.

From its inception, Thomas & Taylor never shied away from political involvement. At interview, successful new recruits demonstrated astute knowledge of the important role government played in women's welfare. They also understood and accepted that in a justice system that routinely sidelined women, they would encounter obstacles rarely mentioned in casebooks at law school and, as such, might expect only occasional, fleeting success.

They would also be joining a firm that constantly monitored governments, not only in the UK, but those abroad, putting pressure on them to amend laws adversely affecting women. Most worrying in recent years, across the Atlantic in the US and Brazil, sister democratic countries, was the scaling back, and in some cases, the dissolution of women's rights. Once Trump and Bolsonaro had assumed power, their first assignment was to slowly dismantle rights feminists in respective countries had been working decades to achieve. Emboldened by these exceptionally dangerous men, closer to home, the Polish and Romanian governments followed their lead, ignoring national and international standards set out by the UN regarding welfare of women.

Responsible for running day-to-day operations, and the firm's global outreach coordinator, Ana. As a young, gay Romanian, she had felt the full force of such invidious agendas in her homeland where, with enthusiastic backing of an actively misogynistic and homophobic Orthodox church, the government had introduced laws criminalising gays and lesbians. With an increasingly right-leaning UK government, and the rise of right-wing governments in Europe, Ana meticulously documented occasions when governments anywhere in the world wilfully turned a blind eye to the abuse of women, updating solicitors first thing at the firm's Monday morning meetings.

"Sorry, sorry," Celia said, rushing in ten minutes late, just as Ana had finished summarising the fallout of the Roe v Wade debacle, and the impact it will have on freedom and equality for American women. "Been dealing with a sick father-in-law. We think it's serious. Sara's up north. She may bring him back down to stay with us for a while. Depends on how he is. I'm sorry for being late. OK, so, who's up first? Stella, what do you have?"

"A new case. Rape. Brutal," she began, flipping through notes. "The girl's fifteen. In a bad way. Under sedation in hospital. Coming home from school, four of them bundled her into a car, drove off and locked her in an old air-raid shelter. In total darkness, underground for four days. No food or water. Two returned, in balaclavas, filmed the rape and uploaded it online. Not the brightest of things. They used first names so we know who they are. I met briefly with the defence solicitor. Real smarmy bastard. From what he saw online, he said the girl didn't struggle so, in some way, may have been complicit. The *boys'* testimony supports this, he says. For a reduced sentence, he'll go for abduction, not rape. They'll be back out on the streets in no time. And, they're not boys. Both are nineteen. Adults. Even if the judge rejects this plea, they'll muddy the waters, argue legal discrepancies between sexual abuse and rape, lean on the judge, appeal for leniency. The press could help us here. I think we should go at this with all guns so to speak."

A collective sigh swept through the room.

Before contacting the press, a group of senior solicitors assessed each case, aware that too much attention on individual cases often worked against victims. For this reason, the firm used the media only occasionally, and always reluctantly.

Seasoned professionals, Celia and Sara, always did the press. Convincing on camera, in addition to talking about specific cases, currently unfit for purpose when dealing with sexual violence towards women and girls, they often called for changes in the country's antiquated laws.

"Stella, let's discuss it some more in detail. We'll talk afterwards," Celia replied.

For the next hour, individual solicitors summarised their cases. Celia brought the meeting to a close, remaining in the conference room with Stella after the others had left.

"Stella, just checking in on the Miller case. If it's a little … close to home, I'm happy to reassign it."

"Thanks Celia," she replied, nodding her appreciation. "I can manage. There's been little progress so I didn't mention it in the meeting. Have you seen the case file?"

"Yes, a real nasty piece of work alright. Cutting the word BITCH into her back. Real psycho. No sexual element?"

"Strangely, no."

"Warped fucker."

"My thoughts exactly."

"So, this new case. Have they a suspect?"

"They think it's the stepfather. What's odd though,

he doesn't fit the profile. Investigators think it might be a copycat. And strangely, there are similarities to the Miller case."

"How so?"

"Well, we've released no details of the case. I carry it in my bag at all times. But, like in the Miller case, he's cut her. But he's only managed the letters B and I, and the horizontal line of the T. The police think he didn't have time to finish. They also think the girl's mother is involved. Apparently she knew where the stepfather was, but refused to give him up. They found him under some old sacks in the shed at the back of her garden."

"And the mother? What's happened to her? Where is she now?" Celia asked.

Stella sighed.

"They took her in. I met with her. Alcoholic. Selfish. Beyond pity. I asked her why she would try and protect a man who's killed her daughter."

"And?"

"She said she didn't believe he did it," Stella said, pausing, shaking her head. "And then, and then, do you know what she said?"

Celia waited.

"She said that it wasn't the first time he'd tried it on with the girl. On the occasion she found him in her room, she threw him out only to let him back in when he promised not to go near her again. She has a record. Drugs. Theft."

Celia shook her head.

"People coming and going, the house is a little drug den. What's strange though, is the stepfather isn't the only suspect. The neighbour who called the police when she heard the screams claimed to have seen a strange man come rushing out of the house. Not the usual type, not like a druggy. Well dressed, carrying a briefcase. She said he looked like a teacher. The police had been to the house many times. For drugs. They arrived this time expecting the same. They found the girl. Mutilated, still alive, just, but she had bled out by the time the paramedics arrived.

"High as a kite, the mother said she didn't know where the stepfather was. They checked her phone to see she'd talked with him shortly after the attack. She kept insisting that he didn't kill her. When the police found him stoned in the shed he could barely talk. At the police station, after he'd sobered up, he swore he didn't kill her. The police think he's lying. They pushed for the confession. I asked the mother again why protect a man who killed her daughter. Do you know what she said?"

Celia shook her head.

"Because she just knew he didn't do it. He wasn't *really* like that. He'd *promised* he wouldn't go near her again. She believed him."

Stella paused.

"And then … and then she said, that, that her daughter, that she had an eye for the fellas. Always teasing him. What sort of woman, mother…? Jesus, a thirteen-year-old girl."

"Listen, perhaps you have too much on right now. I can reassign …?"

"No Celia, no, thanks. I'm OK. It's what we do, huh?"

"It's what we do," she nodded. "You think they'll go for insanity?"

"Most probably. But the strange thing is, how at first, the stepfather was so stubborn, hard to break down. Kept saying he was innocent. Said he wasn't going down for something he didn't do. It took days for police to get a confession."

***

"Good evening, Stella. Glass of the usual?" the waiter asked.

"Thanks Gino, that'd be great," she replied.

"Will Colin be joining you tonight?"

"That's the plan. Must be held up."

Her phone suddenly pinged. Colin was en route. By bus. Northern Line suspended. A young woman on the tracks at Camden.

The venue for their first date, they met at Luigi's often. Here, over long, slow conversations, is where Colin had won her trust, convinced her to confide in him. And she did, where she let unravel deeply intimate details of what had happened to Emma. Except for Dr. Bergeron, and Celia and Sara in the interview, she had never opened up to anyone about Emma.

"Sorry I'm late," Colin said, out of breath, suddenly behind her.

He dropped his briefcase and squirmed out of his jacket.

"I got started without you," Stella replied, smiling, swirling wine in her glass.

"Tough day?" he asked, slumping into his seat.

"You could say that."

"You want to talk about it?"

Stella stared blankly into the flickering flame of a small candle in the centre of the table. Tumbling through her, the image of a mangled, mutilated girl on a slab in the mortuary that morning.

"A girl. Thirteen. He strangled her, then …"

"Then …?" Colin asked.

"He, he cut her first. Then strangled her. A frenzied attack. What, what sort of monster could do something like this? What is it with, with, some men? What the fuck makes them do such things? And the girls. So young. So, so innocent. No matter how long I do this job, no matter how long I pursue such cases, I'll never understand the, the heightened sense of, of, I don't know, rage, fury, in some of these, these ..." she said, pausing to drink some wine. "It's not just, just the rape. It's something more. Something more than just sex. Sometimes not even the sex. For them it's, it's, emotional. Maybe *emotional's* not the word. I'm not even sure it's a power and control thing. The thrill, perhaps. Imagine that, getting kicks from killing girls. Maybe possession? A need to strip the victim of any value. Destroy her. Christ, I don't know. But this monster mutilated the body, he sliced into ..." but again, catching herself, she stopped. "I don't get it. Never will. I read about these wackos. The scheming, the stealth, but he…"

Forcing a smile, she picked up the menu.

"Enough! Enough of that, let's order."

"Stella. Come on," Colin reminded her. "We share.

That's the agreement. We don't bury things. Tell me. What else did he do? Tell me," he insisted.

She put down the menu and gazed across the table at him.

"Stella. What did he do?"

Though they'd never spoken explicitly about it, from very early in their relationship Colin had accepted that Stella's work as a solicitor came before their marriage. And with it came worries he encouraged her to share, if not with him, then a friend. When especially low, he urged her to see Dr. Bergeron.

"He cut her," she whispered. "Sliced her up. All over. And then…"

"And then?"

"He carved the word "bitch" into her back. She was probably still alive. God, I hope not. What, what on earth could she have done to, to …"

"Stella. She could have done nothing to deserve that. Nothing. This is about him. Nothing more. Him. Same old story."

Stella exhaled, regretting offering up details of the case.

"You're right. There is no reason. Perhaps it's that simple. Anyway, enough, enough, enough! Let's change the subject. Your turn. How was your day? What are you going to order?"

Always remarkably uneventful, Colin skipped talk of humdrum meetings to remind Stella of their weekend plans, a trip down to Devon to celebrate his mother's birthday. From the blank expression on her face, he could tell she had forgotten.

"Stella," he said, the tone of his voice suddenly lower. "Mother is looking forward to seeing you. She was a little frosty on that first visit, I admit, but give her time. She'll come around. You just need more time together, to get to know each other. I spoke to her just this morning, she's looking forward to seeing you again. It's only a weekend. Come on, she's getting on. Who knows, she may not be here for much longer," he said, smirking.

"I could smash that line of defence in one cruel swipe," Stella replied, returning his smile. "Well, I suppose as your wife, contractually, I signed up for moments of such unbearable inconvenience. I have a couple of cases I need to look at before Monday. I'll take them with me. What time are we leaving?"

"Around eight thirty. That should get us there just in time for lunch. I'll take Mother out for scones afterwards, leave you in peace to look at the cases. Anything of interest?"

"A couple of women killing their husbands," she replied, smiling. "What shall we get her?"

"For what?"

"Her birthday."

"Oh, yeah. Don't worry about that. I'll pick up some chocolates or something."

Besides his mother, Colin rarely talked about his family. His father made only the briefest of appearances at their wedding. Helen, his twin sister, mother to two young girls, too ill to attend.

As in most families, Stella suspected a degree of discord. On that first visit to his childhood home, she was both surprised and impressed at the splendour of the opulent eighteenth century farmhouse, close to the sea and surrounded by lush, wide-open fields.

Meeting his mother had proven awkward. Greeting Stella with a limp handshake and nervous, uneasy smile, she remained distant the entire weekend. Colin assured Stella that she'd *come round,* then surprised her by confessing that he'd never brought a girl home before.

On Stella's second visit, his mother was warmer, greeting her in the driveway with a smile and a hug. Over a lunch of her signature dish, homemade Shepherd's pie, she was very chatty, detailing the history of the house, of how Colin's great grandfather had once owned a good chunk of the county which he passed on to his son, Colin's grandfather. With no interest in farming, save the farmhouse and a few surrounding fields, just after the war he got married and sold most of the land. When Colin's father took possession, he sold the rest to establish a successful export business in Plymouth, just an hour away.

After lunch, while Colin helped his mother move boxes into the basement, Stella walked up to the top of the cliffs. Resting on an ancient bench, spellbound by a magnificent sapphire-blue sea stretching into the horizon, she was glad that she had come.

An hour or so later, she returned to the house. With Colin in the village running errands and his mother still in the kitchen pottering around, she wandered from room to room, lingering in one with an old, wooden dining table taking up most of the space. Flanked with heavy drapes, light streamed through windows illuminating a large crystal fruit bowl in the centre. In a cabinet on one side of the room, a delicate, porcelain tea set. On the other side, a sturdy sideboard on which rested a framed photograph. Two girls and a boy, perhaps seven or eight. She recognised immediately the boy's gloomy eyes looking coldly at the camera as Colin's. Beside him, two girls. One most likely his sister, Helen. The other, a friend, or perhaps a cousin.

"Is this Colin and his sister, Helen?" Stella asked his mother moments later in the kitchen.

Immediately, she noted a look of alarm in her face.

After washing her hands, his mother sat at the kitchen table and gazed at the photograph. A slow, reluctant smile rose in her face.

"Yes, that's Colin," she whispered. "My husband took this on the beach shortly before their eighth birthday. The girl on the left, yes, that's Helen. She sends her apologies for not being able to make it this weekend. She's unwell, I believe. The girl on the right, that's, that's …"

A tender moment of maternal nostalgia made Stella smile.

"The other girl, that's my Marjory," she continued, her voice trembling. "God bless her. Delightful child, so full of life. She used to drive Colin mad, though. Both of my girls back then, so full of life," she added, her smile suddenly dissolving. "Poor thing. Left us too soon. She was only eight. Not long after this photo was taken. We never talk about it now. None of us. It was such a long time ago. Quite unusual back then, I suppose, triplets."

"Colin's a triplet?" Stella asked, unable to disguise

her surprise.

"Yes, my dear, did he never mention it?"

Stella shook her head.

"Well," she continued, taking in a long breath, "that's not surprising. He never did give too much away. But a nice boy. He finally got his life together. Please, my dear," she said, gesturing for Stella to sit. "Stella, can I ask you something? I don't mean to pry, but, but, you and Colin - you get along well?"

"Yes. Very much so," Stella responded, quickly. "I consider myself very fortunate to have him in my life," she nodded, smiling.

"Colin wasn't a bad boy," she continued. "The perfect gentleman now I know, but I must say, like most boys, when he was young, he did have his moments. He was, maybe, four or five, oh, the wild and worrying tantrums. I thought they'd never end. And Marjory did annoy him. I remember one time she pulled his hair and he slapped her, hard. I tried to console her but she just wouldn't stop crying. My husband, Charles, arrived home to find her in convulsions. We had discussed Colin's temperamental behaviour and both of us agreed he'd grow out of it. Which, of course, eventually, he did. But on that occasion, my husband spanked Colin and only then did Marjory stop crying. Which only made matters worse.

"It was a week or so before we were due to head off on holiday. To France, the Dordogne. I remember the day well, the first week of their summer holiday. It was hot, very hot, so I decided to take the children up onto the cliffs for a picnic. I often took them out, sometimes to the beach, sometimes riding bikes in the countryside, but on that day, we went up on the cliffs. You've been up there, the breeze, the view, just so beautiful. So cool on hot days."

She paused, tapping her fingers on the table.

"I was preparing lunch, and, so used to their spats, I simply ignored the girls' occasional screams. On that day the three of them were playing ball, the girls upset with Colin for throwing it too close to the cliff edge. I thought little of it, they knew not to go close to the edge, and I told him to play fair. But Marjory continued to complain and…"

Again she stopped and stared blankly out through the window.

"As I said, it was, well, normal, to hear the girls complaining. But then I heard the most piercing of screams, first Marjory, then Helen, and when I looked up, she was running towards me, tears streaming down her face, her outstretched arm trailing behind her, pointing towards the cliff, at Colin, sitting with his arms wrapped around his legs, his face hidden between his knees. And, and, I just knew."

She wiped away a tear running down her face.

"I ran to the cliff edge. Below, on the beach, a mad panic huddled around her. Women in tears, men running off in all directions for help. But even then I knew. Falling from that height. There was nothing to be done."

Stella reached across the table and took her hand.

"After the funeral, Charles sent Colin away. To boarding school in Kent. We never blamed him, but, I suppose, he may not have seen it like that. Back then, at that time, Charles could be ... inflexible. He's mellowed with age, but he insisted on Colin going away to school. He required a stricter regime. Flush out the rage, help shape, adjust him. Routine. Discipline. Even the occasional whipping. Key to shaping any boy. Calm his temperamental nature, he said. And so we sent him away. I didn't protest. I should have. I didn't want him to go. And poor Helen. Not a day goes by that I don't worry about her. I think she still sees a therapist. She didn't just lose a sister, she lost her best friend. They did everything together. Like I said, we never talk about that day. Even now, when she visits. Never. And, the poor thing, when she comes to visit, there's something about her, I don't know, a sort of - emptiness. She's distant, she's here, but, but, not quite. It's hard to explain. I'm not really sure she's ever been able to get on with life. Not after that. Having her own family helps. But Stella, my dear, did Colin really never mention anything about that day? Nothing of Marjory?"

A car crunched to a halt on the gravel driveway signalling Colin's return and the end of their conversation. After that last visit, Stella had never mentioned knowledge of Marjory. Had he wanted to discuss such a difficult episode in his life, such a personal, delicate matter, he would have.

Colin's mother was waiting in the driveway, waving as they pulled up. After warm embraces, she showed them inside, offering apologies for her husband's absence, away on a golfing weekend. Helen, Simon and the girls, also away, were camping on the Moors.

Over lunch, very excitedly, she told them of a new *project*. She had taken the *plunge* and joined the village choir. As a girl she had sung in the school choir, a most treasured memory. Now, all these years later, singing again! Praising her most "melodious tone," the choir leader had asked her to perform a solo at the county fair.

After a dessert of strawberries and fresh cream, she showed them round the garden. Charles, now semi-retired, had found solace in planting and pruning, his handiwork making it more colourful than ever, a neighbour had even suggested they enter it into the Pride of Devon Competition. In a clearing at the bottom, space for two large pots bought the previous day in the village. She told them that Colin would collect them that afternoon. Shortly after he left, alone with his mother in the kitchen, Stella asked if she could help her.

"Thank you, dear," she said. "Why don't you take a lie down, and perhaps in a while, we can go for a walk on the beach."

"Yes, I'd like that," Stella replied, sensing a certain subtext in the invite. "Let me know when you're ready."

Sitting comfortably on the bed, she had no appetite for work. Pulling from her bag two files, she opened the first to see a photograph of a woman's face. Sharon. Single mother. Drugs. Housing estate in Tottenham. Two girls. Two different fathers. One three, the other six. Both now in care. Tiny, expressionless eyes spoke of a crushed life, much like the eyes in the faces of most women Stella represented.

She sighed.

She flipped open the second file, immediately intrigued by a woman's eyes staring defiantly into the camera. These eyes told a different story, spoke of a distinctly different life. Though over two decades older than Sharon, this woman possessed the youthful complexion frequently seen in women of a certain age with a Hampstead address. Two sons, nineteen and twenty. Both at university. Clients like Charlotte rarely called on Thomas & Taylor.

Women received feeble representation from lawyers. Early in Stella's career, she had witnessed in court an inept barrister employing age-old tropes, arguing that his client had acted in a "moment of madness," experienced a "momentary lapse" in sanity. On another occasion, another lawyer, much younger, even described his client as "hysterical." So early in her career, this imbalance had provided Stella with examples of the ill-prepared, shoddy defence women regularly received in a two-tier system of defence. And the consequences of women receiving sloppy representation? Much harsher sentences.

Stella was already thinking about the time-consuming footwork required to build a robust defence for both women. Researching precedents, forensic examinations, anything to shine a light on extenuating circumstances in both cases.

"Are you ready for a stroll on the beach dear? It's a lovely day for it," Colin's mother asked, tapping softly at the door.

"Yes, will be with you in a minute," Stella replied,

closing the files.

Glancing at the photographs of the women side by side on the bed, again she sighed, dropping the files into the bottom drawer. But before closing it, she paused. In perhaps a pointless gesture, she momentarily considered the stark imbalances of privilege between the two women, and changed the order of the files, placing Sharon's on top.

A soft breeze wafted up off the sea sparkling a most beautiful blue. Below towering cliffs, arm in arm, Stella and Colin's mother smiled and nodded at people as they passed.

"Stella, my dear," she suddenly said, "please do tell me if, if, I'm being too intrusive. I wanted to ask you something I think I may have mentioned last time you were here, I can't quite remember…"

"Please, anything," Stella replied, warily.

"How is your marriage, love? I mean, are you … content? With Colin?" she added, tentatively.

Stella remembered similar inquiry from the previous visit.

"Believe me, there are no problems at all. We're as solid as the day we married," she replied. "Of course, we're both very different people. We've known that from the start. Work is central to my life. Colin knows this. We spoke about it shortly after we met. If anything, he's always so supportive. He really is. I really couldn't have hoped for a better partner. I feel very lucky. I love Colin, he loves me. We're not only husband and wife, we're good friends. We really are. I'm curious, why do you ask?"

Colin's mother suddenly stopped and looked up at

the cliff face looming above them. Slipping into a fleeting, trance-like state, she gripped Stella's hand.

"Oh, it's nothing my dear, nothing at all. Just checking things are how they should be," she whispered, and they walked on, Stella following her back up the narrow path leading up to the house.

Halfway up, still thinking of how she had gripped her hand below the cliff, she paused and looked back along the beach to where they had stopped, suddenly realising it was the spot where Marjory had died.

"I'll make us tea, dear," Colin's mother said, surprised to see Colin sitting at the kitchen table. "That was quick love," she added, "did you pick up the pots?"

"They said you told them dad would collect them next week," he replied.

"Oh, did I, love? Yes, you're right, perhaps I did. I'm sorry, I'm just so forgetful these days. Not to worry, no harm done. Would you like tea?"

The following morning, Colin's mother waved them off. As she turned to enter the house, the car suddenly skidded to a halt.

"I've forgotten some case files," Stella said, springing out of the car and running back inside.

She opened the drawer, pausing before she took them out. Certain she had placed Sharon's file on top, it was Charlotte's she saw first.

5

Stella often thought Colin overly curious about ongoing cases. Since returning from Devon, the nagging possibility lingered that he had looked at Sharon and Charlotte's case files, putting them back in the drawer with Charlotte's on top, not as she left them.

"Much on today?" he asked over breakfast one morning.

"Off to see a couple of clients. One in Surrey, the other in Peterborough," Stella replied.

"Interesting cases?"

Stella looked up at him.

"A couple of domestic abuse cases."

"Surrey and Peterborough? Good luck on the M25," he said, smiling at her.

"And you? Much on?"

"No, not really - just pulling things together for the conference."

"Conference? What conference?"

"In Manchester. I told you about it, a month or so ago. Remember? You said you had something on with Celia and Sara that weekend."

Stella flipped open the calendar on her phone. He was right. Dinner with the firm's solicitors Saturday evening.

"Oh yes, now I remember," she lied. "The whole weekend?"

"Yes. I'll drive up Friday morning and should be back early Sunday evening. Depends on traffic, the M6."

With unusually light traffic on the M25, Stella arrived at HMP Bronzefield women's prison an hour before the scheduled appointment. One of the better prisons, its rehabilitation programme aimed to help women reintegrate into civic life, offering a wide range of vocational courses and employment opportunities - barista, hair and beauty styling, even work as chaplaincy orderlies.

As she waited in the interview room, Stella opened Sharon's file. Again, looking at her photo, in tiny, lifeless eyes, a pitiful expressionless gaze. Deep inside those eyes, like those of so many of the women Stella represented, swirling and swelling, a permanent well of despair.

Sharon Harris. Age thirty-one. Petty drug dealer. Previous convictions. Theft and drug possession. Two girls. One three, the other six. Different fathers. No support, financial or otherwise. *Helpful.* No record of violent behaviour. *Helpful.* Frequent hospitalisation for domestic abuse. *Helpful.* Confessed to plunging a bread knife into her husband's chest. *Unhelpful.* Likely outcome: first degree murder. Likely sentence: minimum - eighteen years.

When meeting a client for the first time, Stella had a standard set of questions. Had she seen a doctor? A nurse? In Sharon's case, had she been informed of the drug detox programme? To win the woman's trust, additional questions focused on more holistic aspects of her life. Childhood, education, even hopes and ambitions. Based upon her responses, Stella would know if she was stable enough to discuss the crime.

The door suddenly opened and a warden stepped

into the room. Shuffling in behind her, a woman, the dark, purple shadows under sunken, puffy eyes making her appear much older than in the photo. Reminding Stella of old hags limping out of detention camps after World War II, an ill-fitting prison uniform did little to disguise her emaciated, bedraggled state. Here, again, she thought, in one of the richest countries on earth, a shameful reflection, another disturbing reality of systemic disadvantage in human form. Tangled in a system of pitiful neglect and indiscriminate suffering, another woman barely managing, existing in the shadows, little more than pointless, an obsolete cog in a system not designed for her.

As she shuffled to the table, Sharon knew nothing of this. Or of other slow machinations of a criminal justice system about to consume her. Blinking nervously, she sat down.

"Hello Sharon. I'm Stella. Your solicitor. Nice to meet you," Stella said, offering a hand.

Sharon raised a bony hand and shook it.

"How are you? Do you have everything you need?" she began.

"What's 'appened to my kids? Where are they?"

"Your children are with social services. They're in very good care. Have you had a chance to call them yet?"

Sharon shook her head.

"Sharon, I'm here to represent you. To begin with, I'd like to ask you some questions. Questions simply for me to get to know you. I want the court to see you as a person, with attributes, not solely as someone who has committed a crime, but as a person."

"What for?" she replied.

"I'm sorry?" Stella asked, a little surprised.

"Why d'ya need to know who I am? I did it. Ain't that enough?"

"Like I say, to give you the best defence, it's important we know you, the person. You, Sharon. If you don't feel comfortable answering any of the questions, that's fine, just let me know. And, perhaps not today, only when you feel ready, we can talk about what happened. If it's not too distressing."

"I did it. I killed the bastard. And I'd do it again. I'm glad I did it. If you want me to say sorry, or say I didn't do it, it ain't gonna happen. I'm happy 'e's gone. The bastard. Deserved it. 'e won't be able to … well, I'm just glad 'e's gone."

Knee-jerk confessions like Sharon's often came as a relief for many women.

"Sharon. Your kids …?"

"Sara."

"Sara and…"

"Angie."

"Yes, Angie. So young," Stella added, but then paused. "Sharon, from your notes, I think I understand what happened to you. The confession you gave means you are going to prison. I think you know that. But what I'd like to do, it's going to be difficult, but I believe we can reduce the charges. As it stands, you will be tried for first-degree murder. That means a minimum of eighteen years in prison, a sentence I don't believe you deserve. I think I should go with a manslaughter plea. Hopefully, this will reduce the sentence. To do that, however, we'll have to go through some difficult questions you'll most likely be asked again after you've seen the psychiatrist. Is that OK?"

"Psychiatrist?" Sharon asked, looking up at Stella for the first time.

"Expert opinion from a psychiatrist will be fundamental to your case. It will help us get the *real* picture of you. Of your life, of what led to you doing what you did. It will give us the *big picture*, if you like, bring to light all extenuating circumstances. Sharon, again I'm guessing, but, but, on some level, what you did, you did out of duty, not out of malice. Do you understand?"

Sharon nodded.

"What's the difference? In years - between murder and manslaughter?" she asked.

"I can't say for certain. It could be a significant reduction, perhaps six to eight years. Sara and Angie are still so young. You'll be able to be part of their lives again."

"I ain't sorry I did it though," she replied, her eyes suddenly filling with tears.

A solitary drop rolled down her cheek.

"That's OK. I know you had your reasons. I really do. And that's what I want to talk to you about. You have no record of violent conduct which is a really good start. It says much about you Sharon, and will be considered favourably by the court."

"I never 'urt no-one before. Never. I never 'it the kids. Never."

"I know you haven't, and you never would. I can

see that in you Sharon," Stella assured her.

She opened a notebook and fumbled in her bag for a pen.

"Sharon. I'm going to take notes. Do you think you can talk about what happened that evening? Is that OK?"

"I s'pose."

"Try not to leave anything out. Tell me everything you remember. Go ahead."

"He came 'round at about four-fifteen. The kids 'ad just got back from school," she began.

"You mean the deceased?"

Sharon nodded.

"'e was 'appy, smilin'. 'e weren't always 'appy, but that day 'e was. Sometimes 'e was right moody, I knew this when I married 'im. But 'e seemed alright in the early days, they was good. And 'e was always so good with me oldest one, Sara. She wasn't 'is. We used to do normal things. Go out, to the pub, normal things. Like other people. But then one day 'e brought drugs home. I told 'im I didn't want 'em in the house. I used to 'ave a drink before I met 'im, but it was 'im who got me into drugs. Friends tried to warn me, 'bout 'im. I didn't believe 'em. I s'pose I was blinded by 'is attention. 'e said some nice things. No other bloke ever said nice things to me. I guess I thought 'e was alright.

"We got drunk a lot, and then I got pregnant with Angie, me youngest. She's four now. 'e said we should get married, for the baby, so we did. Then, just a week after, 'e got sent down for robbery. I didn't know 'e was even involved in stuff like that, or that 'e 'ad a record. 'e told me 'e was innocent, and I believed him, but they sent 'im down for three an' a half years. Like a fool, I waited. I used to go and see 'im too. And take the girls. 'e loved seein' 'em. 'is face always lit up when 'e saw 'em. I was really lookin' forward to 'im gettin' out, I thought we could make a new start. 'e said so too. With the girls to support, 'e'd get a job 'e said, do anythin'. I was really lookin' forward to 'avin', like, a proper family life, like other people 'ave. It's all I thought of when 'e was inside."

She paused, closed her eyes and shook her head.

"It's alright Sharon. You're doing fine. You just wanted what normal families have. That's what we all want. Please, continue."

"Well, 'e come out. We was waitin' outside the prison for 'im. Me and the girls. And 'e comes home, but 'e don't stay long. Takes me phone and asks for money, says 'e's gotta go somewhere. Wouldn't tell me where. Said it was surprise. And it was. After a couple of 'ours 'e comes back with drugs. 'eroin. I didn't want to upset 'im, but I told 'im I didn't want drugs in the 'ouse. I told 'im 'e shouldn't be messin' with that stuff, that 'e'd be straight back inside if the police caught 'im. 'e said it was good stuff, 'e could 'andle it, and just ignored me. 'e promised 'e wouldn't use in front of me or the kids. I didn't want no trouble. 'e had a bit of a temper, slapped me a couple of times, that's why I was in hospital. I s'pose I just got used to it.

"One night we put the kids to bed and got pretty drunk. It was nice to 'ave 'im 'ome, I enjoyed the comp'ny. I don't know why, the booze I suppose, and

I was 'appy, and so I tried some. 'eroin. Well, after that, I fell in pretty bad. 'ooked. I needed it all the time. I started thievin' to pay for it. Shopliftin'. Got caught a couple of times. 'e never did get a job. 'e 'ad me runnin' around tryin' to score, but then ..."

She suddenly stopped. Stella poured her a glass of water.

"'e, 'e sent me out to score most evenin's," she continued. "After the kids got back from school. I didn't think nothin' of it, I didn't think 'e was, was ..."

Again she stopped. Head bowed, she shook her head and drank some water.

"Are you alright to go on Sharon? We can take a break if you want."

"I'm OK," she replied, sniffling.

She drew in a long, deep breath.

"I felt like a fool. A failure. I didn't suspect nothin'. Especially *that*. 'e always 'ad money. I don't know where 'e got it. I didn't ask. But when 'e got home that day, 'e'd been drinkin'. 'e said I had to go across town to pick up some gear. 'e gave me an address and some money, and I left. But when I got to the bus stop I didn't 'ave me phone, so I went back."

Again, she paused.

"I thought 'e musta taken 'em out, to the park or somewhere. They wasn't in the front room watchin' telly like they normally do after school. I got me phone and was about to leave when I 'eard a noise upstairs. I thought it might be someone tryin' to rob us, so I waited, at the bottom of the stairs. That's when I 'eard Sara, cryin', not like she normally cries though. It was different. I goes up and looks in the girls' room, but they're not there. Then I 'ear them in our room. I open the door, and, and ..."

Sharon covered her face with her hands, and began weeping.

"'ow could've I been so stupid? There 'e was. With 'em. In our bed. Naked. The girls was cryin'. They looked at me. I ran in and grabbed 'em and ran downstairs. 'e shouted after me. 'e said it weren't what it looked like. But I know what I seen. I put the girls in the front room and closed the door, and when I 'eard him comin' down the stairs, I didn't know what to do, I was scared, panickin'. I don't know why, I really don't, but I ran in the kitchen and grabbed the breadknife. And, and, I just waited. And when I 'eard him comin', I didn't know what I might do, I really didn't. But then ... but then, 'e came into the kitchen, smiling, kept saying it weren't what it looked like. It was the way 'e kept smilin', saying I was bein' 'ysterical for no reason. But I know what I seen. And so when 'e comes towards me, I still don't know what to do, but then, then, it 'appened, I just did it, and it went in 'im so easy, and 'e dropped to the floor. And the blood. Loadsa blood, loads. I knew 'e was dead, and, and, I don't know, for a moment, it was like bein' in, in, I don't know, another world, like in a film. 'im dead on the floor, it was like it weren't real. I know I 'af to do time, I know that. But, but, I still think, I do, I still think, 'e got what 'e deserved."

"Sharon," Stella said, looking up from her notes. "Thank you for sharing this with me. I know how hard this is for you, but what you have told me this morning is invaluable. It gives me a solid starting point for building your defence. This is going to be a lengthy process, and so I think this is enough for now. I'll be back to see you many times before we go to court, unless we can come to some agreement before a trial. But we'll cross that bridge later. Here. Call anytime," she added, handing her a card. "Call me if you have any questions. Is there anything you want to tell me before I leave?"

"Can you find out where me kids are? I'd really like to see 'em, talk to 'em. Make sure they're OK. I'm really worried about 'em. Do you think …?"

"Sharon. Your girls are in safe hands. I've already checked with social services. They have both been seen by a doctor. They're perfectly healthy. They may have to go into foster families for a while, I'll call social services again and let you know. Call me tonight, I'll know more then. Perhaps we can even arrange a visit for them. Is that OK?"

Sitting in her car outside, Stella was thinking of previous visits to Bronzefield. Of all the *Sharons* she had represented. Again, for the best defence, she needed to be creative. Maybe start with formative years, her education. Like the hundreds and thousands of girls up and down the country excluded from mainstream schooling, at twelve she was placed in a *special* unit until sixteen, the last of her wilting childhood dreams suddenly crushed as the long and lonely grind of scraping through life on measly state benefits began, and from which there would be no escape.

The prosecution would most certainly dismiss such desperate circumstances. The focus solely on the murder itself. Nothing more. No compassion. No pity. Absolutely nothing to do with his sordid behaviour. Stella could already hear the prosecutor. "Your honour, it is the appellant on trial here, not the deceased." And yet the real deviant was the deceased.

6

Quite unlike most of the women Stella represented, she vaguely remembered Charlotte Cavendish from the flutter of media attention her case had received. In her early fifties, married for twenty-four years, she had two boys at university, Oxford and Cambridge. Surrounded by the capital's academics, artists, and media personalities, she resided in a comfortable six-bedroom Hampstead home. It appeared she had everything.

But for many years, in a marriage to a man she had slowly grown to detest, she hadn't been happy. In public, the perfect gentleman, in private, a brute, subjecting her to a cruel, humiliating indignity.

Now in custody, she already missed care-free mornings roaming the lush meadows and woodland of Hampstead Heath with Henry, her gentle Golden Labrador. She would miss bathing in its swimming ponds in summer months before meeting old friends for cocktails in upmarket brasseries in nearby Parliament Hill.

Cracks in the marriage had first appeared with the boys in secondary school. However, with the patient, stoic aplomb expected of members of her class, she had adjusted to what she considered a *new normal*. But gradually, things got worse. The drinking she tolerated. But the mocking, the taunts, the women, finally proved too much, and returning from a pleasant evening at the theatre, she crushed her husband's skull with a table lamp.

Charlotte and Sharon. Two women, two worlds apart, yet equal in the eyes of a criminal justice system indifferent to their individual circumstances, indifferent to all women.

In the waiting room of HMP Peterborough, Stella glanced back through the case notes. The *lazy* article in the *Evening Standard,* with the headline "Privileged, Educated but Gruesome Killer," annoyed her.

Suddenly, the door opened and Charlotte appeared. Smiling as she approached, she stretched her arm towards Stella and shook her hand.

"Well, I suppose I should inform you that I don't believe there's much hope for me," she began, light-heartedly, in clipped, plummy, private school accent. "Not even with the prestigious, often venerated Thomas & Taylor representing me I'm afraid."

"Mrs Cavendish, you're familiar with our firm?" Stella asked, surprised.

"Please, call me Charlotte. And yes, I'm very familiar with your firm. Many of my friends, ex-friends rather, have used your services. Thomas & Taylor is very well considered in certain circles."

"I'm happy to hear it."

"Have you come far?"

"London."

"I did a little research on you, your firm, rather. I dare say my case is a little different to your usual cases?" she asked.

"Yes, it is rather," Stella confessed.

"Well, I know you will have many questions, but perhaps I should begin. Some context may help," she said, sighing. "I have a law degree. From York. I never practised though. I met … Simon, my husband, in sixth form. And that was that really. We were a good fit, similar backgrounds, both families happy with the match. He was at Highgate, I was just around the corner at Queen Elizabeth's. Even when he went up to Oxford and I was in York, we met on weekends. Kept it going until we graduated and moved back to London. I suppose it was inevitable we'd marry. How could we not?"

"So you were happy then?"

"Yes. I think we were. Certainly for many years. As you can imagine, in here, with time on my hands so to speak, I've been trying to pinpoint the cracks, think about how, where it all went wrong. Our families, friends, always described us as the perfect couple. Mother used to call us unsinkable, like the Titanic. But even in the early years of the marriage, perhaps, the cracks were there. Minor incursions. Like in most marriages. *Irregularities* in his behaviour. But I was busy. The boys were, still are, my world. Simon, working in the city, investment banking, we were all well aware of the rumours. The drinking, the women. I chose to ignore them. Like I say, I stayed focused on the boys. With little to keep us interested in each other, well, like the Titanic, the marriage hit a bloody big rock."

"Mrs Cavendish …"

"Charlotte, please. No doubt this will be the first of many exchanges. We can forego formalities."

"Yes, sorry. Charlotte, you said you have spent a lot of time reflecting on how things began to, to …"

"*Dwindle* is perhaps the word you are looking for.

Yes, it's true, I have. But I must say, unlike my husband's demise, the break-up of our marriage was, perhaps, certainly at first, let's say, subtle. No *lipstick on the collar* moments, only plenty of *working late* excuses. And weekends away. But I managed, kept myself busy, and apart from my ultimate transgression, I still feel that I wasn't failing as a wife. I did what I promised at the altar. Lord, I wasn't about to beat *myself* up. How many women do that? And I had no intention of spicing up the marriage with sexy little numbers from Ann Summers. Or a boob job. Good God, no. None of that nonsense. Besides, always crystal clear in my mind, is that it was *his* behaviour that became intolerable. But ..."

"Go on. But?" Stella prompted.

"But, well, I still don't know why I bother trying to pinpoint exactly *when* things began to slide. When the boys left home, it certainly got worse. Perhaps, then. Yes, perhaps then began the slow hollowing out of my life.

"On the advice of a friend, I saw a therapist. Only the once. More out of curiosity really. In town, Harley Street. Highly recommended. He was nice, polite, empathetic even. But, for some strange reason, I don't know why, I would have been happier talking to a woman. You see, I think that what I was feeling, what I had experienced, *was* experiencing, complex feelings, sometimes impossible to put into words, I think are feelings few, if any, men understand.

In that first, and last, meeting, I held nothing back. Full disclosure. Told him everything. I tried to describe that feeling, the strange, singular feeling lodged inside me. So difficult to describe. Abandonment, or loneliness perhaps. Always with me, even when I was with friends. A sense of, maybe, *emptiness*. But, ultimately, I think what I was really feeling was betrayal.

"With such a detailed confession, I thought he might offer me some insight. Advice on how I might deal with what I was feeling. But he said the most likely cause was menopause. I was *not* impressed. Quite frankly, it felt like a lazy diagnosis. A woman reaches a certain age and then, bang, anything remotely concerning in her life, any worry, voila! - menopause. I didn't, and still don't rule out that it may have had some impact on me physically, but not for a moment did I believe then, or now, it affected the way I viewed my husband's behaviour. Then he added I might have a mild form of depression. Really? What *is* that exactly? Mild depression? Women are well aware of the ups and downs in life. We all feel a little low at times, and yes, even mildly depressed. That's just part of being human. But I had a life outside of the home, outside of the marriage. I met friends regularly. We went into town, to the theatre, to talks at the British Library, the British Museum. No, I had quite the buoyant, interesting life. But ..."

"But?"

"Well, then I had to go home ..."

Drawing in a long, resigned breath, she gazed directly at Stella.

"Well, enough about me. I suppose we should talk about my husband. His, his, behaviour."

"Behaviour?"

"Yes. The reason why I'm here talking to you. His betrayal."

"You feel he betrayed you?"

"Yes, I do. I suppose when people marry, they never talk about the changes that come as they get older. About how they will, ultimately, grow apart. The boys were in school, his business flourishing, breaking into new markets, he was often away. Sometimes for up to a week or two. I had school events, PTA, parents' evenings, our lives had become *functional*. Did I think anything amiss? Of course I did. An attractive, young, middle-aged man with money. Many of my friends were in similar situations. Inevitably, talk revolved around our husbands when we met, endless carping about adulterous men, each meeting a rerun of the one before. All of us, bright, educated women. And yet, no-one ever dared mention that bloody giant elephant in the room. That we'd been conned. We'd fallen hook, line and sinker into the trap of defining ourselves by the men we married.

"It soon grew too tiresome. I withdrew. Cancelled engagements. Timely as it turns out. A couple of close friends were spiralling out of control. Drink, prescription drugs, endless therapy sessions. I've always considered myself strong, mentally. Even when I knew my marriage was on its last legs, I was thinking long term about what I might do after the inevitable split. Travel. Writing, perhaps. It's what I wanted. I even began looking forward to moving on with my life.

"Even now, even after killing him, I consider

myself a rational, balanced woman. Why? Because I've asked myself if I could have done things differently, would I? And I'm not sure I would. You see, above all, despite having committed the most barbaric human transgression, I had to maintain a certain level of dignity, respect. I just had to. Without that, what would I have?"

With innumerable cases as precedents, defence lawyers have many options for building a robust defence for a man. However, it's relatively rare for a woman to kill a man, but when they do, few cases reach trial. Out of court settlement is the norm, and rarely in the best interest of the woman. And motives for women killing men vary enormously. The prosecution would invariably claim Charlotte was jealous, after her husband's money. Or both. In response, Stella would have to provide for the court compelling reasons why Charlotte killed her husband, she would need a strategic *way in*, a credible alternative. Looking down at her notes, she circled the words 'dignity' and 'respect.'

"Charlotte. Are you OK to continue? You don't have to rehash everything at once. I'll be coming again."

"No. I'm fine. Thankyou. I'd like to go on. Perhaps …"

"Perhaps?"

"Well, it may sound absurd, but perhaps there was a moment. When I knew there was no way back. That our marriage was irredeemable."

"Go on."

"On the face of it, certainly for him, it was quite an

insignificant act. But not for me. A s*leight*. I guess that's the word for it. A *sleight* that still weighs heavily in me."

Stella poured her some water.

"It was about six years ago. The boys were still at home. Such an impressionable age. A friend mentioned something that many teenage boys were looking at on the internet. 'Revenge porn.' It sounded horrendous. I looked it up and was horrified to think that my boys might be looking at such sordid material. I didn't want them growing up viewing women, thinking of them as, as something *other*. As their mother, as a woman, it was important for me to give them a *balanced* view of how they should behave. How they should view girls and women. Neither had girlfriends at the time, but as teenagers, they were certainly thinking of girls. I had a duty to provide, I don't know, some direction, about how they should behave around girls. I didn't want their opinions shaped by pornography. I decided to talk to Simon, but he infuriated me, bluntly dismissing my concern, saying it's something "all boys do."

"It was around this time that he became uncommunicative, moody. It was like having another child at home. We argued a lot, I genuinely began to worry about the changes in him. He had become so *different*. His personality. His character. So different from the man I married. I tried talking to him, I even suggested he consider professional help. Which, clearly, was a mistake. He turned, looked at me, and from the rage, the fury I saw in his eyes, I thought he was going to hit me. But, quite possibly, what he said was more painful. "Fuck you," he roared, and stormed out.

"He'd never sworn at me before. Fortunately the boys weren't there. That would have been unforgivable. I felt very protective of them. But one evening, they were at home, in their rooms. We had the most blazing row, loud, it's impossible that they didn't hear it. Things had quietened down, and an hour or so later, we were in the sitting room as if nothing had happened. I was watching television, Simon, as usual, was tapping away on his laptop.

"We often used to have tea in the evenings when the children were in bed. I thought perhaps when he left the room and I heard him in the kitchen making tea, this was his way of easing the tension still simmering between us. As I listened to the clink of the spoons in cups, the pop of the biscuit jar, I remember thinking, I might have even smiled to myself, that still, there were flashes of kindness in the man I married.

"But he returned to the room with only one cup. He didn't look at me. He didn't say anything, just slumped back into the chair and tapped away, occasionally slurping his tea. He knew what he was doing. And I knew what he was saying. Something so simple spoke volumes. I didn't sign up for that."

Charlotte sipped some water.

"From that point on we lived separate lives. As best we could, we avoided each other. It was awkward, but I made sure, for the sake of the boys, we kept things afloat. I still didn't think that he hated me. That's too strong a word. But I sensed in him a certain dislike of me. Irritable, arrogant, yes, but the ability to hate? Me?

Or anyone. I didn't think so. I could never have married a man with hate in his heart. Women see these things. We know. Well, that's what I thought.

"One day the boys were waiting for him to take them to cricket practice. I usually took them, but my car was in the garage. We'd talked the night before and he'd agreed to take them. So, when he didn't show up, I called and left a message. He arrived fifteen minutes later, fuming, screaming that I should have put them in a taxi. As the boys crept into the back of the car, they must have heard what he called me. I still hear it, even now," she said, pausing to draw in a deep breath.

As if praying, head bowed, she sat in silent reflection.

"What did he call you?" Stella whispered.

"He called me a fucking selfish bitch. Then he got into the car and sped off. Never, not even when he was furious, had I heard him use that word before. And in front of the boys. I went inside and cried. I just didn't know what to do, where to turn. He said it with such, such, bitterness. And in front of the boys. There was simply no way of undoing something like that. Such venom. Such disgust, towards me. His wife. And in front of the boys. Perhaps that was the moment. A cliff edge of sorts. Yes, that might have been the moment …"

"Charlotte. I know it's no small comfort, but in most cases I deal with, men use this word interchangeably with the word *woman*," Stella offered. "From what you say, it's clear family was no longer central to his life. These changes - do you think there was, possibly, another woman involved?"

Charlotte drank some water and looked out through the window.

"Not *one* woman. Many," she added, pausing.

"Charlotte. We can continue another day if you wish. Clearly this has been very harrowing."

"No. No, we've come this far. I may as well get it all out now," she insisted. "The women. Yes, there were women. I knew about them simply because he didn't keep them hidden. Sometimes I heard him on the phone, making arrangements. No doubt they were younger, prettier, smilier. Like I say, for quite some time, we had been living separately. He was in one of the guest bedrooms. Some nights he came in very late. Sometimes, he didn't come home at all. I didn't ask questions. The boys knew something had happened between us. Neither, bless them, said a thing. I tried to assure them that all parents squabble, our rows, nothing serious. I only ever wanted to protect them. But the atmosphere at home must have had *some* effect on them. But, listen to me!" she suddenly exclaimed, falling back into the chair. "Me worried that our arguments would harm them! When they finally escape two insane parents, when they finally have their adult lives to look forward to, in cold blood, their mother murders their father."

"Have they been in touch?"

"I'm not sure I can face them yet. I sent them a message - that I needed time before I could talk. I'm sure they'll understand. They'll come and see me. Once it's all sunk in."

"Other women you say?"

85

"Yes. Many. Like I say, he made no effort to conceal them. He took them to dinner in the village. To restaurants we used to go. Word soon got back. But even then I didn't feel jealous. I no longer wanted him. I tried not to but, I guess, subconsciously, I was growing to despise him. When James, our youngest, went off to university, I thought we'd come to some agreement about how best to go our separate ways. I wouldn't contest anything. I just wanted out. A new start. To part in a dignified way. That was the plan."

"You frequently mention dignity?"

"Well, what does a person have if she doesn't have her dignity? And values."

"Values?"

"We came from warm, loving families, we had the best possible start in life. Private school education. Summers in the south of France. Yes, values. Hard work. Family. Kindness. Reliability. Family values, conservative values. I thought we had these in common. Coming from such privileged, similar families, I thought we shared values, values that had shaped us and that would shape our boys' lives. And, then, suddenly …"

"… suddenly it's gone?" Stella said.

"Yes. Stella, I hope you don't mind me asking, but are you married?"

Momentarily surprised, Stella considered if the question had any bearing on the defence.

"Yes. I am. Happily so."

"To a man?"

"Yes."

"Do you trust him? Completely? Can you depend

on him?"

"I can and I do. We must push on though."

"Yes. Sorry. Forgive me. Anyway, once the boys had left for university, he became devious, insidious. Cruel even."

"How so?"

Charlotte closed her eyes and drew in another deep breath.

"He became even more reckless. Drinking more heavily. I think he had a drinking problem. But I daren't say a thing. And he started talking to himself. And then the motorbike. What happens to men mid-life I wondered? Such an awful noise. Neighbours complained. He kept revving it up, it drove me crazy. But he knew what he was doing. He enjoyed upsetting me. Was it something I had done? No! Absolutely not! I had lived up to my promises. I had given up the opportunity of a promising career to raise a family. And though I had opportunities, I didn't take lovers. Like I said, I lived by what I thought were a shared set of values. But, for some unimaginable reason, he was doing everything in his power to destroy them. To destroy everything we had built together."

"What else did he do?"

"Well, let's just fast-forward to the night in question, shall we?"

Charlotte looked at Stella with a steely gaze.

"If you feel up to it."

"I'd had a very nice evening. My best friend, Margo, had taken me into the West End to see a show. She is - was - my closest confidant. I imagine you'll want to talk to her as well."

Stella nodded.

"Well, he'd never brought a woman into our home. I think he knew that that would be a step too far. But he did the next best thing. I'd suspected for some time he was looking at pornography online. Perhaps why he was so dismissive when I mentioned the boys might be watching it. How did I know? Well, sometimes, I heard *noises* coming from his room. I didn't care. I really didn't. But I wanted nothing to do with that side of his increasingly sordid behaviour. Yes, sordid. I'm quite sure he had begun to use women. Escorts, prostitutes, never at home though. As long as he kept them hidden, I got on with life. But things were building to some sort of climax. I don't mean that I was planning anything, certainly not murder. No, that had *never* crossed my mind. No, I suppose I had just accepted that, on his part, there was nothing in our marriage worthy of resurrection. Our ashes well and truly blown to the winds - no phoenix rising for us. So, I sent him an email. I wanted a divorce."

"And he agreed?"

"On the contrary. I waited all day for a response. None came. Before I left for the theatre that evening, I asked him if he had received the email. He said that he had…"

She stopped and sighed deeply.

"… and that I could, I could, well, go and fuck myself. I was quite shaken. I genuinely thought he might see this as a way out. A way to get on with his life. And let me get on with mine."

"So there was no email response?" Stella asked,

thinking of evidence.

"No, none. On the way home from the theatre, Margo suggested I stay at hers. But I thought it best to tackle this head on, try to reason with him.

"The kitchen lights were off when I went in. On the island, his laptop. Open. No sound, just shadows flickering on the wall. He'd left it there deliberately, for me to see it. Pornography."

"A deliberate act of provocation."

"I have no doubt. He wanted to hurt me. I think he really *wanted* me to suffer. I'd sent the email in the hope of reaching a civil, agreeable conclusion. Why he didn't just agree to a divorce I still don't understand. But the laptop was there for me to see. Intentionally. To hurt me."

"So then what did you do?"

"Well, that was a step too far. I needed to let him know I wouldn't be subjected to such unacceptable vulgarity. As I climbed the stairs, again, I heard noises coming from under the door of the guest room. Groaning, panting. In my room the light was on. I'd turned it out before leaving so I knew he'd been in there. But then, what really scared me, I realised the noises were coming from my room, not his. I thought he was in there. Slowly, I opened the door. There, on my bed, another laptop. Open. Pornography. I slammed it shut and stormed into his room. He was sitting up in bed, reading, as if he was expecting me, a menacing smirk on his face. 'Just what are you playing at?' I asked. He closed the book and placed it casually on the bedside table next to the lamp. Yawning, he said that he'd had a long day. I should leave. Then he switched off the light, rolled over, and mumbled into his pillow.

"What did he say?"

"I'm sure he said, 'Are you still here?' I felt so humiliated. He pulled the covers up and nestled into the pillow. And then I heard him laugh. I don't know why, or what, I really don't, but something, deep inside of me, just snapped. Even now when I think about it, it still feels so, so surreal, I can only imagine it in slow motion. Lifting the heavy marble lamp, so heavy, even then, I didn't know what I might do with it. But then he said it again. 'Are you still here?' And he laughed. In that moment, I just, I don't know, I just seemed to implode, and brought the lamp down as hard as I could, and continued to hit him, I just couldn't seem to stop, there was blood everywhere, but I kept on hitting him, again, and again, and again, I don't know how many times, until, until I was exhausted. And, I suppose, that was that," she added, exhaling loudly.

Stella brought the meeting to a close. Musing over her notes in her car, like Sharon, it appeared Charlotte had acted in a moment of extreme fury. But no premeditation. She hadn't intended to kill him. Yet such circumstantial evidence would be of little use in court. The odds were stacked against both women. Here again, a justice system indifferent to what happened to Charlotte and Sharon. Of indifference to all women.

Stella needed to be creative.

7

A self-proclaimed show-off in the kitchen, Colin couldn't decide what to serve Celia and Sara, their dinner guests on Saturday evening. Stella solved his dilemma after a midweek lunch date with Celia at an American diner in Covent Garden. Looking at the gaudy American razzmatazz - flags, bumper stickers, number plates from various states - splattered across the walls, she had an idea.

"What do you miss most about home?" she asked Celia.

"These days, not a whole lot. But I do miss the food. Southern food. Grits, biscuits - the American kind, sweet potato, the taste of the Deep South. And I miss my momma's fried okra."

That afternoon, Stella emailed Colin, suggesting an American-themed evening. A southern feast. Immediately receptive to the challenge, Colin drew up a list of ingredients, and over breakfast Saturday morning, visibly excited, he revealed his carefully-researched menu for the evening.

"For the main course," he bristled, "pan-fried chicken, black-eyed peas and mashed sweet potatoes. They like side dishes so I'll make cornbread, okra, fried green tomatoes and macaroni and cheese. And I'm going to try buttermilk biscuits. Celia will think she's back in Atlanta. Oh yes, and tea, iced tea."

"They put ice in their tea?" Stella asked.

"Yes, Yanks put ice in everything. And for dessert? I'm thinking a pie. They like their pies in the south. I thought about pecan, peach, or maybe pumpkin. But I've gone for a cobbler. It's Georgia, the Peach State, we'll have Peach Cobbler! Here's what I'll need," he said, handing Stella the list.

As she was getting ready to leave, Stella heard a deep, booming drawl coming from the kitchen where she found Colin scribbling away as he watched a YouTube video of a wholesome, cheery chef, slowly stirring what looked like semolina in a bowl. "Grits are key to world peace," he joked, "just give the inhabitants of planet Earth a daily portion of grits and they'll have nothing to fight about. A man full of grits is a man of peace."

"What on earth are grits?" Stella asked.

"Well," Colin replied, "as you can see - some sort of sloppy corn porridge. Apparently in southern states they're a symbol of identity, the source of fierce regional pride. And, I might add, the official food of Georgia."

Insisting he give it a go, Colin took the list from Stella and added cornmeal.

"When you get back, you can try the tea, sweet tea," he said excitedly. "A humble classic of the south. And I've downloaded a playlist. Southern classics, musicians from Georgia. Ray Charles' *Georgia on My Mind*, Randy Crawford's *Rainy Night in Georgia*. I've got this. All I need is the food."

Stella found all the ingredients, including fresh okra and sweet potatoes, at a stall specialising in American classics in Borough Market. On her return, she dropped the bags on the kitchen counter and wished Colin good luck.

That afternoon, while he toiled in the kitchen, she skimmed through Charlotte's case notes. Problematic, annoying even, the elegantly-worded confession. Blind faith in the law would do her no favours. She would encourage her to retract it.

But with little appetite for work, Stella closed the file and switched on the news. She liked the reporter, a no-nonsense woman who asked blunt, probing questions, on this occasion, managing a spat between a seasoned Labour MP and a fresh-faced Tory. She interrupted their bickering with a question about the alarming increase in domestic abuse killings during lockdown, a rise from two to five women a week murdered.

Stella often thought back to those surreal, early weeks of the pandemic when calls to helplines and online services for at-risk women rocketed. Both politicians responded with words like 'sad' and 'unfortunate,' the Tory toeing the party line, issuing a nervous flurry of poorly-scripted rhetoric - that the government had "invested more in the last ten years than at any time." His Labour counterpart scoffed, calling it "pure invention," yet failed to elaborate on what his party would do.

Stella switched the TV off.

***

That evening, Colin opened the door draped in a stars and stripes apron. Celia shrieked with delight as they entered to Ray Charles' *Georgia on My Mind*, barely able to contain herself when she saw in the dining room the table laden with southern delights from her childhood. Over dinner she declared the food exceptional. Especially the fried chicken, and the okra, deep fried in flour, "just like momma's."

Once praise of Colin's culinary skills had subsided, Sara enquired how the pandemic had affected life at UCL.

"Well, we're certainly in a transition period. Virtual learning it appears is the future. Many courses are now only offered remotely online, the older staff dread it. Some have even taken early retirement. I suppose the greatest concern after lockdown is funding. Most universities get a good chunk of their funding from overseas students, their numbers have dropped sharply, and though they're picking up, not nearly the numbers from before the pandemic. So we're expanding our networking, reinvigorating overseas trade so to speak. For promotion purposes, we're talking about potential trips to China, India, maybe even the States. Basically, to those countries with the strongest economies. I'll know more in a couple of weeks. We'll learn of how desperate the situation really is at the UCAS conference in Manchester. There's even talk of the academic year starting in January. Mind blowing," he said, smirking, getting to his feet. "OK. I'll leave you ladies to it. But, before I go, coffee, anyone?"

Stella had just opened a bottle of wine, they declined, and so he bid them goodnight.

"Stella," Celia said, a little tipsy, slipping into a familiar southern drawl. "You lucked out there, honey. Good-looking, kind, great cook. The girl did good!"

"No more wine for you," piped in Sara, smiling.

"All OK between you hon?" Celia added.

"Yeah, yeah. Everything's fine. It really is … except …"

Stella paused, swirling the wine in her glass.

"Except that, I don't know, sometimes, he can be a little, what's the word?"

"*Distant*?" Celia offered.

"Perhaps. *Suspicious* isn't the right word. Maybe, *elusive*. Yes, maybe that's the word. *Elusive*."

"*Elusive*? In what way?" Sara asked.

"I don't know really. We're a couple, we do well together, very well. Yet, sometimes, I just feel like there's something missing. It's hard to explain. He probably thinks the same, that I'm the *elusive* one. And, sometimes, I am. Especially when we have a lot of work on. Like now. And, and, sometimes, I just feel he's a little too inquisitive about cases I'm working on. He knows I can't discuss them in great detail. He can't help it though, he's just … interested, I suppose. But he does like to … pry."

"Stella," Celia said. "You got a good one there, hon. You're just overthinking things. He shows interest. That's gotta be a good thing. And with the greatest of respect, I think much of what you're talking about here is, well, him just being a man. My daddy, he rarely spoke to momma. He was what you might call *distant*, or *elusive*. I call it *secretive*. That's just how some men are. They have secrets, insecurities. Which, I guess, gives us our careers."

"I know, I know. He is good," Stella replied. "And

he knows me well. Too well sometimes. Anyway, enough about Colin. Tell me, do you have any summer plans?"

"Well, now that you ask. Yes, we do," Sara said.

"We do?" Celia asked, turning and looking at her quizzically.

"Stella," Sara added, smiling, "this evening of southern delicacies couldn't have come at a better time," she said, turning her gaze on Celia. "I just booked flights to Atlanta this afternoon. We're off to see the mother-in-law!"

"You did?" Celia said, beaming at her. "Thanks hon," and leaning over, kissed Sara's cheek.

"That's great. How old is your mother now?" Stella asked.

"She's ninety. Fit as a fiddle. Still drives. Still going strong."

"That's great."

"How about you guys?" Celia asked.

"Well, we've been thinking about Corsica. Apparently, lots to do, real Mediterranean buzz. Colin's very keen, been doing lots of research. Apparently Napoléon was born there! Good food, excellent wine, beautiful beaches. Sounds about perfect. Talking of wine, can I top you up?"

"No, no, we must be getting on," Sara said, getting to her feet, tugging Celia's sleeve. "Stella, this has been so, so nice. Thank you so much. It's our turn next time."

"That okra," Celia said. "Just so, so fine. Reminded me of when I was a girl. Be sure to thank Colin. And when you guys come over, I'm gonna return the favour - make some of the Yorkshire Puddings y'all adore," she added, laughing.

After clearing the table, Stella loaded the dishwasher, poured a glass of wine, and at the kitchen table, opened Charlotte's case file. Circled in her notes, a solitary word. *Mariticide*. Killing a husband. Beside it, a question: why do women kill? Below the question, a list of possible motives.

Money? Even if Charlotte had come out of a divorce settlement badly, she had her own resources, family money. Love? She no longer loved him. She wanted a divorce. Jealousy? She had turned a blind eye to other women. She wasn't vindictive.

She'd also circled the word, *values*. Charlotte had talked passionately about shared values. Hard work, family, love, kindness, reliability. Values central to her life, the building blocks of their marriage, all of which he had wilfully abandoned. A starting point for a defence, perhaps?

***

First thing Monday morning, Stella arranged with social services for Sharon's children to visit their mother in prison. Until lunchtime, she reviewed Charlotte's case, growing increasingly confident that she should build her defence on what she had said about "shared values."

Passing a sandwich bar on her way to Covent Garden for lunch, someone tapped the window. Moments later, Colin met her outside.

"Where are you off to?" he asked.

"To get lunch in Covent Garden."

"Come on in. Join us, I'm with Maria. I think you met her once when you stopped by the office."

How could Stella not remember Maria? Young, early twenties, Spanish. Striking eyes. Perfect skin, small hands. Adorable.

Colin joined the queue and Stella sat down opposite Maria.

"Lovely to see you again Maria," she began, wondering momentarily if Colin was seducing her. "You're looking very well. How are you?"

"I'm very well thank you. So happy the pandemic is over."

"Aren't we all. What a nightmare that was. Spain was hit hard I believe. All your family are fine?"

"Yes, thank you. We are from a small village, Sagunto, just outside Valencia. My parents are fine. They live in the countryside. I think the big cities, Madrid, Barcelona, they suffered most."

"I'm glad to hear your family are fine. How is work going? Colin doesn't work you too hard I hope," she said, jokingly.

Maria smiled.

"Colin is the perfect boss. He is very easy-going," Maria said, smiling, just as he returned.

"Was that my name I heard being denigrated?" he asked, placing before Stella on a small tray, a bottle of sparkling water and salad.

"Maria was just telling me what a monster you are. A proper micromanager - unsmiling, lacking in any form of charisma or social skills, and next to no understanding of leadership or the fragility of the human condition. Yes, quite the monster," Stella replied, smiling, winking at Maria.

"Oh no! My cover's blown! Maria - you're fired!" Colin replied, laughing. "Stella, did Maria tell you her good news?"

His eyes shifted towards her stomach.

"Are you …?"

"Yes. Six months."

"Congratulations. You must be excited?"

"Thank you. We are very excited. We have just bought our first home. I think we are ready. My mother will come and stay when the baby arrives. Yes, we are all very excited."

"So you're busy feathering the nest?" asked Stella.

The metaphor left Maria baffled.

"You're decorating your home," Colin piped in.

"Yes, yes. It is very hard work. We have the upstairs almost ready. Downstairs is still too messy. But that reminds me, we are painting this weekend. We need, how do you say in English, the tape to cover things you do not want to paint? I must buy it."

"Masking tape?" Stella replied.

"Yes. This is it. Thank you. Stella, it was lovely to see you again," she said, getting to her feet. "Colin, I see you back at the office."

"Lovely to see you Maria. Don't let him work you too hard!"

As Stella ate, Colin returned to the queue for coffees.

"There you go," he said moments later. "Flat White. No sugar."

"Thanks. Maria's very nice."

"Yes. A real sweetie. She only came to London for a month, to learn English. But then she met James. Investment banker. She did well worming her way in there."

"That's a bit harsh. *Worming* her way in. Is that what we women do to men? Worm our way in? Looks like it's James who won the lottery," Stella said.

Colin changed the subject.

"Busy morning?"

"Intense."

She sensed he was waiting for details.

"It's the case I mentioned," she continued, "rich woman. Hampstead. Bludgeoned her husband to death."

"Why?"

"Well, that's what I'm working on. More frustratingly, she doesn't appear to know either. Yet. It happened in what appears to be a moment of *insanity*."

"It happens."

"What do you mean, it happens?" Stella asked, looking up at him.

"You read about it all the time, women killing their husbands. There are programmes on television, dramas."

"The reality is that it's very rare for a woman to kill her husband. Normally it's the man killing the wife."

"I suppose you're right. So, not much hope for her then?"

"Well, she confessed. That doesn't help matters. She'll have to serve time. I'm trying to work out how to reduce the charge. From first degree murder to manslaughter. That should halve her time."

"What was he like?"

"For the most part, a very good provider. Oxbridge. Fancy house. Nice holidays. Private schooling for the kids, boys, two. But once they'd flown the nest, he became a prick, going off the rails. Women. Staying out. Very much your male midlife crisis. He got quite nasty towards the end."

"Did he hit her?"

"No. As men are wont to do, he just tormented the shit out of her," she said firmly, touching his hand, adding, "present company excepted. You'd never torment me, would you?"

"And I thought I did! God, I'm going to have to up my game here! We're still relatively young - plenty of time to show you how big, bad and mad I can be!" he responded, playfully.

"OK Hannibal, calm down. Listen, I best get back. Any ideas for dinner?"

"I've got it covered. Call me on your way home and I'll have it ready."

Sitting on a bench in Lincoln's Inn Field, Stella was thinking of Charlotte's case. It was all about evidence. Nothing more. Cases failed in both Crown Court and Courts of Appeal due to insufficient evidence. The prosecution would ignore the years of mental abuse. They would paint her as the vindictive, jealous wife, killing her husband because he slept with other women. Stella wanted to present the *bigger picture,* drive home extenuating circumstances, show that Charlotte wasn't solely responsible for the crime. Perhaps even point to her as the victim? But this required irrefutable, ironclad evidence. What she needed was an expert witness.

**

Celia suggested that Stella contact trusted forensic social worker, Dr. Waters. A little eccentric, but a brilliant mind, playfully referred to as Dr. Google by many of the firm's solicitors. Stella sent him an email, his swift response proposing they meet that afternoon.

As she made her way to Dr. Waters' office, uppermost in her mind was Charlotte's confession, and possible ways of limiting its impact. And she wasn't happy with the responses she'd given in the questionnaire that all inmates entering prison for the first time must complete, specifically the question alluding to 'abnormality of the mind.' In strange surroundings, under such grossly unreliable conditions and with insufficient time to reflect on her actions, she had ticked the box declaring herself of sound mind. Still dealing with the trauma of killing her husband, she clearly wasn't. Stella hoped Dr. Waters would conduct a reassessment.

"Thanks for seeing me so quickly Dr. Waters," Stella said, shaking his hand.

She glanced around the room at files heaped on window-sills and in piles along walls.

"I know, I know - looks like a tip, but I can assure you I know where everything is. And please, call me Allan. A pleasure to meet you Stella. And do take a seat. Would you like tea? Coffee? Water?"

"No thank you, I'm fine," Stella replied, sitting

down.

"Well Stella, I've taken a quick look through Charlotte's notes you sent, and I see your dilemma. Clearly, the confession doesn't help. This, at present, is our major hurdle."

Stella nodded.

"I suspect you're going for damage limitation here?"

"Yes, I think that's the best option," she replied. "I'm looking to reduce the plea to manslaughter. That's where I thought *you* might be able to help. Perhaps you can assess her? She's been through hell, and unless we can do something about the confession, the prosecution will steamroll her. When I first met her, I don't know, there's something I can't quite put my finger on, just something about her. An innocence perhaps. I see it in a lot of women. I want to show that what she did was a direct result of the torment she suffered. She doesn't deserve to disappear, possibly for the rest of her life for just, for just, I don't know, having nowhere else to turn. She just snapped. So much shit, so many years. It just doesn't seem ..."

"Fair?" Dr. Waters said.

"Yes. Fair. Do you think you can help?"

"Well, I can certainly try. Send me the completed case file over and I'll take a look. Then I'll get up to Peterborough next week to assess her. Stella, I understand your frustration. With us, men, I mean. Though we may appear rather one dimensional, Luddite even, we are complex apes. Did you know that the expression the 'fair sex' also used to refer to men as well as women? The bard himself, in Hamlet,

103

a tad long in my opinion, when he questions the ghost of Hamlet, describes Horatio as 'fair.' "Who art thou that usurp'st this time of night together with that *fair* and warlike form in which the majesty of buried Denmark did sometimes march? By heaven, I charge thee, speak!

"Oh dear, listen to me. Stella, do forgive me. My point, what was I saying? Oh, men, yes, that's right, and fair. Dear me, I do get myself in a muddle sometimes! I suppose what I might be trying to say is that, as we both know, men can be wretched, cruel, and unfortunately, murderous. Perhaps it's those secrets we toy with deep down that drive us mad. Who knows? Stella, forgive my babbling, I digress, a character flaw I hope not too bothersome. Where was I? Oh, yes, once I've met Charlotte, I'll send you my evaluation. Leave it with me. I'm in court all this week. Next week? Yes, I'll pop up next week to assess her. In the meantime, from what I've read so far, I'd probably consider coercive control. I think that's your best bet."

Only a few years old, the Coercive Control Act had come into law as a direct result of men "threatening, humiliating, intimidating and abusing women in any way so as to harm, punish, or frighten them." As in Charlotte's case, the abuser is usually known, often intimate, and behaves in a terrifying manner which leaves the victim emotionally fragile, and in most cases, totally defeated. In dealing with the incredibly complex power dynamics seen in coercively controlling relationships, antiquated Common law had proven toothless, and so hearing Dr. Waters advise a strategy similar to what she had been thinking, Stella felt confident about building a solid defence.

8

Dr. Waters emailed Stella on the Friday morning Colin left for the UCAS conference in Manchester. He had been to see Charlotte and, as he suspected, believed she had been subjected to serious emotional abuse, coercive control the main contributing factor. He also agreed that her confession had been taken under duress. In his opinion, she was not of "sound mind" and so he would make a return visit for a further, more comprehensive assessment.

An email from Celia provided details of the monthly gathering of the firm's solicitors in a city restaurant the following evening. Always a boozy night, she anticipated the inevitable hangover on Sunday, and so spent Saturday working on Charlotte's case.

At midday, she paused for a light lunch of soup and fresh sourdough bread she had bought that morning at the market. Unable to find the breadknife, with a serrated steak knife she cut off two uneven slices and squeezed them into the toaster. After lunch, she worked until five o' clock then began preparations for dinner that evening. As the tub filled, she scrolled through her phone for the music she always listened to in the bath.

In their final session before Stella moved to London, Dr Bergeron gave her a Nina Simone CD. "Simone had her own design for living," she said, and that "all women understood her roar." Also a fan, Celia had seen her in concert. Germaine Greer described her as "constant inspiration whose music provided evidence that female genius is real." Stella had since downloaded all of her albums, and so with that alluring, raspy melody echoing all around her, she slid slowly into the warm water.

Dinner that evening at a quiet Lebanese restaurant in the city involved lots of wine. Various rounds of shots followed, resulting in festivities continuing on a dancefloor of a gay club below Tottenham Court Road station. Stella stumbled out onto the street at three-thirty and hailed a taxi, waking on the sofa fully clothed the following morning, head throbbing.

At around midday she received a text from Celia. Its main gist - enquiry into the severity of her hangover, but also attached, a BBC link. Stella opened it and read of a story just breaking - the murder of a woman in Norfolk. She switched on the news, and from a country lane on the outskirts of Norwich, a woman provided details.

"An apparently random, fatal stabbing just outside Norwich took place last night here in this quiet lane at approximately ten-thirty. Not far from the popular Dunston Hall Hotel on the Ipswich Road, this stunning wooded parkland the most unlikely setting for such a gruesome act. The young woman, in her early twenties, walking her dog, lived nearby. Detectives from the Specialist Crime Unit leading the investigation, along with the Norfolk Constabulary, are urgently appealing to the public for help in tracking down the man responsible for this senseless murder. Anyone with information that may lead to the man's identity should contact them. They are keeping an open mind as to any motive for the attack, and as yet unable to release details other than to say the woman died from multiple stab wounds. Next of kin have been informed. The police are not currently linking the murder to other investigations, but first on the scene, and with me here now, Detective Inspector Yvette Marshall from Specialist Crime Command. What can you tell us so far about the investigation?"

"Well, clearly a pointless act of violence. We'll be working tirelessly to identify and apprehend the very dangerous man responsible for this despicable killing. I'd like to appeal to members of the public to contact the police if they have information, or if they knew the victim. Forensics are on site and police are conducting door-to-door enquiries. All help, no matter how insignificant may be of importance, so please contact us."

Stella called Celia.

"Hi Celia. I've just seen the report of the murder in Norwich. What's the connection?"

"The Miller case you're working on. We think there's a link. Well, we're pretty sure."

"The detective just said it's not linked to other cases."

"Yes, I know. DI Marshall, Yvette, the detective you saw on the news, the chief investigator, she's a friend. She called this morning. She's familiar with the Miller case and thinks there are very striking similarities. She wants to dig a little deeper before making any public announcement."

"What sort of links?"

"The Norwich murder has a similar MO to the

Miller case. Except for strangulation."

"Did he cut her?"

"Yes. But it's what he cut. The word *bitch* into her back. As in the Miller case. If for no other reason than to eliminate it from the investigation, Yvette wants to see if there is a connection."

"A copycat?"

"No, we don't think so, it's a bit too early to tell. Few details of the Miller case have been released. Can you go and meet her, Yvette, in Norwich, tomorrow?"

***

That afternoon, Stella strolled through the winding paths of Hampstead Heath. She stopped in a familiar, secluded spot, spread out a blanket and pulled from her bag a short story she'd read many years before in secondary school. For a writer best known for children's literature, Roald Dahl's *Lamb to the Slaughter* explores the more ominous reaches of his imagination, the shrewd protagonist, a lonely housewife, creating immediate intrigue by killing her errant husband, a high-ranking police officer, cracking his skull with a frozen leg of lamb. Colleagues of her husband arrive and search high and low for the murder weapon, but find nothing. Knowing the men well, the woman provides lunch, simultaneously eliminating from suspicion both herself and the murder weapon by serving them up a delicious Sunday roast, a sizzling leg of lamb.

Colin arrived home from the UCAS conference in Manchester that evening. Traipsing into the kitchen, his eyes lit up when he saw that Stella had dinner prepared.

"You, wife, are a life-saver," he said, kissing her cheek. "The food at the conference was inedible."

"You look tired," she said. "How was it?"

"Let's just say, I'm happy to be home. I didn't get much sleep."

"Well, let's eat. I'll take this through," she said, slipping on oven gloves to carry a dish of steaming lasagne into the dining room. "Bring the wine."

Cutting the lasagne into squares, she heard the sudden clunk of the washing machine door open and Colin fumbling in his bag.

"Colin, leave your clothes. I'll take care of them after dinner," she said.

"They're in now," he replied.

The washing machine gave a kick and whirred into action.

"Don't forget the wine," she added.

A drawer rattled open. Moments later, a cork squeaked and popped from a bottle.

"Oh, and Colin, bring the bread too. There's a fresh loaf by the kettle. I think I lost the breadknife somewhere, the stainless steel one from Selfridges. We'll have to use a steak knife."

Again she heard him fumbling in his bag.

"Colin?"

"Yes, yes, one moment, I'm coming," he said, his voice trailing off.

A sudden draft blew through the house.

"Colin? What are you doing?" Stella asked, getting up and going into the kitchen.

110

Through the back door she saw him coming out of the garden shed.

"What were you doing in there?" she asked.

"This," he said, holding the steel bread knife aloft. "You didn't lose it. I left it in the shed. I was using it to cut up some plastic piping the other day."

"Oh, OK. Come on, the food's getting cold."

Over dinner, again Stella commented on how tired he looked. He'd not slept well, was very tired, and so directly after dinner went to bed. After washing the dishes, Stella poured another glass of wine and looked online for details of the murder in Norwich.

***

From the news report the previous day, Stella immediately recognised the woman waving at her outside Norwich Thorpe station.

"DI Marshall?" Stella asked. "Pleasure to meet you."

"Yvette," she replied, shaking Stella's hand. "Celia called and gave me your arrival time. I thought we could discuss the cases over lunch."

As they drove through lush, flat green fields of the Norfolk countryside, DI Marshall, about the same age as Celia, provided Stella with a summary of her career to date. Joining the Metropolitan Police in 1983, along with one or two other women recruits, male colleagues, including superior officers, made little to no effort to curb casual sexist commentary, some actively encouraging it. She recalled one occasion, as her team prepared for an important operation. With not enough radios to go round, the superior officer threw a couple of ten pence pieces across the table at her and the only other female officer on the team, dismissively suggesting that if they required back up, they should find a phone box.

Her first transfer into the drugs squad excited her, especially working on the first case, close monitoring of a notorious gang, chief suppliers of cocaine to London and the south east. She volunteered to go undercover, infiltrating the inner sanctum of the gang, gathering vital information about plans to transport a large haul of cocaine from Holland up the Thames Estuary for distribution in the capital.

On the day they planned to seize the boat, her superior officer made it clear that Yvette was to remain in the car and take no further part in the operation. After capturing and impounding the drugs, some of her colleagues, mainly younger men, made it clear to him that they were not happy about Yvette's exclusion. His curt response typified the lingering attitude towards women in the force at that time - that in the "highly dangerous and delicate" final stages of the operation, he wanted no women involved.

Slowly the force began to change, opening up, women occasionally promoted to positions of responsibility. Earning several commendations, Yvette was one of these women, rising through the ranks to her next post as tutor at Hendon Police College. From there she moved into her current role, Detective Inspector in Norwich, a rank and position allowing her to conduct criminal investigations, the type of police work she found most satisfying, like the case they discussed over lunch in a pretty country pub.

"Have you seen the body?" Stella asked.

"Yes," Yvette replied. "When I saw how he'd cut her up, the MO looked so similar to what I knew about the Miller case. That's when I called Celia."

"So it's just these two cases? No others with similar MOs?"

"As yet, no. My team are trawling through the records as we speak. But in both cases, the cuttings are so distinctive, more or less the same. If it is the same man, it's as if he's leaving a message. As if he's toying with us."

"Any connections between the women? Did they know each other? Family members? Any connections at all?" Stella asked.

"None that we can establish so far. One of my officers has been to London and talked to the Miller family. But nothing of note. We'll continue to dig, but it appears this murder, like the Miller case, is completely random. I'm seeing the pathologist this afternoon. You OK to see the body?"

Based on her experience, Yvette conceded that finding the killer would be very difficult, adding that a lurid fascination with killing women had become universally glamorous, a potential money-spinner.

"Misogyny institutionalised. Think of Jack the Ripper. Over a hundred years later, this notorious killer of women still an irresistible enigma. Documentaries, films, East End pub tours. The attraction? Perhaps, that he got away with it. We have to ask ourselves: how many others like him are there out there? But, fortunately, things are improving. Mainly down to science, but also a shift in thinking on the part of the police, a desire to not only solve cases of murdered women, but to prevent them from happening in the first place. I'm hoping this guy will make a mistake and then we'll have him."

At the morgue, the heavy smell of disinfectant hung in the air. Dr Assad, the pathologist, paused before pulling open the drawer.

"I've sent off samples to forensics. I'll have them back in a day or two. I must say though, this is a strange case. Brutal. No sexual assault. If I had to guess, I'd say the man, and I think it is a man, was quick. He probably surprised her, cut the jugular before stabbing her, directly into her heart. She would have died in seconds. And, I must say, the first time I've come across this. He removed her shirt to leave a … signature. Are you ready?"

Stella suddenly felt a strange uneasiness. If this case was connected to the others, a psychopath was on the loose. And he'd strike again.

Dr. Assad pulled open the drawer and unzipped the body bag. As if in homage, the three women stood silently. When she turned the body, Stella drew in a sharp breath when she saw the word *bitch* carved into the torso, almost identical to that on Lisa Miller.

"You think there is a possible link to the case in London?" Dr. Assad asked.

"We're still working on that possibility," Yvette replied. "The MO is similar in each case. I've only ever read about killers who feel compelled to leave a *signature*. Yesterday I met with a criminal psychologist to discuss why some killers leave them. She believes that men with an insatiable desire to control and humiliate their victims carry out such brutal crimes. These desires often stem from childhood trauma. Not necessarily physical abuse, but almost certainly a degree of emotional abuse. These men tend to continue killing until they're caught. Catching them is extremely difficult. Many appear, well, let's say, *normal*. They live in plain sight, among us, concealing from those close to them their sick fantasies."

Stella thought of the similar comments by Dr. Waters.

"It looks as if our man selects his victims randomly," Yvette continued. "He takes pleasure in the post-mortem act. Leaving the *signature*. He *has* to leave his mark, leave something personal. Perhaps he wants to tell us something? His needs, compulsions? Perhaps, anger? I've read that many killers possess obsessive quirks. One in Slovakia always left the body in the same provocative, sexual position, as if posing. Another in India left beer cans next to his victims. In Greece, the killer targeted prostitutes, stabbing them exactly four times, always in the neck. Most intriguing, perhaps, an American case in the 1970s, shows us just how well these men assimilate. On this occasion, the killer had a preoccupation with eyes, which he always removed. Largely down to astute investigation, detectives narrowed down potential suspects to eye doctors which in turn led them to the country's leading ophthalmologist who, incidentally, had operated on the First Lady's eyes just days before."

***

Yvette and Stella made plans to meet the following week in London. As she boarded the train, a text from Dr. Waters flashed up on her phone. He'd finished Charlotte's report and after a final edit, would email it, in half an hour or so. If she wished, she could drop by that afternoon to discuss it.

As the train pulled into Liverpool Street station, Stella's phone rang. Ana's name flashed up on screen.

"Hi Ana. I'm just pulling into the station. Is it something urgent? I'll be back in the office later if it can wait."

"No. Nothing urgent. I'm calling to remind you about tonight. The talk at UCL."

"Talk? What talk?"

"The Women's Equality Party talk."

"Ah! OK. Yes, I remember now. Wait for me at the office. I'll get there as soon as I can. Around six-thirty," she replied, and hurried to Dr. Waters' office.

***

"Can I get you anything? Tea? Coffee? Water?" Dr. Waters asked as Stella sat down.

"No, I'm fine, thank you," she replied.

"Well, I must say this is a very unusual case," he began. "Charlotte really is a rather most likeable woman. Quite charming in fact. Coincidentally, we were at university, in York, at around the same time. Our paths never crossed. Indeed, a very level-headed woman."

"It's hard to believe she actually . . ."

"Yes. I agree. As you'll see, I mention this in the

report. I think my findings will serve you well in court. Though no overt sexual aggression from the husband, there's persistent, repetitive assault. He flaunted his brazen promiscuity and subjected her to abject humiliation, often in front of her boys. Clear and nasty provocation. Makes you wonder what he really wanted. The marriage had broken down irretrievably, Charlotte had actively sought a way out, via an amicable solution, divorce, I don't know why he just didn't agree to it and get on with life. As Charlotte had clearly wanted. He seemed to revel in his mistreatment of her, he simply wanted to control her. And so, as suspected, I recommend you build your defence through the lens of coercive control. Stress Charlotte's noble restraint, how she sought a solution. But keep the focus on him. The recklessness, the warped emotional exploitation, the cruel manner in which he tried dragging her into an unfamiliar, murky world of degradation, embarrassment, deprivation. He craved control, effectively reducing Charlotte to a "bit part" in a family she had tenderly, almost single-handedly, raised on her own. Stress his refusal to accept the divorce. And Charlotte, at her lowest, incapable of making rational, and clearly, ethical choices. *This* is why she murdered him."

Dr. Waters paused and thumbed through the report.

"Stella, had this happened ten years ago, you wouldn't have had much of a case. Fortunately, in these more enlightened times, with new laws like the Coercive Control Act, December 2015 I believe, long overdue for women like Charlotte, I think you have a very strong case. Even so, the term "coercive control" is still very much misunderstood. I can't stress enough the importance of you highlighting the constant assaults, the threats, the humiliation, the intimidation - all premeditated. He wanted to terrify her, make her life hell.

"You mentioned that you would like to see this case used as a precedent for future cases. I agree. As you deliver your defence, keep the language clear, easily understood, logical. Clarity counts. I describe his behaviour as extreme - be sure to mention this, as I will if called to testify. She felt like a hostage, trapped, but even then, in the depths of despair, like any mother, she felt duty bound to protect the boys. And she never sought vengeance. No, no, she is clearly not a vengeful woman. She chose to endure his constant, emotional manipulation for the sake of the boys, to keep her family intact. Convince the court of this."

***

With all seats in the main UCL auditorium taken, Ana and Stella made their way up to the second level where a flurry of eager, young women in party T-shirts handed out glossy flyers. Once they'd found seats, thinking Colin might still be on campus, Stella tried to call him, but the battery in her phone had died.

Printed in capital letters across the front of the flyer, the fledgling party's commendable mission statement. "To unite people of all genders, ages, backgrounds, ethnicities, beliefs and experiences in the shared determination to see women enjoy the same rights and opportunities as men - so that all can flourish." On the back, in smaller print, strategic ambitions to create a society with a buoyant economy and a workforce made up of *all* of its human resources. Full use of women's potential ensured "active integration" at all levels of industry, from the shop floor to boardrooms. Running along the bottom of the flyer, a final soundbite. "Equality means better politics, and a society at ease with itself."

Stella sighed. Though noble in its intent, why, in 2022, did women still have to gather to demand equal rights? She thought of Charlotte. How if, in another life, how she might have pursued a meaningful, fulfilling career. Perhaps in politics. She would have enjoyed gatherings such as this.

The agenda for the evening suddenly flashed up on a screen above the stage.

Domestic Abuse
Intersectionality: Domestic, Sexual and Intimate Violence

Media and Equality
The Shadows within the Shadow Pandemic

Successive governments had failed to put forward meaningful legislation to tackle domestic abuse. Controlled by a small cabal of media tycoons, exclusively men averse to upsetting the status quo, the media provided a green light for violence against women. With the means to make or break a party, a fledgling party pissing off the gatekeepers was either very brave or extremely foolish.

The hall suddenly erupted into thunderous applause as four women strode onto the stage. As three took seats, the other stood behind a lectern centre stage, smiling, waving and clapping along with the audience. She put on her glasses and a hush descended.

"Ladies and gentlemen," she began, pausing to squint into the audience. "Yes, I've been reliably informed there are one or two gentle men with us this evening," she added.

A solitary man's muffled voice provoked a short-lived ripple of applause.

"Ladies and gentlemen," she repeated. "Thank you for coming. It really is a pleasure to see so many of you here this evening. As you see on the screen behind me, we will discuss two pressing issues that every day adversely affect women's lives. And, by extension, all of society. Firstly, domestic abuse. As we all know, cases spiked during the Covid 19 pandemic. Yet again, our government failed to address this shameful menace among us. And when I say "our" government, I do so reluctantly, simply because this government, time and time again has ignored us, and here, this evening, we will assess the fallout their apathy has for so many women. Secondly, as you all know, so detrimental to the struggle many women face, we examine the role the media plays in reflecting our roles in society."

She paused for a drink of water.

"If you will, let's cast our minds back. To that horrendous experience that began in the spring of

2020, the residual effects of the Covid 19 pandemic still very much with us today. I must make special mention of our tireless NHS staff. Heroes and heroines all, who, day after relentless day, battled in atrocious conditions to save so many lives."

Rousing, spontaneous applause and whistles suddenly erupted.

"They were brave, unflinching in their care for others, while as we now know, this despicable government partied in Number 10. They took the nation's sacrifices for granted. Faltering with each very dodgy decision they took, they failed the NHS, they failed the citizens of this country. The worst and most serious of their shortcomings? Leaving these brave men and women, NHS staff, to deal with this deadly disease without adequate equipment. It really is down to their commitment, their professionalism that we can gather here tonight. And we must spare a thought for those we lost. We must not, and we will not forget them.

"At the height of the pandemic, the public proved resilient. Ladies and gentlemen, you followed the rules. As a country, as communities, frequently reducing us to tears, we witnessed daily so many random acts of generosity and kindness, we saw the true spirit of the people of our country. Meanwhile, the government sipped champagne, ignoring not only frontline workers of the NHS, ignoring the thousands of terrified, vulnerable women locked in homes with abusive partners.

"But their inaction has only served to embolden us. We are gathering strength, and we will continually hold to account a government which simply takes for granted staff who work in our public services, in the NHS, care workers, sectors made up with disproportionately high numbers of women. Still very much in the early stages of gathering data, we demand an independent investigation into the government's appalling performance.

"In an island nation, we had the highest number of deaths in Europe! An increase of over 120% for women trapped in homes with abusive partners, many with criminal records, killed in their own homes. Frontline services were unable to respond to the record-breaking numbers of calls from women living in constant fear with nowhere to turn. Dr. Alexander, our first speaker this evening, will talk more succinctly about this and elaborate on how, as a country, we are failing in our duty to protect vulnerable women.

"Then, once again, we turn our attention to the media. Its biggest failing? How it consistently fails to report what we women contribute. In times of society's greatest need, women always step up, as we did during the pandemic. And yet, its failure to report, shine a light on the the numbers of women murdered at the hands of violent men is in itself criminal."

Stella sighed in agreement.

"Our esteemed guests, each an expert in her field, will address how this party aims to reduce violence against women. We'll take questions from the audience at the end, but before we begin, I'd like to read out a letter that our party sent to Number 10 some time ago, available on our website. We have yet to receive a response.

"Dear Prime Minister. Study upon study shows that when women are confined to homes with abusive men, their lives are in danger. During the pandemic, as reports first surfaced about the increase in violence against women, your response to these dangers was negligible. You failed in your duty of care to protect women. Again. For vulnerable women desperately needing help, cutting funding to support services meant some women paid with their lives. The police did what they could, but after years of underfunding, women who needed their intervention were not served. They were not a priority. We in the Women's Equality Party will never fail in our efforts to protect women and girls in this country. We are watching you."

Applause rumbled through the hall.

"But now, I'd like to introduce our first speaker, Dr. Alexander. A forensic criminologist and former police officer, her focus this evening, exploration of the root causes of domestic abuse."

A tall woman rose to her feet and approached the lectern to a ripple of applause.

"Good evening. A killer's work is methodical and calculating. His methodology is strategic. He knows how to stalk, abuse, and control. He knows how to murder. Control is everything to him. And more often than not, he is a shrewd and cunning expert in what he does. And what does he do?

"Well, first he normally declares his love before gradually weaving himself into a woman's life. He tightens his control of her to get what he wants. And what is this? Most killers want absolute submission.

"As already mentioned, lockdown was a particularly difficult time for at-risk women. Confined to homes alongside unstable men with extremely violent tendencies, this unpredictable trigger event suddenly had many women existing in a state of constant terror. Threatened with their lives, many were brutally raped. Some murdered.

"And many women had babies. Even in times of celebration, like the imminent birth of a baby, these women had to endure months of confinement with dangerous men, a period of unimaginable anxiety. Try for a moment to imagine how they must have felt when the baby arrived, the new-born seen as competition, and in behaviour all too familiar to victims of abuse, men felt ignored, and no longer the focus of attention, they became aggressive and lashed out.

"Even today, post-pandemic, with resources for women so alarmingly underfunded, they have nowhere to turn in moments of dire need. Even those lucky enough to escape their abusers, many continue to receive cruel, manipulative texts often threatening to inform the police, or social services, a particularly sensitive area of concern for women with children.

"Unlike other parties, I believe this party can make a *real* difference in improving the lives of women. I'm very familiar with the woeful policies this government has when it comes to supporting women. Shameful. A party created by women will not sanction the same empty rhetoric mainstream parties churn out on issues affecting women. Why? Under this government

80% of frontline support for women's organisations has been reduced. A pledge last year from the Home Office of two million pounds for domestic abuse services is, quite frankly, laughable. A drop in a very, very deep ocean. Central to this party's ambitions, a cornerstone if you like, is to ring-fence funding for the protection of vulnerable women."

For twenty minutes or so, the remainder of the presentation delved further into such concerns. The next two speakers, experts in media, echoed similar sentiments, both ending their talks offering unequivocal support for the Women's Equality Party. When overhead lights suddenly flickered on, the leader sprang back up to the lectern.

"And so now, we'd like to hear from you. You'll see dotted around the auditorium a number of young women with microphones. If you wish to ask a question, please stand up so they can see you."

Arms shot up, and for the ten minutes or so, all four women responded to a range of questions. When the leader momentarily returned to the lectern to ask if any men in the audience had questions, a lull descended, the only sound, a low, inquisitive hum. But then, from somewhere in the front row of the auditorium, a commotion. Holding a microphone aloft, almost bent double, a young woman shuffled across the front of the stage.

"Ah, there's a brave soul. Over there, at the end of the row, quick," she said to the young woman. "Quick, quick, before he changes his mind," she added, laughing.

Curious to see this brave soul, Stella leant forward,

stunned to see Colin on his feet, microphone in hand.

"I know this may not be the most pertinent, or popular question you'll take tonight," he began, pausing to clear his throat, "but I was just wondering if you would ever consider a man for leader of the party?"

Hisses rippled through the auditorium. The leader turned and looked at the other speakers smiling at her nervously.

"As you know, a party's policies, and values, play an important role in promoting equal representation in all spheres of life," she began, turning back to Colin, pausing her preamble to pour some water. "We are no different to other political parties in this respect. In both local and national elections, we put forward candidates who believe passionately in the aims of our party. For us, the bedrock of the party is equality for all women. We know from experience that any form of social progress is incremental. Women's political participation and representation are on the rise, but there really is so much more to achieve. In 2019, women held just 24% of all parliamentary seats and only 20% of ministerial positions. Such unequal representation excludes us in decision-making bodies in which privileged posh boys, who have kept women in the margins for centuries, are intent on maintaining this exclusion. For this reason, and in answer to your question, we are looking for more women to assume posts in government in order to add their voices to the decision-making process. If a man were to lead the party, he would have to be truly committed to achieving gender equality. Would our members elect someone who hasn't felt what it's like to exist in the shadows? Any candidate would certainly have to make a case for understanding how exclusion has affected women, how we perceive the world, and why wanting to make government more inclusive benefits everyone. If a man were able to convince party members he really does understand how we feel, and they vote for him, then yes, it would be possible for him to lead us.

"However, historically, no party led by men in any country has ever been responsive to women's needs. We've simply not been included. Just look at gender equality measures in other parties' manifestos. All the evidence shows that these parties, led by men, fail in providing equal and effective political participation to women, either in their parties, or in society. Women bring to the table new ideas, new strategies, new ways of doing and seeing. Women from all walks of life must be offered opportunity. The more women in a party, the stronger that party. The more effective a party is, the better off the country will be. Like I say, if a man steps up and persuades party members he can achieve this, we welcome him. Our members will decide. If they put their trust in a man, then we must adhere to what our members want."

Muted applause brought the evening to an end. Hoping to find Colin, Stella rushed downstairs, waiting with Ana outside for ten minutes or so before she made her way home.

"Stella?" Colin called from the kitchen as she closed the front door. "Is that you?"

"Yes."

"I've just put a pizza in the oven. Is that OK?"

"Sure," she replied, entering the kitchen, dropping her bag on the island and glaring at him.

"What?" he asked, opening a bottle of wine. "What have I done now?"

"So. Would this party ever consider a man to lead it? You got some balls Colin."

He smiled.

"You were there?"

"Yes, with Ana."

"You should have called. We could have had dinner in town."

"Phone died. What did you think of her response to your question?"

"Usual political rhetoric. She could have just said no and taken more questions."

"And that would have worked for you? Exclusion of men?"

"It would have been honest."

"Would your stake in the patriarchy permit you to vote for a party led by a woman then?"

"Not sure. Doubt it. You?"

Stella momentarily reflected on the frenzied excitement in the hall. As if they are on the precipice of something really possible, large gatherings of women never fail to generate a feverish buzz. However, even with praiseworthy but untried political ambitions, a new political party, a new entity with little political clout, or visibility, the stark reality is that it would be operating in such an established, broad political landscape which men have controlled for centuries.

"Touché," she responded. "How long will the pizza be?"

"About fifteen minutes. You say you went with Ana. How is she? Has she found the love of her life yet?"

"She's fine. She did mention she's seeing someone. They're taking it slowly. We'll see."

"I've got something to ask you," he said, his tone suddenly changing.

"Should I be worried?"

"Probably not."

"Ask away."

He drew in a deep breath.

"Well, it's not really a request. More of an order."

Stella folded her arms and looked at him sternly. He smiled.

"Yes, yes, an order. That's the word. And after that rally, after that most patronising mauling, and in spite of such public humiliation, I feel inspired. As such, I'm afraid I must lean on my male privilege. In fact, you have no option to refuse me in my humble request."

"OK Zeus," Stella replied, "let me have it."

"We've been talking about a holiday. Well, today I booked us a week away in France. Well, almost. Corsica. The dates are set. We leave in two weeks. I called Celia and she said with so many weeks of annual leave remaining, she was quite insistent that you take a holiday. She thinks you're working too much. I agree."

Colin filled two glasses with wine. Still smiling, he handed Stella a glass. Timelines, appointments, meetings flashed through her mind as she raised her glass.

"Oh husband of husbands," she said. "Merci beaucoup."

9

In its desire to break away from France and win recognition for the national rights of the Corsican people, the National Liberation Front of Corsica took a foothold on the island in the mid-1970s. However, ambitions for self-rule guaranteeing and safeguarding its people's citizenship, language and culture, came with costs. Civil disobedience, violent protest, people dying. Fortunately, today, the organisation's forty-year struggle is over. All military operations have now officially ceased, and though still keen to fulfil its mandate of winning independence, the island's governors now prefer compromise to chaos. As a result, this enlightened approach to self-rule has been of great benefit to an idyllic Mediterranean island noted for its spectacular beauty, climate, home to around 300,000 people, and in recent years tourists have come flocking back.

Landing at Ajaccio airport, Stella and Colin picked up a rental car and headed south through spectacular verdant, undulating hills. Refusing to provide Stella with even the smallest detail of their destination, an hour later they pulled into the wide gravel driveway of an old, isolated stone cottage draped in vines. Stella sprang from the car, running up onto the terrace stretching the length of the cottage, at one end a view of the glittering Mediterranean, on the other, row after row of olive trees stretching into the distance as far as the eye could see.

"Well?" Colin asked.

"It's beautiful, I absolutely love it. It really couldn't be any more perfect," Stella replied, beaming at him.

"I think, maybe it could," he said, taking her hand and leading her to the rear of the house.

"Colin!" Stella cried, barely able to contain herself when she saw the swimming pool, its crystal clear water sparkling in the midday sun.

"Nice, huh?"

"More than nice. This is so, so, perfect she said," hugging him. "Come on, let's unpack, I'm ready for a dip."

While Colin prepared lunch, Stella put on her bathing costume and slipped into the pool.

"How's the water?" Colin asked moments later, placing on the table under a large parasol small bowls filled with hummus and olives.

"Perfect, just perfect. Everything is perfect. Thank you so much."

"You're most welcome. Come and have some lunch. The owners left a welcome gift in the fridge, a nice bottle of local white wine."

After lunch, Colin went for a drive, to get the "lay of the land." Stretched out on a sun lounger, Stella studied the Corsican guidebook she'd picked up at the airport. Propriano, a small village just a short drive away, with its small harbour and an "array of tempting restaurants and buzzing café terraces lining the marina," sounded perfect for dinner.

That evening, just as the sun was setting, they parked in the village marina and strolled back along the harbourside admiring the modern, glossy yachts bobbing on the water. In the warmth of a beautiful evening, on the patio of a small restaurant, sipping wine, they watched the last vestiges of the sun slipping below the horizon. Above them, high on a hillside, the twinkling lights of a tiny village. In a moment of fuzzy appreciation, Stella looked at Colin. So aware. Of her, what she needed, when she needed it. He gave her space, time, solitude. And for his kind, gentle thoughtfulness, what did she provide in return?

"So, will you give your French a go?" he asked.

"I will," she replied, with a giggle. "Let me see. Je voudrais. I would like. Je veux. I want. Nous voudrions. We would like. And then we'll point to the menu!"

"Looks like we're set then," he replied, just as a pretty young waitress appeared at their table.

"Bonsoir Madame et Monsieur. Souhaitez-vous tous les deux manger ici?" she asked.

A little embarrassed, they looked up at her blankly.

"Pardon, je ne comprends pas bien…" stuttered Stella.

"Oh, you're English," the waitress replied, smiling. "I just wanted to know if you would like to order something to eat. The food is very good."

"Why not?" Colin replied, looking across at Stella.

"Yes, why not?" she replied.

"Your English is really rather good," Colin said, smiling at her.

"I am English. From Somerset. Well, I should say half English. My mum's from here. My uncle owns this restaurant."

Colin and Stella looked at each other and smiled.

"I'll be right back with some menus," she said.

Stella noted Colin's eyes follow her inside.

"Well, stroke of luck that," he said.

"What a sweet girl. This wine's very good."

"Isn't it? We'll ask her what it is when she returns. Oh, here she comes."

"I'll let you take a look and be back in a couple of minutes," she said, placing a small basket of freshly-cut bread on the table and handing them menus.

"Any recommendations, perhaps something typically Corsican?" Stella asked.

"We're surrounded by the sea so the fish is very good, fresh each day. But the signature dish of the island is the wild boar, Civet de sanglier. They cook meat really well here. It's like a casserole. Onions, carrots, garlic, chestnuts, fennel, and eau de vie, a colourless brandy with a light, fruity flavour, lots of red wine - it really is very good. But if you don't fancy boar, we have good veal, or the Agneau Corse, Corsican lamb, a favourite with the locals. I'm Amelie by the way."

"I'm Stella. This is my husband, Colin."

"Lovely to meet you. Your first time in Corsica?"

"Yes, and it won't be our last. Absolutely stunning. We arrived today. Do you know the island well?" Stella asked.

"Yes, very well. This part at least. As a girl I spent every summer here. We'd come over as soon as school broke up. I have cousins and friends here. Second home really. I do like it in the summer. Somewhat duller in the winter."

"What do you do back home?" Stella asked.

"I'm at university. Bath. Second year. I'm studying French and History."

"How is your French?" Stella asked.

"I can speak it perfectly, no problem at all. But writing - well - that's a work in progress. At the end of the season, I'm staying in France for my year abroad, in Lyon. Really looking forward to that. I'll be back in a moment, just have to deliver an order."

Smooth, golden bronze skin, gentle, tender manner, Amelie reminded Stella of her younger self, alone in Barcelona for a month one summer without a worry in the world.

"I'm going to have the boar," Colin said. "Why don't you choose another dish and we'll share?"

Amelie returned, took their orders, recommending a bottle of red Sciacarello, popular with meat dishes and unique to the island.

Dusk gave way to a starry night and diners filled the terrace. Excellent food, quality wine, Stella and Colin agreed they would return before leaving. At eleven o' clock the kitchen closed and Amelie arrived at their table with another bottle of wine.

"On me," she said, holding it up. "OK if I join you?"

"Please do," Colin said.

"How was dinner?" she asked, topping up their glasses and pouring herself a glass.

"Excellent recommendations," Stella said. "We're here for a week. I think we'll be back! Any suggestions on what to see while we're here?"

"You're staying near here?" Amelie asked.

"Yes," replied Colin, "just a short drive north from here - we could have walked."

"This part of the island, the west coast, is wild, rugged. Inland is very pretty, quite like our national parks at home. Forests, stunning valleys, hills, lots of waterfalls and rock pools. The island is very sparsely populated, even the capital, Ajaccio, has only about 70,000 people. You won't see many people, perhaps a few shepherds. The Corsicans are a proud people, they treasure their land and wouldn't dream of cashing in on it like in other countries. At Easter we took a family holiday to Spain, to Almeria, not too dissimilar to parts of this island. Mum said what developers had done to the coastline there, destroying it with thousands of high-rise apartments, all empty, was vulgar. That simply couldn't happen here. They consider the land an inheritance to cherish. Quite refreshing really. And be careful on the roads, especially during the day. Mountain roads have very sharp bends the higher you go."

Colin and Stella glanced at each other and smiled.

"The flag," Colin asked, pointing up at the pole above them. "It's all over the place. What is it? Rather sinister looking."

"That's the island's flag. You'll see it hanging above most cafés and bars wherever you are on the island. A proud emblem for all Corsicans. You rarely see a head on a flag, I suppose the Moor's head on ours is quite distinctive. It's a symbol of enormous pride - all political parties display it at rallies."

"And that up there?" Stella said, pointing up at the tiny village on the hill.

"That's Olmeto. Well worth a visit. You look down on Propriano from up there. Very quaint, old, cobbled streets, gabled houses, a few cafés. Quite typical of the villages on the island. And you must explore the beautiful coastline on this side of the island. Secluded tiny bays, white sandy beaches, crystal clear water. On my days off, Tuesdays, Thursdays and Sundays, I go to a tiny, very secluded inlet just up the road. I have it all to myself. It's what I miss most about the island when I'm home. If you have any questions while you're here, you can call me."

Well after midnight, the terrace had thinned out. Amelie's uncle brought to the table a *digestif*, a liqueur very popular on the island, a blackberry Mirto. Before leaving, they made a reservation for dinner on Friday, their last day, and the following morning rose early and headed inland to explore the interior of the 'L'Île de Beauté' - the Island of Beauty.

Winding mountain roads took them up through a labyrinth of dense pines giving off not only a most pleasing fragrance, but the most spectacular views of the island and surrounding sea. In remote, dusty villages they sampled exceptional local wines and regional cuisines, wholesome natural dishes cooked with herbs growing wild in the surrounding shrubland known to locals as *maquis*.

Purely by chance, they discovered one of the island's hidden gems. Built by French engineer Alexandre-Gustave Eiffel in 1891 - he of that most iconic Parisian structure - the impressive Pont du Vecchio, a railway viaduct of ornate ironwork, originally linked Bastia in the north with Ajaccio in the south. Nestled between two sturdy granite cliffs dropping into deep gorges of emerald-green waters on either side, for half an hour or so, they lingered below it taking pictures, before spending the remainder of the afternoon swimming at a secluded cove Amelie had mentioned.

On Thursday, they stayed in the cottage. Stella lounged by the pool re-reading Sophocles' *Antigone*, a play she had studied for A level. Again the eponymous protagonist's principled stance and fervent unwillingness to submit to tyranny at any cost impressed her. Thinking it ideal advice for any young woman about to make her way in the world, she would give her copy to Amelie when they returned to the restaurant the following evening.

To escape the intense mid-afternoon heat, Stella moved inside, napping on the sofa until seven-thirty when she woke to find a note from Colin attached to a bottle of wine in the fridge. He'd gone for a drive and would pick something up for dinner on his way back.

Returning to the pool, Stella slid slowly into its warm water, floating on her back and looking up into a vast purple sky. Suddenly flashing through her mind, another life a world away - London, Charlotte, Sharon, Thomas & Taylor. Sucking air deep into her lungs, she sank slowly to the bottom of the pool.

After showering, she took a cool glass of wine onto the terrace, the snickering sound of cicadas filling the air, the rolling hills hazy in the setting sun. One day, she promised herself, she would return to see again the spectacular beauty of this island.

At eight o'clock Colin still hadn't returned. Thinking of the sharp bends and winding roads of the interior, she called and left a message. At eight-thirty she left another, and at around nine-fifteen, about to call Amelie for advice, the sudden crunch of tyres in the driveway signalled his return. Moments later, Colin entered the kitchen looking noticeably dishevelled.

"Are you OK?" Stella asked. "You look a little shaken."

"I'm fine, I'm fine. Some lunatic nearly ran me off the road," he said, dropping the keys on the counter.

"Did you pick up anything for dinner?"

"Oh," he stuttered. "No, no, nothing was open. Anyway, we can go out. Let's try another village, one we've not been to."

"If you like. But tomorrow night we're seeing Amelie, remember. I want to give her a book."

"I need a shower," he replied. "I'll take a dip in the pool first."

"Why don't you do that. Looks like that lunatic really rattled you."

At breakfast the following morning, Stella sensed an unusual restlessness still lingering in him. She suggested they visit one of the secluded coves Amelie had recommended, or perhaps a picnic in the forest. Colin preferred another day by the pool.

"Are you OK? Something the matter?" she asked over lunch.

"I'm fine," he said, forcing a smile. "I didn't sleep well. I think I might have something coming on. It's nothing. It'll pass."

Late that afternoon, Stella woke from a nap to find him face down, asleep on a lounger, his back a deep lobster pink.

"Colin, Colin, get up, get up. Your back is red raw," she called, nudging him awake.

"What? What is it?" he said, dazed, pulling out his earphones.

"Your back. It's burnt. Get out of the sun."

Rolling onto his side, he winced.

"That's going to be sore. I'll put some cream on it."

"It'll be fine, I'll jump in the pool, cool down," he said, slipping into the water.

By eight o'clock, a deep red shadow had crept up over Colin's neck and into his hairline.

"Listen. We can have dinner here," Stella suggested, rubbing moisturiser gently into his back. "I'll pop into Propriano first and say goodbye to Amelie. I want to give her a book. I'll get us a takeaway."

"Why don't you just send it to her when we get home?" he suggested.

"No, I want to say goodbye. I shan't be long, half an hour or so. I'll have a glass of wine while I wait."

In Propriano, the village buzzed with people huddled outside restaurants and bars. As Stella drove by Amelie's restaurant, a large sign announced in English and French it was closed.

"It was closed," she said to Colin on her return. "Strange, the other restaurants were very busy. Suppose I'll just have to send the book when we get home."

"Closed?" Colin asked, mildly surprised.

"Yeah. Locked up. No lights on, nothing. And I was so looking forward to seeing her. Anyway, we'll have to make do for dinner. There's some cheese and ham in the fridge, I'll make some sandwiches."

10

Sheltering from torrential rain below a canopy at Holborn station, Stella was flipping through holiday photos on her phone, now over a month ago. A little drunk, big happy smiles, arms around each other, the selfie taken of her and Amelie on that first night made her smile.

The phone suddenly pinged. A message from Colin. Nursing a heavy cold for a couple of days, he was feeling better. Did she want anything special for dinner? As she tapped a reply, a woman interrupted her.

"Hello again," she said, shaking an umbrella.

"Oh, hi, … uh," Stella replied, unsure of who the woman was.

"Maria. I work with Colin," she said, pulling down her hood.

"Oh, of course. Maria. So sorry, I was miles away. How are you? My," she said looking down at the bump below her coat, "any day now?"

"About 2-3 weeks," she responded with a sigh. "I'm ready to *not* be pregnant. I think this is the first and the last time!"

"Well, nearly there," Stella said, making a mental note to send her a gift when the baby arrived. "How's the house coming along?"

"We've moved in. A lot to do. My mother will be here soon, so she can help. Everything is just about ready. It's just a matter of waiting now," she said, gently tapping her bump. "How is Colin?"

"Just a cold. Or perhaps Man flu!" she said, laughing. "He'll be OK in a day or two, I'm sure. I just got a message from him and he's on the mend."

"You had a nice time in Corsica he told me. You look very well."

"Thanks. It seems like centuries ago now though."

"Lovely to see you again, but I must go. I'm going to the doctor. We must meet for lunch some time. Tell Colin not to rush back, and that I emailed him just before leaving the office. Documents, expense forms he has to sign for HR. I have left them on his desk. If he wants, I can drop them off at your office nearby?"

"Are they important?" Stella asked.

"No, not really. Just payroll. They need his expenses from the Norwich conference by the end of the week."

"The UCAS conference?"

"Yes."

"In Manchester you mean?"

"No. This year's conference was in Norwich. I made the arrangements."

"Strange. Manchester must have been another trip. Yes, of course I'll let him know. Good luck with, with the…" she added, pointing to the bump.

"Thank you. See you soon, and we will meet for lunch soon," Maria replied, then disappeared down the escalator.

**

"Colin? I'm home," Stella said, closing the door.

"I'm in the kitchen," he replied, his voice still a little

hoarse.

"How are you feeling?" she asked, lingering in the dining room.

"A little better. I slept til about ten. I needed it. Hungry?"

"Yes. Very," she said, taking off her coat.

But why had she thought the conference was in Manchester? She'd simply got it wrong.

"Colin?" she asked, tentatively.

"Yeah?"

"I just ran into Maria at the tube station."

"I just got an email from her."

"About expenses?"

"Uh ... yeah," he said, pausing. "She told you?"

"Yes. For the UCAS conference?"

A drawer rattled open.

"You want some wine?" he shouted.

"OK."

"She looks well," Stella continued as Colin came in with two glasses of wine.

"She does, doesn't she? She'll be off on maternity leave any day now," he said, handing Stella a glass.

"Her mother's coming."

"Yes. You know what the Spaniards are like. Family, family, family," he replied, and returned to the kitchen.

"She said something about expense forms for the UCAS conference. For some reason I thought it was in Manchester?"

"Uh ... no, Norwich. Did I say Manchester? You must be thinking about last year - I was in Manchester last year at another conference. Do you want bread?"

143

"Yes," she said, sighing.

"I might go in tomorrow, I'll see how I feel in the morning," he said, returning with the bread. "Do you have much on?"

"Tomorrow I have a meeting with Elizabeth."

"Dame Campbell?"

"The one and only."

Many of the senior solicitors often described the 1970s as the 'Dark Ages,' a period in which Dame Campbell had battled her way up through the ranks to become the country's most distinguished female barrister and formidable speaker. In packed auditoriums up and down the country, she railed against the shocking, insensitive treatment women received from the Criminal Justice System. Her message simple: that women should be treated with dignity, respect and receive equal justice under the law.

Unshakeable in the courtroom, she knew the loopholes prosecutors all too often used to defend men who abused women. In addition to work as a sought-after barrister, even with retirement nearing, she continued to lead a small team whose sole purpose was reviewing policy that directly affected women's concerns. In more recent years, she had made it crystal clear to the new generation of law graduates of their obligation to continue pursuing equality by dismantling antiquated procedures that required overhauling.

Stella fondly remembered meeting Dame Campbell for the first time. Pushing her way through the crush of a busy pub one Friday evening, she saw this legendary woman sitting between Celia and Sara, drinking wine and laughing. In this and many such social gatherings that followed, she learnt of Thomas & Taylor's difficult, early days, of Celia and Sara's tireless work, of Dame Campbell's guidance and encouragement, instrumental in helping shape the firm's philosophy. She understood the obstacles they would encounter, not only as young solicitors still learning their trade, but of the virulent opposition they would face from other firms unhappy about women entering *their* domain. Always available to the firm's solicitors, before agreeing to take on a case, she insisted on thorough investigation, meticulous preparation, and robust evidence.

"Stella, lovely to see you," Dame Campbell said, hugging her. "I'm sorry to rush you, but I have to be in court at midday. I've reviewed the cases, and I must say, it's time you came to work for me!" she added, smiling. "Most pleasing is the comprehensive evidence you've gathered. In Charlotte's case, I agree with you, going with coercive control is the best route. I hate to speak ill of the dead, but that bastard had it coming! A cautionary note. Many judges have been slow in getting up to speed on this new law. In their defence, they have had a flood of abuse cases since lockdown, and Dr. Waters' affidavit, David, I know him well, he knows his stuff, his testimony will certainly add weight to our defence.

"Sharon, poor thing - just trying to protect her kids. I suppose, like Charlotte, she just reached the end of her tether. We'll do our best. Yes, I think I have enough to begin, I'll let you know when we have court dates. Please let the women know of our progress."

Sighing, she looked up at Stella, holding her in a curious gaze.

"I'm serious about you coming to work for us," she continued. "You'd make a fine barrister. With your experience and my reference, as you prepare for the bar, you'll be exempt from most of the required courses. Please think about it."

"Thank you, Dame Campbell," Stella replied, flushing a little. "I'm flattered. But I still feel I have much to learn. What's your gut feeling on these cases?"

"Well," she said, drawing in a deep breath. "In Sharon's case, with the kids involved, by reason of diminished responsibility, I think we can reasonably expect manslaughter. Charlotte may be a little trickier. As we've agreed, we'll argue coercive control, but the prosecution will hammer us with her privileged background, arguing she had the means to leave. We'll see. Once I have a court date, I'll go and see her. In your notes, you say she is perfectly rational, understands what she's done, bright?"

Stella nodded.

"When you meet next, brief her on how we intend to proceed. Explain in detail what coercive control is. She's met Dr. Waters, give her a summary of his report. She may not agree with it, so convince her that for any woman who kills her husband, her judgement has to be substantially impaired. Drive that home, she needs to know our strategy, know the risks, inform her exactly how we intend to proceed. With regards sentencing, first-time offenders are often seen as less blameworthy, and so sentences are significantly lower than those for repeat offenders. With no criminal record, the undiagnosed medical condition Dr. Waters has clearly detailed in his report, well, I'm optimistic we can mitigate the length of sentence. Much depends on how the court assesses her level of responsibility - high, medium or, - what we're aiming for - low. You've established her ability to exercise self-control, a key characteristic, and so proving momentary mental disorder is pivotal. But first, as usual, we'll review the evidence and highlight every potential detail that might convince the court of diminished or mental disorder at the time of the offence. And, of course, we're hoping for a modicum of mercy. Perhaps the prosecutor is a woman. She'll understand where we're coming from.

"Sharon's case, however, a little trickier. Drugs. Previous convictions. Leaving the girls with a paedophile. I think there is little hope of her keeping the children. I'll go with social degradation, low educational levels etcetera, but I think we're looking at ten to fifteen years. Clearly no breaks for the poor. Again."

***

Stella returned to her office, called the prison and made an appointment to see Charlotte. On her desk, an unmarked manilla envelope. She called Ana.

"Ana. An envelope, on my desk, a yellow one?"

"Yes, with the sticky note. It's from Maria. Works with Colin? Pregnant?"

Stella looked on the floor beside her desk. On the carpet, a bright pink sticky note.

"OK. Got it. Yes, I know who it's from. She said she might stop by. Thanks."

Inside, Colin's expense forms for the UCAS conference. Two nights. Dunston Hall Hotel, Norwich. The name had a strangely familiar ring. She put the papers back inside the envelope, sealed it, and headed home.

Colin greeted Stella with the news that Maria had given birth to a boy that morning.

"We should buy her a little gift," Stella suggested. "Do you want me to look for something?"

"Would you? I wouldn't know what to get," Colin replied. "I'll call Rob, her partner, and ask him when's a good time to visit."

The following morning Stella received an email from Yvette. There had been a development of sorts in the Norwich case. A possible French connection. A detective from Paris was travelling to London on Friday to discuss the cases. Would she like to meet her? Stella suggested they meet for lunch. She'd make arrangements and email the details.

That evening at the hospital, Maria's face lit up when she saw Stella and Colin. Next to the bed, hands in lap, a gentle, unassuming woman sitting by a baby's cot.

"Hola! Hola!" cried Colin, kissing Maria on both cheeks.

"Hola, Hello," Maria replied, clearly surprised. "This is my mother. She doesn't speak English. Mamá, estos son mis amigos. Stella y Colin."

"Hola," Colin said again, nodding.

Stella smiled at the woman and looked into the cot at a little bundle wriggling below a blanket.

"Encantada," Maria's mother replied, nodding shyly.

"Oh, he's so tiny," Stella said. "So beautiful. Have you named him yet?"

"Yes. Leonardo."

"How lovely," Stella replied, handing Maria a small bag.

"Oh, this was not necessary," she said, pulling from inside a light grey cashmere blanket.

She shook it out to reveal a large white star in its centre.

"Oh, how beautiful!" Maria said, holding it to her cheek. "Thank you so much. Mamá, mira, que bonita," she said, handing it to her.

"Si, si, niña. Muchas gracias. Muy agradable."

Stella suddenly felt her phone vibrate, Yvette's name flashing up on the screen. She stepped into the corridor to take the call.

"Hi Stella," Yvette began. "Sorry to call so late. But I'm going to have to bring forward our meeting. I'll be in London with the French detective tomorrow, not Friday. Apparently strikes in France at the weekend are causing disruption to travel, so she's coming tomorrow instead. Are you available?"

"Yes, yes, of course. No problem. I'll call the restaurant and change the booking. I'll text you the details. About one-thirty. Is that OK?"

"Perfect."

"Yvette. Before you go. You said it might have

149

something to do with the Miller case? An officer from Paris? What's the connection?"

"Well, chances are there isn't. She read something about the Norwich murder and got in touch. That's about as much as I know right now. I guess we'll get the full picture tomorrow."

***

A message from Yvette informed Stella they were just minutes away. From the terrace of the Italian restaurant on the Thames, just below Tower Bridge, she looked up and saw her with another woman.

"Hi Stella," Yvette said, moments later. "I hope you've not been waiting long."

"No, not at all."

"This is Detective Simone Dupont."

"Pleased to meet you," Stella said, shaking the woman's hand.

"Pleased to meet you too. You must pardon my English. For many years now I don't speak English. But enough I think to discuss the case. And thank you for choosing such an impressive restaurant," she said, looking back up at the bridge looming over them.

The city had changed a lot since she was fourteen, when she had come to London to study, studies interrupted when, quite unexpectedly, she fell in love with an Italian boy on the course.

A waiter arrived, and once they had ordered, the conversation turned to the French murder.

"Simone. Can you brief Stella on the case?" Yvette began.

"We are still very early in the stages of investigation and have little information. This afternoon I will meet the family of a British woman murdered in France. Yvette has told me about the cases of the young women here, in London and Norwich, the methods the killer used, and so I think there can be connections."

"Why do you think the cases are connected?" Stella asked.

"There are similarities," Simone continued. "I think it can be a copycat killing. Men, killers, they see movies, go on the internet, and see things about murder. I read the report of the Norwich case first, the way the killer leaves a, a … what is the word, a sign …"

"A signature," Yvette said.

"Yes, yes, a signature. In Norwich, and in London, the killer has left a signature."

"So, the connection is that the killer in France carved a word into the woman's body too?" Stella asked.

"Yes, I think so. All three cases have this. But there is a difference. In the language. In Norwich, and here, the killer has cut in the word *bitch*, the English word, no? In France, he has used the French word *salope*. Cut into the woman's back. Maybe to confuse things, I don't know. But why we think it may be a copycat murder. I have a picture."

Simone took from her case an envelope, pulled out a photograph and passed it to Stella. Face down on a mortuary slab, a woman's grey body. Stella recognised the familiar straight lines sliced into the woman's back immediately, Simone's assessment that

151

the cases might be connected very astute. Signatures in both the Norwich and Miller cases easily could have been done by the same man.

"I showed the pictures to a graphologist," Yvette said. "From a psychological perspective a sustained use of capital letters is often used simply to draw attention. A sort of taunting. Most likely suggests the killer reaps pleasure from the act. The crude and clumsy simplicity of the signature is his way of saying that once the victim is dead, his work is done. The murder is his work. Much like an artist signing the bottom of a canvas, he leaves his mark. He wants us to see it. However, though the signature styles are similar, as the murders took place in different countries, it's highly unlikely it's the same man. I think it's probably the work of a copycat."

"Yes, the signatures are very similar," Stella added. "But Paris is not that far these days, closer than Edinburgh on the Eurostar. Perhaps it's someone with connections to both London and Paris. Just a train ride away."

"The case is not in Paris," Simone interjected. "In fact, it's not really in France."

"Not in France?" Stella replied, clearly baffled. "I don't follow."

"This murder was in la Corse," Simone replied.

The name sounded unexpectedly familiar.

"Where?" Stella asked, a tremble shivering through her.

"la Corse," repeated Simone.

"Corsica," Yvette said. "The island of Corsica."

"Corsica?" Stella repeated, looking again at the

photo trembling in her hand. "When, when was this woman killed?" she asked impatiently, her face suddenly pale, her voice quivering.

"Stella? Are you OK?" Yvette asked.

"When was she killed?" she repeated.

"We have been working on the case for over a month now," Simone replied. "So we think maybe five or six weeks ago."

Stella stared blankly out over the Thames.

"Stella?" Yvette asked again. "Are you OK?"

"I was in Corsica around that time. The murder could very well have been committed when I was there. Do you have more photos? Perhaps of the woman? Of her face?"

Simone pulled another photo from a manilla envelope and handed it to Stella.

"No! no, no, no, no," she suddenly gasped, reeling back in her seat, her hands covering her mouth. "NO! No, it can't be. No, please God, no. No, this isn't possible," she repeated, tears welling in her eyes.

A waiter appeared at the table, Yvette motioned for him to leave.

"Stella? What? What is it?" she asked.

"I know this woman. This girl. This is Amelie," she whispered, her voice cracking.

"Yes, Amelie. This is correct," Simone confirmed.

"Here, look," she said, wiping her eyes, fumbling for her phone.

She pulled up a photo of her and Amelie together, smiling, arms slung around each other's shoulders.

"We met her on our first night on the island. She was a waitress at her uncle's restaurant where we had dinner. She was, was, so full of life. I sent her a copy of *Antigone* when I got back. I wanted to give it to her the night before we left, but, but ...."

Suddenly quiet, lost in thought, her eyes again wandered out across the river.

"Our last night there. I went into Propriano to give her the book. But the restaurant was closed. That must be the night, the night it happened ..."

"Yes, near Propriano. Do you have the dates that you were there, on the island?" Simone asked.

Stella pulled up the calendar on her phone. Simone confirmed that the day Amelie died Stella and Colin were on the island.

Stella wept silently.

"I'm sorry," she said, trying to compose herself. "This really has come as quite a shock. Let's go back to the office. I'll make a statement there."

***

Holding Stella's hand as she gave a statement, Celia recalled her mentioning a young English girl she had met on holiday.

"Stella, I'm so sorry, hun," she whispered once Yvette and Simone had gone. "This is really fucking shitty," she added, caressing her back.

"Celia, she was so young, so alive," Stella spluttered. "We met on the first night. She came and sat with us, we drank wine. She was adorable. Precious. With such a, such a future ahead of her..."

She wiped tears from her cheeks.

"I know, I know," Celia said, passing her a tissue,

releasing a frustrated sigh. "Honey, I know."

Words, thoughts, prayers, nothing could undo this senseless act of such vile barbarity. The girl was dead. Like Emma.

"Does Colin know?" Celia asked.

"No, I'll tell him when I get home."

"Let me call a taxi. Best you go home now."

Stella drew in a deep breath.

"No, thanks Celia. I'll manage. This is what we do, right?" she said, standing up.

"Yes, baby, this is what we do," Celia replied, hugging her. "Listen, I'll leave you be for now. Be back in a while."

***

Colin found Stella in the garden. Her eyes rubbed pink, he approached slowly.

"Stella?" he whispered, softly.

Kneeling in front of her, she withdrew her hand as he tried to console her.

"What's the matter?"

"It's horrible," she said, her voice breaking, her eyes unable to meet his gaze.

"Tell me," he replied, calmly.

She drew in a sharp breath.

"Amelie. The girl we met on holiday in Corsica. She's dead. Someone killed her."

"Not the Amelie we …"

"Yes, yes," she said, suddenly angry, looking directly at him. "Who the fuck would do that? Why? She was so precious."

"How, how did you find out?"

"I met with a French detective investigating the case. She came to London, she thinks they're connected to other cases."

"Other cases? What other cases?"

"What does it matter?" Stella snapped, suddenly on her feet. "Someone killed Amelie."

"Yes, yes. Of course."

"No matter how long I do this job, I will never understand the kicks these fuckers get out of killing girls. The lives they destroy. I will never understand it. Why? Why? Why?"

"I suppose …" Colin began, but stopped.

She wiped her eyes and waited for him to continue.

"I suppose it's, it's . . . complicated."

"Complicated!" Stella sobbed. "Complicated? Tell me Colin, how the fuck is murdering an innocent girl complicated? And then, cutting her up? Tell me, tell me! Just how the fuck can that be so complicated?" she yelled, and stormed into the house.

Like she had felt after Emma's death, lurking deep inside her, twisting, spinning, a strange and dangerous sickening despair.

She thought of her early sessions with Dr. Bergeron. Could she have done more to help Emma? Could she have saved her? And now, Amelie. Sweet, precious Amelie. And an unknown woman in Norwich. Women's lives wiped out.

She sensed Colin lingering by the door.

"I'm sorry," he whispered.

Stella, however, had nothing to say.

11

A gift from Dr. Bergeron given to her shortly before she left for university, Stella looked up at the painting of Boudicca on the wall opposite her desk.

She picked up her phone.

"Hi, it's Stella."

"Hi Stella," came Dr. Bergeron's usual bubbly reply. "It's been a while, how are you?"

"Actually - not so well."

Two hours later, Dr. Bergeron was sitting opposite Stella in her office.

"Tell me, what can I do?" she asked, her tone serious. "Speak to me Stella."

"I think I might need direction. To, to, I don't know. Maybe, focus. I'm struggling, in here," she said, touching her head. "I don't know, I'm not sure I can manage what's happening right now. It feels so personal. Like, I don't know, like I'm being attacked. Someone I knew. Not like Emma. I knew Emma as a friend. Someone I met only once. But still, I knew her. And, and, now she's dead. I'm not sure I can manage this."

"A case you're working on?"

"Not directly, no. Protocol doesn't allow it. But I want, have to do something. I want to help. But I feel so helpless. Lost, I suppose. I feel like I'm sinking, like I'm under a dark, dark cloud."

"Can you tell me anything about the case?"

"Just that we think two, perhaps three, cases are connected. It might be the same man."

"A serial killer?"

"Possibly."

"What do you know about serial killers?"

"Not much really. Besides, that's a social forensic focus."

"Well, why don't you find out? What is it that motivates men to kill women? You deal with this daily. It's part of your life. You've invested so much already. This is something you *can* do. Push yourself. Get busy, active. Push yourself through this."

"But I don't know how. Where should I start?" Stella asked.

Dr. Bergeron glanced up at the painting of Boudicca.

"You say the cases are connected. Perhaps now is the right time to think about your work from, say, a more forensic angle. If this is a serial killer, you're dealing with a callous, unemotional psychopath. Men like this have extremely complex profiles. Neurologically speaking, there are problems with reduced connections between the prefrontal cortex and the amygdala. In my training we looked at a wide range of trigger points - what sets psychopaths off, so to speak, what I think you're looking for. I'll go back through my notes and send you what I have. That should get you started.

"Stella, think of our early sessions. We talked about how, in low moments, it's important to get busy, find a focus point. And you found one. You got through it. It helped then and it will help now. Take a look at the forensics, learn what motivates psychopaths. This will not only give you a focus, but provide insight into the psychology of killers which will help you in your work."

That afternoon, Stella looked at the first of the many articles Dr. Bergeron sent. Men kill for a variety of reasons. Many are sexually aggressive, angry, they focus on acts of abnormal psychological gratification. Others possess "visions" of superiority, some are on a "mission" to rid the world of women. Most alarming - those who kill simply for the thrill of it. The common denominator, the thread that connected virtually every article - men who kill because they feel that, in some way, women have undermined their sense of *ownership*.

Many articles angered Stella, especially those with stark inaccuracies. Like those that claimed current statistics of domestic abuse were overblown, that minor incidents of violence rarely led to murder. Others, clearly gratuitous, provided unnecessary graphic descriptions of how women were killed.

Another observation was the disproportionate attention on men's feelings, so much focus on what motivated them to kill, yet nothing about women's deeply-entrenched feelings of self-worth, their dignity, or of the humiliation, or terrifying experiences they had endured. And beyond disgraceful, those articles that lurched into baseless speculation about women's personal lives, even of those women who had taken their own lives, vague generalisations lazily referring to them as *unhappy*, or *lost*, patronising language that, again, only served to mitigate the behaviour of men.

Once again, Dr. Bergeron's advice had been more

than instructive. Following a week of intense research, Stella had a focus. But she also had questions. What she needed was expert opinion, so she called Dr. Waters who suggested they meet for lunch.

"Dr. Waters, thank you for meeting me on such short notice," Stella said.

"Please, call me Allan. And no problem. Anything for Celia and Sara. Always happy to be of service to Thomas & Taylor. I did talk to Celia after you called, we're old friends you know, helped me get started back in the day. She told me about the French case, your connection to it. I'm sorry for your loss. How are you?"

"Well, to be honest, it's really knocked me back. And, well, yes, it's personal. I knew the victim, Amelie, a young woman we met on our first night on holiday in Corsica. I was with Colin, my husband, we had dinner at her uncle's restaurant where she worked as a waitress. She was just getting going in life. And then, someone, some monster, stepped in."

"I am so, so sorry Stella. Please, tell me how I can help."

"Allan, I don't mind telling you that my coming here, meeting with you today, is probably outside of my remit as a solicitor. A psychologist, a friend, helps me out from time to time. She advised me to keep busy, so I've been looking into forensics, profiling, researching how men who kill women think, how they try to justify deeply-rooted misogyny, the violence, the warped sense of power, control issues etcetera. I suppose what I'm looking for is your insight into the twisted satisfaction murdering women gives men. What is it that triggers a simple dislike into that next fatal step, what turns angry, often violent men into callous murderers? Tipping points."

"I see," Dr. Waters said, drawing in a deep breath. "Well, encapsulating over lunch the more ominous nature of men is somewhat a tall order. But I'll give it my best shot. To begin, permit me to ramble. Stop me if I'm not making much sense, or babbling, I'm told I tend to *wander*."

"Your insight and experience are invaluable. Do you mind if I take notes?"

"By all means. Well, I suppose I could start with lockdown, a period in which rather dreadful numbers of women were murdered by abusive partners. I'm sure at Thomas & Taylor, like me, you're playing catch-up with the numbers of domestic abuse cases. Thank God for the vaccine. Incidentally, in the context of this investigation, the virus killed more men than women, the number of men dying 2.4 greater than women.

"But I digress. As you say, the perversion that literally forces men to murder women is indeed very much rooted in misogyny. My own view is that it begins with systems."

"Systems?"

"Yes, systems. That shape expectations and attitudes from the moment we are born. At the very core of each system, of course - good old patriarchy. Like a parasite, it buries itself deep inside us as toddlers, incubating, before it gets to work, clawing away at us from cradle to grave, furtively assigning norms, foisting upon each of us skewed beliefs that women and girls are inferior to men. I'm not a neuropsychologist, but in many men, I believe that these systems shape desires that simply lay dormant, kept in check through other systems such as the law. This is just my view, quantifying evidence for such a claim is impossible, but, perhaps, in some cases, more than we'd like to admit, to limit extreme acts of violence against women, men themselves must simply employ a degree of self-control. Perhaps a tad extreme, I accept, but we often talk of women as *survivors*. What then is it they have survived?

"Historically, serial killers have got away with it. Operating with clinical stealth, the numbers of unsolved cases are too numerous to mention, and only relatively recently, in the last decade or so, have sentences really caught up, matched the crime. Like I say, misogynistic values continue to weave themselves into all of our lives, somewhat ironically, via institutions - systems - created to keep us all safe. The family, church, education, the law. Institutions at the heart of every culture systematically turn a blind eye to the abuse of women, keeping it invisible, not only making the relegation of women and girls appear normal, but making their inferior status seem acceptable.

"It's from within these systems that serial killers have not only emerged, but thrived, often finding safe haven. One might argue that they have been given permission, throughout the centuries sanctioned by little men in lofty parapets, proclaiming, insisting, affirming that age-old deception of a *natural order*, that men are superior, an idea which, sadly, continues to persist. In short, institutions that purport to keep us all safe, when it comes to protecting women, do little but perhaps, occasionally, add fuel to a raging bonfire.

"Take for example enforcement, the police. More specifically, the policing of women. Let's think back to the case of that young woman in Clapham, a while ago, during lockdown I think. Sara…"

"Everard."

"Yes, thank you. Sara Everard. Murdered by a serving police officer. Once again, her murder provoked much debate on violence against women. A splash of outrage, *illegal* demonstrations on Clapham Common during Covid, followed by a swathe of promises to change, improve things to make women safer. But really, what action has been taken? None. Here we are, today, *back on track* so to speak. As you've seen from your research, the focus reverts to sordid intrigue into the perpetrator's complex nature, his behaviour, his aggression, but rarely do we see sympathy for the victim. And the Plymouth case?

"Plymouth?"

"Again, a while back, the young man with links to incel groups. Killed five people, including his mother. Permitted a gun licence which the police had previously revoked. How, we must ask ourselves, can people like him slip through the net? It remains very clear that though we make grand fanfare about the dangers of misogyny, we do very little to combat it. Token gestures from time to time. A flash of media coverage. And what about where it really counts? In law. What about legislation? I personally believe it's shameful that successive Home Secretaries, male and female, refuse to make violence against women and girls a priority. And with escalating cases of rape - why the reluctance to establish rape units throughout the country? And what of despicable landlords who pressurise women into having sex to pay their rent? Few if any prosecutions. And the result? The government stubbornly refusing to consider misogyny a hate crime. What is it about women governments fear?

"You mentioned trigger points. Again, no psychological proof for this, but I often wonder if there is, lurking within men, an *innate* desire to control women. Many boys grow up frustrated, reckless, but it's only the few who harm women. But those who do, do so brutally. Unfortunately, what triggers in adulthood such macabre desires, such despicable acts is very often impossible to detect. You often hear women talking about men as grumpy, quick-tempered, believing that this is just how *they are*. They grow accustomed to living on a *knife-edge* so to speak, unaware that a sudden shift in circumstances, such as lockdown, or a whole range of indefinable trigger points, ignites impulsive, unpredictable violence."

Dr. Waters paused.

"I read that rates of rape and murder fluctuate with societal wellbeing," Stella said, glancing down at her notes. "Does this suggest that during economic recession the numbers of men killing women increase?"

"Precisely what the statistics show."

"So why doesn't the government ring-fence organisations that try to help these women?"

"Yes, good question. You think this would be the case, certainly with the evidence at their fingertips. Again, this is where it all gets a little fuzzy, I'm afraid. You see, it appears that, in fact, the reality is that the *opposite* is true and those organisations seeking to help women are always the first to be targeted for funding reductions by any new government. In the UK, it's subtle. However, across the pond in the US for example, it's often more explicit. In that great, self-proclaimed beacon of global democracy, Trump's first instruction to his administrative heavies was to target women. Do you recall that new judge he appointed to the Supreme Court, that dreadful religious loon? I forget her name. A woman brought in to do his dirty work, to wield the misogynist axe. We've now seen the result. The repeal of Roe v. Wade. Imagine how women in that country feel now. And the judge, she's young, in her forties, she'll be there for as long as she chooses, so I'm sure she hasn't finished turning the screw on women's rights. American women will continue to suffer. Whether future administrations can stem the tide, undo some of the damage recently inflicted on women, only time will tell. But what is clear, women there are under attack, direction of travel is worrying, not just for women, but for all Americans.

"When governments fan the flames of intolerance it only emboldens violent men. No level of debate or reasoning can change deeply-held irrational feelings of which they are so certain. Especially those men who find women an infuriating substandard part of the whole. What happened in their childhood for them to develop perverse fantasies, frustrations, they believe can only be resolved by killing women? And to think many of these killers had caring mothers, sisters.

"Studies suggest that it's in formative, the early years of childhood, when feelings, attitudes, values, often described as *innate*, are subconsciously shaped. A period in which, perhaps, when the conviction that women are expendable takes shape, when potential psychopathic tendencies emerge and, as I mentioned earlier, are aided by institutions fostering attitudes in the home, at school, and through religious organisations.

"And the gatekeepers of these institutions? Those expected to shine a light on this imbalance? Well, billionaires, all men, who have bought up and control the media. Men in positions integral to society who I believe delight in the constant, simmering intolerance in any field of human conflict from which, ultimately, they profit. *Automatons* is perhaps a more accurate descriptor for them. The Zuckerburgs, the Musks, the Murdochs. In reality, they do very little but pay lip-service to concerns of inequalities in society. I have no doubt they are currently monitoring what I describe as a *slow creep*, the shifting attitudes in central Europe and the US to women's reproduction rights. These men allow politicians to easily and quickly access the electorate to achieve their ultimate aim - to gain and maintain power and control.

"They attack women through messaging that routinely dismisses them, ever more frequently, explicitly insisting that they alone cannot make informed choices on what they do with their bodies.

How is this still possible today? Just think for a moment, imagine this if you will, if the tables were turned, even for just a day, the uproar, the revolution, if women had control over what men did with their bodies. I know, I know, preposterous. Even hypothetically, it is pure nonsense. Yet even here in free-thinking Europe women must constantly monitor how powerful men place limitations on their freedoms. Again I ask, how in a *progressive* society like ours, is this possible? Clearly, there remains a simmering, residual misogyny in men that provokes an irrational fear of losing control of women. Which takes us back to systems.

"In the last fifty years or so, though long overdue, women have progressed in all areas of society. But we have seen how men don't like it, how they consider *their* spaces, *their* spheres of control, out of bounds for women. Corporations, government, religion, the law - even sport. Think of Celia and Sara, the frustrations they felt in the early days of establishing Thomas & Taylor. Today, thanks to women like them, there are more frequent and notable success stories of women excelling in positions of influence traditionally reserved for men. Those who immediately spring to mind, though now retired, Merkel in Germany, Ardern in New Zealand, women who led their countries through a global pandemic making wiser, speedier decisions than their male counterparts in other countries such as our own, and as a result, saving many lives. Yet despite their successes, despite their wisdom and shrewd decision making, despite them proving themselves, excelling in the most testing of times such as during the Covid pandemic, who do most people *really* expect to replace them when their term in office comes to an end? Men. Resumption of the *natural order*? Women as leaders again reduced to mere anomalies, their contributions perceived as *exotic*, perhaps lucky, mere blips. Sometimes, when I see these impressive women, at G7 meetings for example, normally the only flash of colour amid a sea of grey suits, as they rub shoulders with incompetent, petty men, I often wonder if they are thinking of who will replace them, inevitably a man, and if he will simply lean on, or slip back into systems of archaic patriarchy that have always failed women."

Stella looked up from her notes.

"So, are you implying women might be fighting a losing battle?" she asked.

"No, not at all. Well, perhaps. You see, it really is rather quite confusing. I do think we must applaud the tireless work, the sacrifices women have made and continue to make in effecting change. The achievements of the suffragists for example. And the work you continue to do at Thomas & Taylor. Very, very important work. But, rather unfortunately, firms like Thomas & Taylor are rare. And, perhaps, occasionally, you may feel like you are constantly swimming upstream?"

"All the time."

"Which begs the question. Why? Why is it that more isn't done to create true equality for women? It appears it's just so much easier to skip along to the same old drumbeat we've been listening to for hundreds of years. Perhaps we're all *automatons*.

Resisting change. Resisting thinking. Everyone terrified of upsetting the apple cart. All of us complicit in maintaining the status quo. Doing nothing is just so much easier. Thus, easier to keep women in their place.

"And muddying the waters? Well, perhaps, women themselves. Though all around them they see the damage, the harm, the indignity that men constantly inflict on them, many continue to believe men are better suited to lead. Duped from birth into seeing men as part of that natural order. And so here we are again, back to systems. It's difficult to even bear thinking about, but somehow, women are often complicit in men's vile behaviour. Think of Epstein's sidekick, Ghislane Maxwell. Born into privilege, best private schools, Balliol College, Oxford. Why did she feel compelled to support his perversions? On the other end of the privilege spectrum, working-class women voting for right-wing governments when the evidence clearly shows their rights will be curtailed, their lives made worse. Like those who gushed over Boris Johnson. Or the sycophantic white women who voted for Trump. How is this lunacy possible? Even within women it appears that misogyny is so deeply ingrained, stirring the passions of the downtrodden and privileged alike. In fact, someone coined a word for it. *Himpathy*. Can you believe that?"

Stella rolled her eyes.

"One of the articles I read mentioned *lone wolves*."

"As I briefly mentioned, many men feel a simmering, low-level misogyny women often recognise as man's *natural* condition. The *grumpy* husband - a *boys will be boys* mentality we have heard all our lives. Again, casual, accepted acknowledgement that early in boys' lives, certain behaviours, attitudes, often very aggressive, are tolerated, simply because they are boys. They are excused. Forgiven. Sometimes, even praised. Aggression appears to dissipate as boys and men age, but is it ever entirely extinguished? Clearly some boys continue to wrestle with feelings of frustration and dissatisfaction stemming from childhood well into adulthood. Often associated with genetics, most notably, the X and Y chromosomes continue to spark interesting debate. Some believe the Y chromosome, passed by men on to their sons, is responsible for turning boys into serial killers as men."

"Childhood experience? Nature-nurture?" Stella asked.

"Here, again, there are certainly lots of theories. Mainly Freudian. However, in my humble opinion, a more enlightened figure who investigates links between a boy's childhood experience and murder is Peter Vronsky. A little known Canadian, still alive, he has spent the best part of his professional life looking at every aspect of serial murders, his research stretching back to accounts of serial killing in Roman times. He suggests that isolation in childhood has some effect. Loneliness, bullying, exclusion. Of course, one might argue that most boys experience a degree of these at some stage in childhood, but perhaps, in some cases, severely distressing episodes in a minority of boys spark aggressive fantasies which they then carry furtively into adolescence, on into adulthood which, for some, turns them into killers.

"Many psychologists believe the mother/child relationship is key. But, here, again, the evidence becomes a little hazy. Even rather speculative. Especially if you examine evidence given by killers themselves. Many have described their mothers as controlling, overprotective, in some cases, both physically and emotionally abusive. Broad generalisations that, again, unfairly point to men killing women as a failing in the women who raised them. In my opinion, utter claptrap. More excusing men. More blame on women."

"Tired old trope," Stella added.

"I agree. Freud talks about the unconscious personality in early childhood that influences behaviour later in life. Personally, I think this may be a little too hypothetical, yet…"

"You think there might be something in this?" Stella asked.

"Well, for some men, quite possibly so. We still know so little about the primitive period of childhood. For decades psychologists have conducted tests on children, exploring how feelings are manifested. Some killers, as children, repress certain feelings. Some point to feelings of being stifled as having a direct effect on their behaviour as adults. Freud describes three aspects of human personality. The *id*, the *ego* and the *superego*. During the *id* stage, passive and active impulses develop, including the impulse of *mastery*, a period in which children can be extremely cruel. As they clamber into the *ego* stage, again, another very difficult period, as they try to disentangle formidable,

171

complex feelings, impossible to unravel, they struggle with conforming to societal norms, a period in which many psychologists believe the *real damage* occurs. At the next stage, the superego, the teenage years - when important values and morals are formed. For many adolescents, a most confusing time. Indeed, a period in my own life I wouldn't like to repeat. Throw into the mix *unconscious* drives, another wholly speculative field of work, and you see how, at best, when searching for specific triggers, well, we're back to mere, bleary speculation. Like I say, we're left guessing. I'm sure you've heard much of this before?"

"Some of it, yes. But such profiling gives us *something* to go on?

"Well, yes, I believe it does. But not much that can reliably be used as evidence in court."

"So, where do we go from here?"

"Well, fortunately, today, the numbers of serial killers are in decline. Better policing, more women involved, education, leaps and bounds in science and technology - CCTV, DNA testing et al. As you know, cold cases of rape, murder, and other crimes, are now regularly solved with DNA evidence. The most complicated part is the gathering of irrefutable evidence.

"A final point if I may. Many leading psychologists believe that psychopaths, including serial killers, mingle among us daily. Often described as, shall we say, astute *actors*, they *operate* in plain sight as respectable, functioning members of society. As such, psychological profiling is still considered risky, certainly as a form of reliable evidence. They know how to avoid capture. They know what to hide. Like us, they have access to information, technology. Stella, who's to say I'm not a modern-day Jack the Ripper!"

Stella's eyes searched for his hands.

"Yes," he continued, smiling, holding them up. "Pure giveaway. These, thankfully, have seen very little heavy lifting. Mother wanted a pianist son, like Mozart, a prodigy. I'm not sure how big his hands were, but these tiny digits can barely manage to straddle a 9th on piano. Rachmaninov and Liszt, the masters, hands the size of dustbin lids. Now I play purely for pleasure. Oh, but again, forgive me, I digress. You'll simply have to take my word for it, I'm no killer!

"I suppose the most famous example of the charming serial killer mingling among us is Ted Bundy. Exceptionally good looking, an unemotional demeanour and keen intellect that made him not only a remarkably effective predator, but provided a very compelling smokescreen. His interviews, quite chilling, most notable for what is often absent in most serial killers. Any sense of empathy. Bundy simply didn't care about the women he murdered. Callous, indifferent, brutal, he showed no pity, no remorse. Like I say, exceptionally gracious, but in reality, a cunning psychopath, targeting victims in public places, tricking them into trusting him then luring them to secluded spots where he raped and murdered them. He got away with it for so long as those closest to him didn't suspect a thing. Which begs the question, how do we prevent men like Bundy from doing what they will, inevitably, feel they must?"

Stella stopped writing, looked up, a quizzical look on her face.

"In everyday intermingling with others, you say Bundy was able to function, go undiscovered? That he simply didn't care about murdering women? What then do you think was his primary motivation?"

"I suspect, simply put, to dominate and torture. In interviews, in rather disturbing detail, he describes how he found great satisfaction in the actual murder. A most "satisfying, final expression of power and control" he called it. It's what he craved. His success, if we can call it that - getting away with it for so long. This, he says, was down to patience. Another common trait amongst serial killers. When, how, and under what circumstances he committed his next murder, planned with exact precision. But that was the 1970s. Today, with advanced methods of investigation, I'm not sure that even he could remain hidden for as long as he did then.

"But Stella, I must be getting back. Think of what I said about laws and systems. The way men have manipulated them. And finally, food for thought. As human beings, as cultures, do we *really* want to improve women's lives? Many men wielding authority remain stubbornly reluctant to accept women as their equals, refusing to believe they are *entitled* to the same moral, material and social benefits as them. Indeed, very wearisome. Believe me, I understand women's anger, their bewilderment, their frustrations. How for a magic pill to change men's delusions of power! To make them realise how we could all do so much better by letting women live freely."

***

Snowed under with reports due at the bursar's office by lunchtime the following day, Colin called to say he'd be home late. In the garden Stella looked back through her notes. Her discussion with Dr. Bergeron and Dr. Waters had certainly helped, but also, unsettled her. Opened up something inside her. Something that for now, at least, like one of those clever psychopaths, she would have to keep hidden.

12

Stella had been in bed an hour when Colin arrived, shortly after midnight. Wide awake, her heart was pounding heavily in her chest. Feigning sleep as he crept into the bed, she listened, waiting for the familiar, shallow breathing drift slowly into a soft snore, and then she slipped out of bed and quietly descended the stairs.

In the kitchen, the microwave timer flashed one-ten. Outside, black and silent night. A busy day just hours away, she was being irrational, absurd even, she should return to bed. But at the foot of the stairs, she looked up into the darkness of the landing and suddenly froze.

In the living room, she stretched out on the sofa. Wayward specks of dust floated in and out of a silver shaft of light piercing the darkness from a streetlight outside. She *had* to keep at bay, murky, perilous thoughts ready to rise and stir.

"Wake up! Stella, wake up! You'll be late."

Looming over her, Colin, smiling.

"Morning," he said, handing her a mug of coffee. "Are you OK?"

"I'm fine. Fine. Cramps again," she lied, sitting up. "Didn't want to disturb you. What time did you get home?" she asked, taking a sip of coffee.

"About eleven I think. Did I wake you?"

"No, no. Didn't hear a thing. Did you get all the reports finished?"

"The what?"

"The reports. Today's deadline?"

"Oh, uh, yeah. More or less. Listen, must rush. If you're not feeling so good, why don't you work from home today?"

"Yeah, I just might just do that."

The door closed behind him. Slowly swelling, dreary, dangerous imaginings returned. The cup trembled in her hands.

"Get going," she said to herself, "up, up, stay busy."

Climbing the stairs to the bathroom, she stopped on the top step and looked up at the small hatch in the ceiling, entrance to the attic. She often heard Colin up there rooting around, she'd only been up once, when they moved in.

Pulling open the hatch, a retractable ladder clattered down. She climbed up and turned on the light. Below dusty sheets, old boxes stacked haphazardly. She lifted one out, its fading yellow sellotape seal curling up at its edges. Scrawled in thick black felt tip across the top of a box, the word SCHOOL.

The seal gave way easily and she pulled out an exercise book. On its cover in blue ink, Colin's name and that of his primary school teacher, Miss Anderson. She flicked through the pages impressed by neat penmanship disturbed occasionally by splashes of smudged ink. An essay titled *King of the World* underlined in thick, red felt-tip pen had a commendable opening line which made her smile. *When I grow up, I will be king of the world and put an end to poverty and war.* Thumbing on through the pages, she stopped again, on another title. *Big Brother.* Here, the main character, a boy, undoubtedly Colin, longed for a brother, a big brother, who he could turn to when his sisters annoyed him.

She pulled out another book, a sketchpad from secondary school. Fortunately, he had developed a talent for words, as clearly evident from the sketches inside, a series of one-dimensional matchstick men, he had little artistic imagination. Perhaps a little too harsh, cruel even, candid comments from his teacher expressed disappointment, bluntly informing him that he wasn't good enough.

In an old shoebox, some old photographs, mostly of Colin alone, but a couple of him standing next to his mother at home in Devon looking warily at the camera. In another, an old school photo of row upon row of solemn-looking boys, Stella found Colin at the end of the second row, just behind subdued-looking masters decked out in gowns. About to pull out another box, her phone rang. Probably Ana calling. She returned the books to the boxes, threw the sheets back over them, and climbed down the ladder.

In the shower, she was thinking of the photos, of how unhappy Colin looked. Then, on a most unexpected whim, she decided not to go into the office that day. Instead, she called Colin's mother, telling her she had important documents to collect in Plymouth, and if convenient, she would drop in and see her around lunchtime.

***

"Absolutely delighted to see you again my dear,"

Colin's mother said, hugging Stella warmly. "What a wonderful surprise. There's a fresh pot of tea brewing. Come, come inside, I'm making us lunch."

Moments later, Stella was sitting comfortably at the kitchen table.

"So, documents in Plymouth you say?" she asked as she poured the tea.

"Yes. Important documents for a case," she lied. "I guess I could have used a courier, but it's nice to escape the city. When I saw the address, in Plymouth, so close, I thought I'd bring them myself. And come and see you. I do so like this part of the world."

"Well, I'm so very glad you did, my dear. It's such a lovely surprise. And how is Colin?" she enquired.

Opening the oven, she slid in their lunch, a large Shepherd's pie.

"He's fine. Working hard. Was out late last night - busy working," Stella replied.

"Well, I shall send some pie back with you for him," she said, smiling.

"Actually," Stella added, pausing. "I didn't tell him I was coming. He was still asleep when I left. Like I said, he got home late last night, he has no idea I'm here. I'll let him know when I get back."

"Well, not to worry," she continued. "Stella, I'm sure you know this already, but husbands don't need to know everything their wives get up to, do they? Only God knows what they get up to!" she said, breaking into a smile. "If Colin doesn't know, well, he doesn't know. I think it's best we leave it like that. My dear, you must be hungry after such a long drive?"

"Starving," she replied, smiling.

Over lunch, Stella received step by step instructions on how to make a magnificent Shepherd's pie.

"Chop and sauté onions. Grind the lamb. Add parsley, thyme, rosemary, and of course plenty of salt and pepper. Then, after browning the meat, throw in garlic, a splash of Worcestershire sauce and butter. Mash the potatoes, add a dollop of cheese, it really does work wonders you know, and then to finish, pour into a casserole dish, top with potatoes and bake. Voila!!"

Conversation during dessert shifted to Stella's work. As examples of the often-tangled complexities that come with preparing a defence, she offered cursory details of Charlotte and Sharon's cases.

"My dear, such business must have its pressures. Please, Stella, if ever you need a break, do come and visit. Consider this an open invitation," she replied, patting the top of Stella's hand.

Momentarily moved by this spirited little woman's heartfelt gesture, Stella watched as she made tea, trying to imagine how, as a young mother, she had managed the trauma of losing a daughter.

"Stella, you haven't mentioned your holiday. France wasn't it?" she asked, the tone of her voice changing as she poured the tea.

"Yes, Corsica, the island," Stella replied.

"Oh yes, that's it. How was it?"

"Well, certainly at the beginning it was magical. The island still has that rugged, old-world charm - there are still some parts of the world unspoiled by man's obsession to destroy. We stayed in the most beautiful cottage on the side of a mountain overlooking olive groves. The weather was ideal. Yes, it really was, well, for the most part, ideal, but ..."

"And Colin? Did he enjoy himself? Did he behave?" she asked.

Memories of a smiling Amelie suddenly plummeted through her. She thought of that Thursday evening, when she woke and Colin wasn't there.

"Apart from frying himself in the sun on our final day, yes, he behaved," she replied, noting the puzzled look on his mother's face.

"Corsica you say? You know, I read about Corsica just last week. I was on a trip with some women from the village, OAPs. We went to Bath for the day. Lovely city, you must visit. Yes, I saw Corsica mentioned in a local paper there. You were already back, so I wasn't overly concerned. A rather distressing headline, something about a local girl, tragically murdered there."

Bowing her head, Stella sighed.

"My dear, is everything alright?"

"Yes, yes. Oh, I'm sorry. So sorry," she said, drawing in a deep breath. "It's just, just, hearing you say that. About the young girl. You see, we knew the girl, we met her on our first night. Her name was Amelie."

Colin's mother's face grew suddenly dark.

"I think I still have the paper. One moment," she said, leaving the room, returning moments later with a newspaper. "Here it is, Yes. The body of a local student was found murdered. Bath University student. Amelie Harris, 20. Didn't show up for work at her uncle's restaurant. Her killer still at large. Oh my, Amelie, you say?"

Stella nodded.

"I'm so sorry my dear, I didn't mean to break …" she added, taking Stella's hand as tears welled in her eyes.

"No, no. It's OK, really. I already knew. The French police are investigating. A detective came to London and I gave a statement. She believes it may be linked to other cases."

"My dear, how can you possibly be involved?" she asked, a concerned look suddenly in her eyes.

"A couple of cases I'm dealing with here in the UK share similarities with Amelie's murder."

"Oh, I'm so sorry you have to deal with this business. So sorry, my love."

"Thanks. It's OK. It's, it's all part of my work. It's what I do."

Colin's mother poured more tea.

"I was up in the attic, this morning in fact," Stella continued, trying to lighten the mood, "and stumbled across a box of Colin's old schoolbooks. I read a couple of stories he wrote in primary school. An extremely ambitious young man."

"Primary school? Yes, as a very little boy, he was so very happy, very - I suppose the word is, loving. He was rarely out of my lap. But then, well, after Marjory, he left us for boarding school. Not the wisest decision to send him away. But my husband …"

"A tough time for him then?" Stella asked.

"Yes. I think so. It all came to a head years later, in

182

fifth form. He was nearly sixteen, home for Easter, and informed us that he would not be returning to school. Caused mayhem. Quite terrifying the arguments he had with his father. Surprising too. You see, until then, aside from the spats with his sisters when he was young, Colin had always been so mild-mannered. But, on this occasion, he simply wouldn't back down. We saw another side of him. I didn't realise he had it in him, that he possessed such, such - anger - I suppose is the word. But it appeared Charles got what he'd hoped for. Toughened him up. Boarding school did the trick. I think ..."

She paused. Momentarily lost in thought, she sipped her tea.

"I think it was at that point that the Colin I knew, the boy I knew, had *left* us. Something changed in him. A sense of, I don't know, it's hard to describe. He lacked energy, passion, for anything. I suppose he found saying goodbye to his childhood very difficult and withdrew, spending most of his time alone, in his room, reading. Wallowing in adolescent solace, gloomy teenage life. Fortunately, he went to London, university seemed to get him back on track. And then, his greatest fortune, and I must say, it really did come as a surprise, when he told us about you."

She took Stella's hand.

"Stella," she continued, "you are just so good for him. We really are so very grateful."

"Thank you. But it's quite common for teenagers to dwell on those darker moments, especially boys."

"You say you found a box of his schoolbooks?"

"Yes. Up in the attic."

"Well, there's another box in his room, under his bed. From his schooldays, I think. Maybe from university. Shall we take a look?"

Stella heaved the box up onto the bed.

"Listen," his mother suggested. "Why don't you take them with you? Put them in the attic with the others. Colin might even enjoy looking through them again."

"I think I will," Stella said. "I've had a most wonderful visit. And the pie - simply delicious. But I really must be getting back. Thank you again for everything."

Stella carried the box out to the car and put it on the back seat.

"Stella, please come back soon my dear. It really has been delightful to have you here. To see you so - *safe*. Remember what I said, you're welcome anytime."

As they hugged, Stella felt the genuine warmth of her embrace.

"I'll come back soon. Very soon. I promise," she replied, getting in the car.

"Drive safely my dear. I doubt I'll hear from Colin. He rarely calls these days. But if he does, let's just keep this little visit between us?"

***

At around six o' clock, still a couple of hours outside London, Stella sent Colin a text to say she was working late. But two long and lonely hours proved time enough to stir in her thoughts she had refused to let surface, and as she entered London over the Hammersmith flyover, the most acute sense of dread suddenly overwhelmed her, forcing her to pull over.

"Stop it! Stop it! Stop!" she screamed, thumping the steering wheel.

She flung open the door, got out, and pacing back and forth, tried to rein in the increasingly disturbing delusion spinning through her. One thing of which she was certain, she just couldn't go home. She thought of sleeping in her office. Or, perhaps, check into a hotel. She got back in her car, took deep breaths to compose herself, and called Celia.

***

"Come in sweetie," Celia said, opening the door.

"Listen, I'm sorry for barging in like this," Stella replied.

The short drive had given her little time to rehearse a reason for this sudden intrusion.

"Stella. Can I get you a drink?" Sara asked.

"Do you have wine?"

"Coming up," she replied, disappearing into the kitchen, returning with a bottle and three glasses.

Unsure where to begin, Stella looked at her two trusted friends.

"Are you OK, honey?" Celia asked.

She drew in a deep breath.

"I don't know," she confessed, looking down into her glass.

Sara and Celia glanced at each other.

"Is it to do with … Emma?" Sara asked, sensitively.

Stella shook her head.

"No. Well I don't think it is. I hope it isn't."

"Everything OK at home?" Celia asked, gently.

Stella remained quiet.

"I don't know," she stuttered.

Celia and Sara glanced again at each other. A minor spat with Colin. Constant, reliable, her pillar of support. They knew Colin. One of the good ones.

"Can I stay here tonight?" she asked.

"Of course you can, hon," Celia replied.

"You can stay as long as you need. As long as you want," Sara added.

"Thanks."

"Honey, let me call Colin for you," Celia suggested. "I'll tell him your phone died, and we're up to our necks in case work we need for tomorrow. Is that OK?"

Stella nodded.

Moments later, she returned from the kitchen smiling.

"All good," she said.

"In your own time Stella, no rush," Sara said.

Stella sipped her wine nervously.

"I don't know where to start, I really don't," she began, sighing deeply. "I just keep doubting myself. It feels so constant. I have these thoughts, irrational thoughts. Small things, more recollections really. Somehow, I don't know, recently, they just keep, I don't know, kind of exploding - in my mind. Irrationally. I can't seem to shake them."

"Is it anything to do with work?" asked Sara.

"No. Well, yes. Yes and no," she replied, again

sighing deeply. "It's connected. Yes, it is. To the Miller case. And possibly the Norwich case." Then, tentatively, added, "and maybe the case in Corsica."

Celia and Sara sat up, baffled looks on their faces.

"The similarities in all three cases suggest these women were killed by the same man," Stella continued.

"Yes, we discussed this with Yvette and Simone," Celia said, still confused.

As if embarrassed, Stella again looked down into her glass.

"Listen, Celia, Sara, I'm tired. I'm not quite up to this right now. I'll explain more tomorrow, I promise. I really will."

***

Over breakfast, Stella apologised. She was feeling better. Just a *low* moment, nothing to worry about, she lied.

At work, she tried to stay busy. Dame Campbell had finalised a court date for Charlotte, so she took a final look through the evidence, making sure everything was in order. A message from Colin shortly before midday, the type of message he sent most days, served only to rekindle irrational, unsettling thoughts from the day before. Enthusiasm for work suddenly dwindled, she skipped lunch and strolled in Lincoln's Inn Fields, again trying so hard to banish from her mind feelings she simply couldn't let surface.

Before returning to the office, she sat in her car, on

the back seat, next to the box full of Colin's schoolbooks. She pulled one out, a History book. On the first page an account of the *Battle of Hastings*. Stella had only vague recollections of the battle, but Colin's account enthusiastically detailed how after a long and bloody battle in October 1066, William, the Duke of Normandy, decisively defeated Anglo-Saxon King Harold II, establishing the Normans as rulers of Britain.

On the next page, a drawing of the battle. Harold, unsteady on his horse, loyal soldiers around him either dead, dying or fighting to the last. Above the drawing in Latin, HIC HAROLD REX INTERFECTUS EST. Below, a translation. *Here King Harold is slain.* Strangely familiar, the simple straight lines for the curves of each letter reminded Stella of a similar scene from a copy of the Bayeux tapestry she had seen somewhere. She flicked through the pages, stopping to read a half-page summary of the beheading of Charles I. A rudimentary, gruesome drawing accompanying it depicted slouched over a bucket, on his knees, a headless man. Stella slapped the book closed, tossed it back into the box and returned to the office.

Passing through reception, she smiled and nodded politely at a woman sitting in reception. Just as she sat down, Ana called.

"The woman in reception. A Mrs. Flynn. She's here to see you."

"Mrs Flynn? For me? I've nothing scheduled. Is it in the calendar?"

"No, it's not. But she was quite insistent. Says it's

important."

"Really? OK. I'm on my way."

"Mrs. Flynn, very pleased to meet you," Stella said, moments later in reception.

Almost immediately, she was struck by something familiar in the woman's face. An old school friend perhaps.

"Hello Stella," the woman replied, smiling anxiously as she rose and offered her hand. "I'm Helen. Colin's sister."

Hoping the polite smile had disguised the sudden panic rushing through her, Stella showed her into her office.

"I am so sorry for barging in unannounced. I really am," Helen said nervously as she took a seat.

"No problem, no problem at all. In fact, it's very nice to meet you at last. Does Colin know you're in town? We can meet for dinner if you like?"

Helen shifted awkwardly in the chair.

"No, he doesn't. And if you don't mind, I'd rather he didn't know. The truth is I came to London to see you. Not Colin. Mother told me that you visited yesterday. She's grown very fond of you Stella."

"And me of her."

"It's no secret, you must have noticed, there's a certain tension in our family. My absence at family gatherings. The wedding?"

"Yes. But in what I do, I've discovered that, in reality, most families have disagreements, tension of some kind that makes gatherings uncomfortable. It's really quite normal. But, clearly, your mother holds it all together, she's the rock?"

189

"She most certainly is. But with everything she's had to deal with, I do worry about her. The truth is, I've thought of coming to see you on many occasions. When she called me last night and mentioned you had visited, I decided to come today. She was quite cross, we argued. She said it would be an intrusion. If so, I do apologise. She also said that you would *sense* a problem if there was one."

"I'm sorry Helen," Stella replied, "I don't follow. A problem?"

Helen drew in a sharp breath.

"Stella," she replied, a tremor in her voice. "I'm here, I'm here to talk to you about Colin. Please, forgive me, this is very difficult. But I could never forgive myself if anything happened, and, and, I just sat idly by. But I came really to, to make sure that you, that everything is, is, as it should be. Between the two of you, I mean. That he is, that he treats you well?" she faltered, a deep flush rising in her face.

"Helen, let me assure you," Stella replied, trying to find the words she no longer believed. "Colin has always treated me very well. I'm aware he had a difficult childhood. Your mother told me about Marjory, your sister. About the accident on the cliffs. It must have been very hard for all of you," Stella added sympathetically.

"Accident? She called it an accident?" Helen asked.

"Well, yes. After all, it *was* an accident?" Stella replied, suddenly very curious.

Helen grew quiet, her lower lip trembling.

"He hated Marjory. Hated her," she suddenly blurted out.

"Helen," Stella protested. "I'm not sure I need to hear ..."

"He frightened me. Still does," she continued. "He has done, for as far back as I can remember. Marjory stood up to him, she never let him get away with anything. I know we were only children, but there was something, something very, very, strange about him. Even as a child. Father was quite harsh on him. That's true. Perhaps he recognised something in him, something, I don't know, something not quite right. Something spiteful. But more than that. It's hard to describe, perhaps, something controlling. I saw it in him. Especially when he screamed at Marjory, often for no reason. It used to really upset her. It terrified me.

"I remember one day, we were in our room, just the two of us, playing with our dolls. Colin suddenly rushed in and began punching and kicking her, he wouldn't stop. If Mother hadn't come in and pulled him off, he would have caused her serious injury ..."

She sighed and drew in another, nervous breath, shifting again in the chair.

"Helen," Stella interrupted, "I can assure you I have never seen anything remotely violent about Colin. Ever. Really. I admit, with regard to certain aspects of his childhood he has been guarded, secretive even. Like never mentioning Marjory. I just always assumed he was a twin. Your mother told me what happened. But, as I'm sure you yourself understand, perhaps his way of dealing with the trauma of Marjory's death is by blocking it out, erasing from his memories a most traumatic episode in his life."

"He never mentioned Marjory to you?" Helen asked, searchingly.

"No. He mentioned you, but never Marjory."

"And Mother, what she said happened to Marjory, she described it as, an . . . *accident*? She's never mentioned Marjory since, we never speak of that day. But last night, she mentioned it. She cried."

"It was really only by chance that I learnt about Marjory," Stella replied. "When I found the photograph, the one in the dining room - of the three of you when you were eight. I asked her about the other girl, and that's when she told me - about the accident on the cliffs."

Helen looked up and gazed at Stella.

"It was no accident," Helen whispered, as if to herself, her lower lip beginning to tremble again.

"Not an accident? What do you mean? Your mother . . ."

Suddenly lost in thought, Stella stopped abruptly.

"As far as I know," Helen continued, "Mother has never spoken to anyone about what really happened on the cliffs. Not to me, and I very much doubt my father. What goes through her mind when she thinks about what happened that day, as I'm sure she does, well, I just don't know how she has got through all these years. I don't know how... how she balances it all out. I don't even know if she knows what *really* happened. I don't know what she said to the police. Or what Colin said to them. We were only eight."

"What *really* happened? What Colin did?" Stella asked apprehensively, "I don't follow."

"Stella, I have told only my husband what I'm about to tell you. I suppose the reason I came here today is to tell you what I witnessed on the cliffs that day. What I saw. You see, and I know this sounds ludicrous, and I so hope I am wrong, but I feel I have a *duty* to tell you. Quite possibly for, for your own ... *safety*."

The way she whispered the word *safety* provoked in Stella a sudden feeling of dread, reminding her of a similar concern expressed by Helen's mother the previous day.

"It was a beautiful day. Mother told us we were going to the cliffs for a picnic lunch, something we often did in fine weather. But that morning, Colin had got into trouble. With his favourite knife, one he got for Christmas. I think he had a collection of them. He had stripped a sapling of its bark and quite unexpectedly, for no reason, he rushed into our room and lashed Marjory with it, breaking the skin, blood trickling down her leg into her sock. When Mother saw the blood, she took him by the arm, slapped his legs, and took away his knife. He begged and pleaded with her to have it back. She refused. In tears, he stormed through the house, screaming at Mother, threatening to take one from the kitchen if she didn't give it back to him.

"Around lunchtime, still a little moody, he seemed to have calmed down. On our way up to the cliffs, trailing behind us, he bounced a tennis ball. We reached the top, and while Mother prepared lunch, he asked us to play catch. I thought he was trying to make up with Marjory, but right from the start, he kept throwing the ball too high, way over her head. We complained to Mother, she told him to play fair, but he ignored her, deliberately throwing the ball high over Marjory's head, ever closer to the edge. Like I said, she had a temper, and finally, she'd had enough. She grabbed the ball and ran towards him, throwing it at him, striking him square in the eye. He fell to the ground holding his face. But then, suddenly, he was on his feet running at Marjory, pulling her hair, dragging her towards the edge. I turned and ran screaming to Mother and, and…"

She paused, drew in a breath and closed her eyes.

"I was running towards Mother, and I saw her look up, and, and, I'll never forget the expression on her face, the horror in her eyes. No, I'll never forget her eyes. Screaming Marjory's name, she sprang up, rushing towards the cliff edge ..."

She lowered head.

"But she had gone," she whispered. "Near the edge, holding his knees to his chest, Colin looked up and stared at me. And in that moment, I knew, we both knew, what he had done. I'll never forget it."

She looked up, directly at Stella.

"After the funeral, Father packed him off to boarding school. When the school holidays approached and Colin was coming home, I begged Mother to let me stay with my aunt. She never refused, always driving me there herself the day before he returned.

"Stella, what happened to Marjory that day was *no* accident. I can't be near Colin. Not after what he did. Just the thought of seeing him terrifies me. To this day, the sinister, yes, that's the word, the sinister way he looked up at me, it continues to haunt me. He knows that I know what really happened. What he did. I think he may have told the police Marjory had - *slipped - losing her balance* - as she chased the ball. An account satisfactory for the police report. Mother didn't make me talk to the police. Stella, I came to see you to let you know what Colin did. What he was, and perhaps, still is, capable of. I apologise if you feel I have overstepped the mark here. But, we, Mother and I, thought it only fair you had the *full* picture. Of what really happened to Marjory. Of what he did. Of what he was capable of then. As a child. He may have changed. I hope he has. I really do."

Helen got to her feet.

"Stella, I think I've taken up enough of your time. Despite the circumstances, I really am very pleased to meet you at last," she said, shaking Stella's hand before leaving.

Standing up, Stella could feel herself trembling. Pacing the room, she drew in long, deep breaths. Helen's confession couldn't possibly be true. It was so long ago. And she had freely admitted that she didn't see, definitively, what had happened on the cliffs. Perhaps Marjory did slip. Colin the man didn't reflect that boy she had described. There was nothing violent in his character. He could never be capable of, of, murder. She would have picked up on something so, so portentous. How could she not? No, no, it was simply inconceivable that he could have killed Marjory.

And yet. She had opened up to him about Emma. Full confession. Why had he never mentioned

Marjory? Or what had happened to her on the cliffs that day? She thought of Helen's closing words. *He may have changed. I hope he has. I really do.* Words that suddenly sounded like a warning.

Everything was suddenly so hazy, her mind swirling with such disturbing, troubling possibilities. Obligations. Solicitor. Wife. Woman. And Amelie. Sweet child. What really happened in Corsica? She *felt* - no - she *knew* something wasn't right. Colin, the lonely boy, cruelly banished by a harsh, bitter, unsympathetic father. Why had he never spoken about Marjory? What now? Talk to him? Tell him about her conversations with his mother? And Helen?

She didn't know what to do.

But she couldn't ignore the evidence.

13

Stella had summoned Celia and Sara to the conference room. Looking across the table at them, she sighed. Once uttered, there was no way of unsaying what she was about to tell them.

"Stella, in your own time," Celia said, calmly.

"I'm not sure if I can," she replied.

Springing to her feet, she walked to the window and lingered there, staring blankly up into a heavy bank of gloomy, grey cloud.

"I think what I'm about to tell you, will, will, make you think I'm mad," she said, turning to face them.

"Stella. Whatever it is, we're here," Sara replied. "Anything."

She returned to her seat and drew in a deep breath.

"Celia, Sara, we've known each other a long time. You know me well, my story, my history. How I've pushed through, with your help, for which I'll be forever grateful. But those dark days, that episode in my life, was personal, something I had to deal with, for the most part, alone. Despite some very low moments, it never affected my work. I managed it. It affected only me. Me alone. But what I'm about to tell you, is, is, different. It's not only about me. It involves others, and when I tell you, it will draw you in. And, quite possibly, the reputation of the firm. It may even have you questioning my soundness of mind."

"Stella. Whatever it is, we're here," prompted Celia.

"Colin?" Sara asked.

Stella sighed.

Celia and Sara had dismissed the possibility of Colin and another woman. Now they weren't so sure.

"You will think me deranged," Stella continued. "You'll think me some mad cow who's completely lost the plot. Sara, Celia, I'm going out on a fucking seriously dangerous limb here and, and, I don't know if I should. And yet, yet, I can't let this go on, let it continue to fester. It's pulling me in the, in the, the, wrong direction. Into the dark. I have to do something before, before, it destroys me. And others."

Celia and Sara waited patiently.

"It's Colin," Stella confessed. "But, but, I'm not sure how to, to say what I'm thinking. What I suspect. Like I say, when I think about it, just the idea of saying aloud what I'm thinking, what I'm about to share with you, sounding out such ludicrous thoughts, thoughts that ..."

She paused.

"What I'm about to tell you will certainly spell the end of my marriage."

Again, on her feet, she walked to the window. With her back to them, she began.

"Something *has* happened," she said, softly. "Something has been, been - uncovered. Brought to my attention."

Celia and Sara glanced at each other.

"Yet, it may be nothing, groundless. Simply my mind straying into places it shouldn't. Or it might just be me - overthinking. I hope to Christ it is, because it feels, it feels as if what I'm about to say, reveal, well, I don't know if I *should* be going there."

"Stella, please," Celia urged. "Talk. Give us the facts. This is how we solve this thing."

Stella returned to her seat.

"Do you remember the night you came to dinner?" she began. "When Colin made southern food?"

"Yes, yes. Of course," Celia said. "A lovely evening."

"Well, he said something that night, that in passing, I think, has turned out not to be true. I'm sure, or at least I think I am, that he said he was going to a conference in Manchester. Do you remember him saying that?"

Celia and Sara looked at each other puzzled. Neither remembered any mention of Manchester. They shook their heads.

"Well, he did. He said the conference was in Manchester. I thought I might have been wrong, but I'm not. I'm certain of it."

"So he went to a conference in Manchester. And? Surely this is more than minor miscommunication Stella?" Sara asked.

"But there was no conference in Manchester. He lied to me."

"Well, certainly, that would be out of character for Colin," Celia conceded. "But he doesn't come across as someone to mislead. Has he done anything to make you think he lied to you deliberately? Did you ask him?"

"Yes, but he brushed it off."

"And you don't believe him?" Sara asked.

"Perhaps."

"Another woman?"

Stella didn't seem to hear her.

"OK. Close me down if you think what I'm about to tell you is too impossible, just too, too absurd," she rushed out, sucking in another long breath. "Please, pull me back out of this very fucking deep hole that's about to swallow me up, but yes, I think he lied to me deliberately. And he had his reasons. And no, it's not another woman. Frankly, that wouldn't concern me," she said, pausing. "There was no conference in Manchester. The conference was in Norwich. He was in Norwich that weekend. I only found out by chance, when I bumped into a colleague of his. She told me the conference was in Norwich, not Manchester."

"Norwich? Manchester? So, perhaps he got the cities wrong," Celia said. "Slip of the tongue. He does go away a lot, up and down the country. Lots of different cities. Maybe you just heard him wrong Stella? You've had a lot on lately. But anyway, there must be more to this than a simple mistake?"

"The weekend he was in Norwich is the weekend the woman was murdered. The case Yvette is investigating. The one with the possible connections to the Miller case."

Celia and Sara sat upright. Hesitatingly, they looked at each other, then across at Stella.

"Oh, honey," Celia said, suddenly on her feet shaking her head. "Stella, hon. No, no, no, no, no. Colin? No way. That just doesn't fly. Honey, do not go there. No!"

"Colin is one of the good ones," Sara added. "That's what we've always said. That's what you've always said. Stella, no. Your Colin? Gentle Colin.

That's what you always call him. There's simply no way. No way."

"The French connection. The girl in France, Amelie," Stella continued. "The case Yvette and Simone are working on."

"How can Colin possibly be connected to that?" Celia snapped, sitting back down.

"You know we met the murdered girl. On our first night in Corsica. Amelie. The waitress. She came and sat with us. She drank wine with us. We knew her."

"But you were with Colin the whole time. How can you think he could have done such a thing? It's just not possible," Celia replied.

"One afternoon, the Thursday, I was sleeping. When I woke, he was gone. I called him but he didn't pick up, and when he came back, late, he looked, well, shaken. Said he'd nearly been in a car accident. I thought nothing more of it. But then, the following night, our last night there, we'd planned to return to the restaurant, to see Amelie. But that afternoon he got badly burnt, I think deliberately so. He never goes in the sun. Hates it. He could barely move, so we had to cancel dinner plans. I wanted to say goodbye to Amelie, so I drove into the village alone, but the restaurant was closed. I now know why. Because Amelie had disappeared. It was the day after she was murdered."

Celia and Sara sat quietly.

"And there's more. I think," Stella continued. "When I first had these suspicions, I read up, on serial killers …"

"Honey, no, no, please, don't go there," protested

Celia, again on her feet. "Honey? Colin a serial killer? Really?"

"Hear me out. I met with Allan, Dr. Waters, for advice. He doesn't know anything about what I'm telling you, I told him I was seeking advice for another case. We talked about traits psychologists ascribe to killers, traits shaped in childhood. Colin has always been so very guarded about his childhood, he's never opened up. Yesterday, I went to see his mother, in Devon, at the family home. Picture postcard, near the sea, quite beautiful. What she told me about something that happened to Colin as a boy, something very disturbing, is why I called you here."

She paused.

"Colin told me he was a twin."

"He is a twin, we all know that Stella," Celia said, her tone impatient.

"But he isn't. He's one of three. A triplet."

"A triplet? Really?" Sara said, surprised.

"Yes. His mother thought it odd he'd never mentioned it," Stella added.

"Yes, that is odd. You've mentioned a sister before. The other triplet? A brother? Sister?" Celia asked.

"He has, had, two sisters. Helen lives near their mother. The other, who Colin has never mentioned, is dead. A sister. Marjory. She died when she was only eight. A tragic ... *accident*. She fell from cliffs onto the beach."

"Poor thing," Sara said. "Well Colin must have taken it badly. Really affected him. Him not telling you about her is probably his way of blocking the accident out, dealing with what was clearly a traumatic episode for him. That makes sense."

"Possibly," Stella replied. "And yes, I agree the incident did affect him, but not because he lost a sister."

Again, Celia and Sara appeared puzzled.

"I think it's because he killed her. He pushed her off the cliff."

"Stella, no, no, that's not possible," Celia protested, thumping the table. "Hon, I think, I think, no! That's just a step too far. Honey, you're over-analysing all this. Colin? A killer? How can you possibly assume this? His own mother said this?"

"No. Not the mother."

"Who then?" Celia countered, momentarily perplexed.

"An hour ago I had a visitor. Colin's sister. Helen. I'd not met her before. She didn't come to the wedding. She came to London today specifically to tell me about what happened on the cliffs that day. She witnessed it all and has avoided Colin ever since. For most of her life. What she revealed about him, about what happened on the cliffs that day, has only added weight to my initial suspicions that he had been, that he is, hiding something. This is why I need your advice, your help. She told me about Colin's early life, about how as a boy he had extremely violent tendencies. Marjory stood up to him. Yes, she annoyed him, often riling him to distraction. On the day she died, Helen saw them arguing at the cliff edge. Only briefly, she turned to tell her mother, but when she turned back, Marjory was gone. She's convinced Colin pushed her over the edge."

"OK. I think I've heard enough," Celia said, thinking, tapping her finger on the desk. "Firstly, you will be staying with us until we decide what to do. We must play this by the book. I'll call Colin. Tell him that we have important cases pending and need all hands on-deck so to speak. That should give us a day or so. I need to think this through. Stella, I still have reservations about this, but from what you have told us, we have a duty to investigate. For Marjory."

"And Amelie," Stella added.

***

That evening, Celia called Yvette and Dr. Waters. As a matter of urgency, she invited them to meet with her, Sara and Stella in the conference room the following morning.

"Let me just say up front, that this is an extremely delicate matter," Celia began. "Stella, bringing this to our attention is absolutely the right thing to do. Wherever this goes, whatever the outcome, you have the full support of everyone in this room. And so, before we begin, perhaps it's not necessary to say, but I will anyway. What we discuss here, stays in this room. Until we agree otherwise. There's enough experience around this table to work this thing out. It's a most unusual predicament, certainly unexpected, very sensitive, both personally and professionally. But we can and will resolve this. Yvette, thanks for coming on such short notice. I'll pass this over to you."

Yvette nodded.

"Stella, firstly, I'm sorry to see you again under

such circumstances. However, I agree, I think you have done the right thing in bringing this matter to bear. So where to begin? To be frank, we have little to go on. In these initial stages of the investigation, we can only focus on the cases in Norwich and France, and the links that Colin may have to them. He was in both places at the time of the murders. This in itself is not evidence, and so for now we keep the focus on these cases. Let's see how it goes, and if need be, we will of course bring in the Metropolitan Police. Until then, we go on only the evidence. What's important now, is that we don't let Colin suspect he's under investigation. We'll take things slowly, see what turns up. Not shake the tree too hard. Stella, what do you think?"

"You want me to be the eyes and ears," she replied. "I can do that. Carry on as if nothing has happened. Like you say, we don't want to arouse suspicion."

"I think that's a good start," Yvette continued. "Whatever you can provide will be useful. Anything that lets us start building a profile. Allan, is there anything that Stella might want to be alert to?"

Dr. Waters nodded.

"Stella. It's clear that you are very perceptive. Indeed, your perception is what has brought us here today. So, at home, take a look at things with, dare I say, fresh eyes. For things you may have simply overlooked. For example, you made mention in your statement something about Colin's old schoolbooks?"

"Yes," Stella replied. "I mentioned the books, it's probably nothing, but in one of his history books he recounts the Battle of Hastings. I know this in itself is

205

nothing strange, virtually every child in the country studies this part of our history, but alongside his description of the battle, he sketched a battle scene. What caught my eye was the shape of the letters in the title. They reminded me of, well … they had a passing resemblance to the shapes of the letters cut into the victims' backs. It may simply be nothing, something he copied from a book, I'll bring them in and we can take a look, even if only to dismiss such a tenuous possibility. Perhaps it can give us an idea of what Colin was like as a boy."

"I agree," Celia said. "We double check everything. I think for now, we're all in agreement on how we proceed. I propose we meet again in a week. In the meantime, Stella, it's important you don't put yourself in danger at home. Take no risks. Is that clear?"

"I'll be fine," she assured them. "Those of you who know Colin, know him as the most gentle of men. Part of me hopes I'm wrong, that this all collapses into nothing. But, potentially, women's lives may be at stake. I feel as if we have no other option than to pursue this. Whatever the outcome, whatever the cost."

"We'll meet again in a week and discuss next steps," Celia replied, bringing the meeting to a close.

***

Stella and Colin often chatted during the day. Under normal circumstances she wouldn't have given calling him a second thought, but on this occasion, after leaving a message for him to meet her at Luigi's at seven-thirty, she replayed the conversation over in her mind. Had she said anything out of the ordinary? Had the tone of her voice evoked suspicion? This, she thought, is how things would be until the matter is resolved.

When Stella arrived at the restaurant, Colin was already there scrolling through his phone.

"God, it seems like forever since I've seen you," he said, greeting Stella with a gentle kiss on the cheek. "You have a lot on then?"

"Tons," she replied, taking off her coat. "We have a run of cases pending. Mostly fact checking. One very big case, overseas clients. Celia asked us to muck in," she added, smiling.

"Anything interesting? The international case?" he asked.

"Trafficking," she lied, surprisingly easy.

The waiter took their orders, and as they chatted about Maria and her baby, it reminded Stella of the early days of their relationship, she even found herself enjoying the evening. But, perhaps a little too relaxed when, quite out of character, she mentioned the possibility of another holiday. She never talked about taking time off work.

"Another holiday?" Colin queried, clearly surprised.

"Well, once we get through this backlog of cases, I think I'll need one," Stella responded, trying to make light of the suggestion.

"Perhaps Sardinia? Must be fairly similar to, to . . ."

He suddenly stopped.

"Yes, Italy. Why not? Perhaps Sicily - I hear it's beautiful," she replied.

"How's that case you were working on?" Colin asked, changing the subject. "The woman who killed her husband. Charlotte, I think, was her name?"

Casually dabbing her mouth with a napkin, Stella disguised her surprise. He knew her name. Solicitors at the firm only ever referred to cases using clients' surnames. Never first names.

"The Charlotte case?" she asked.

"I think that's the name. I overheard you talking with Celia one evening, on the phone. I'm sure you said Charlotte."

Had she let her name slip? She couldn't be sure.

"Oh yes, Charlotte, that's in court with Dame Campbell," she replied, still mildly alarmed.

He *had* looked through the files in Devon, returning them to the drawer with Charlotte's file on top of Sharon's, not how she had left them.

"We're confident we've got the charge down to manslaughter. We'll know next week, we hope," she continued.

"Manslaughter?" he asked.

"Hope so," Stella replied.

"Did she mean to kill him?"

"I think she did. But he was a real bastard. Put her through hell. But she knows she has a price to pay."

"Does she regret killing him?" he asked.

In their meetings, Charlotte had never mentioned remorse.

"I'm sure she does," she replied. "They had two boys. They'd built a life together, but he destroyed everything. Even so, she must have regrets. Surely anyone who takes another life must have regrets," she added, again regretting such a rash, provocative comment.

"But like you say, if the husband was a real bastard, making her life hell, perhaps deep down she has no regrets. She sees killing him as justified," Colin suggested.

"Can murder ever be justified? Under any circumstances?" Stella asked, again, a little too briskly. "Well, it's up to the courts to provide justice."

"Yes, yes, of course," he replied, nervously. "Of course not. Anyway, come on, it's time we were off," he said, raising his arm for the bill.

***

The following morning, Celia informed Stella that the prosecutor in Charlotte's case, a young female barrister, had agreed with Dame Campbell that a minimum sentence was not unduly lenient. In summing up, the judge declared a murder charge unviable, that the defendant had clearly suffered from an "abnormality of mental functioning," and her mental state "substantially impaired her from making a rational judgement or exercising self-controllability leading to the nature of her conduct." Key to the verdict, Dr. Waters' compelling testimony that Charlotte had killed her husband in a moment of diminished responsibility brought about by persistent coercive control. With no previous convictions and submission of an early guilty plea, Charlotte was found guilty of manslaughter and sentenced to two years in custody.

14

"Firstly, I'd like to welcome Simone," Celia began, opening proceedings at the next meeting. "I think you've met everyone, apart from Dr. Waters I believe."

"Enchanté. Allan," Dr. Waters said, smiling as he shook Simone's hand.

"I think the best way to start," Celia continued, "is to assess what we currently know. Yvette, you have a couple of potential leads I believe?"

"We have the CCTV footage from the hotel in Norwich on the weekend of the murder. And the guest list for those at the conference. I can confirm Colin was there. My team has gone through the tapes a number of times, and while he appears in the footage on many occasions, there's no sign of him leaving the premises on his own. Stella, do you recognise this?" she said, passing her a photograph of a small blue handkerchief.

"I can't say I do. Why?" she asked.

"We found it snagged in some bushes on land near the perimeter of the hotel. Near to where the murder took place. It's a bit of a long shot I know, but we've sent it off for DNA testing. We may need a DNA sample from Colin," she continued, hesitantly, looking at Stella.

Stella shifted uncomfortably in her seat.

"Listen, I think I know what you're asking, and I don't want to hinder progress," she said, "but acquiring DNA without permission is a line I feel very

210

uncomfortable crossing. Besides, somewhere down the line, such evidence might compromise the case if it's obtained without consent."

"I agree," Celia interrupted. "We have to tread carefully here, Yvette, no cutting corners. Do things by the book. Besides compromising Stella, I must think of the reputation of the firm."

"I understand," Yvette replied, drawing in a deep, frustrated breath. "Like I said, once we have DNA results from the handkerchief, then we can come up with something that doesn't compromise Stella or the firm. Simone has a possible lead I believe?"

"Yes," she began. "I have just returned from Corsica. It is a big island, not many people, not even in tourist season. I spoke with detectives investigating the case, but they know little, maybe nothing. However, they believe Amelie was killed a little north of Propriano, a small village where she was working at her uncle's restaurant. This is where I believe Stella met her?"

Stella nodded.

"I interviewed the uncle. He informed me that on the day she disappeared that she had gone swimming in a small cove, north of the village. She often went there, sometimes with cousins. On the day of the murder, she was alone. No personal belongings were found, so we cannot say for certain she was killed there. The body could have moved with the tides."

"Did they say exactly what day she disappeared?" Stella asked.

Simone flipped through her notepad.

"Yes, on a Thursday."

Stella closed her eyes.

"Stella? Are you alright?" Sara asked.

"That's the day Colin went for a drive. Late in the afternoon, alone. He returned at around eight-thirty."

"Did he say where he'd been?" Yvette asked.

"Not that I recall. He said something about nearly being in an accident, with another car, a near miss. The roads there are narrow, it made sense. I never thought anything more of it. But he looked very shaken, agitated."

"And so this was Thursday?" Simone confirmed.

"Yes," Stella replied.

"And you say Colin was not with you around seven p.m.?"

"No. He wasn't. I remember, it was after eight. It was just getting dark when he got back. Yes, I'm sure it was about eight-thirty. Why is seven important?"

"The detectives spoke to an old man. Very old. Ninety-one years. A shepherd who lives in the hills above a cove north of Propriano. Near where Amelie swam. On that afternoon he was taking his goats back into the hills, along the road, a common sight on roads in Corsica. He said he saw a car parked near the cove, but couldn't remember details, only that it was silver."

"Our rental car was silver, a Peugeot," Stella said.

"There are thousands of silver Peugeot rental cars in Corsica," Simone replied. "And the memory of the old man is a little unsure, too. At first he said the car was white. Stella, do you know which company you rented the car from?"

"Hertz."

"OK. We will contact them, find the car, inspect it.

Maybe this can be a DNA lead. I think this is all from me."

"Thank you, Simone," Yvette said. "Allan?"

"I think at this point it might prove useful for me to provide a simple overview of possible characteristics of our killer, whether or not it's Colin. None of us can say for sure what someone is thinking. Or say for certain that someone may be inherently incapable of evil. And though we all like to think that we know our nearest and dearest better than anyone else, in many cases involving serial killers, time and again, it comes as a complete shock to family members that their father, son, husband is a cold-blooded murderer. Many of you have showered Colin with compliments, attesting to the upright nature of his character. If indeed it is Colin who has committed these murders, those of you who know him, well, perhaps you may well be wondering if he really is capable of such an act. Deception acts as a very effective smokescreen for serial killers who, until caught, are often found to be upright standing members of communities. Such subterfuge hinders investigations and slows down arrests. Stella, I apologise for the blunt nature of my description here."

"Please, Allan, continue," she said, nodding her appreciation.

"Study after study shows that many serial killers are adept at keeping this darker side hidden. In effect, they are experts at living double lives. Like I say, to those around them they appear to be fully-functioning members of society. School fêtes, team players at work, contented husbands and fathers. Yet, lurking beneath this veneer of respectability, a sadistic murderer with a lurid, perverse appetite to kill. Very often, when he's caught, even with indisputable evidence, those closest to him refuse to believe him capable of such crimes.

"An example. One woman, the veritable Stepford housewife, had what she thought an idyllic life. Including the perfect husband. Wholesome family man, solid job, weekends away camping with well-adjusted children all doing well in school. But, he got sloppy, made a mistake, and after his arrest, when questioned, the wife was adamant that nothing during their courtship was amiss, all seemed perfectly normal. When asked to try and recall any slightly *strange* incidents, she mentioned that the house he was renting when they met had no carpets, no bed, just a mattress on the floor. But she was young, blinded by love, so of course she believed the story that the landlord had ripped out the carpet before he moved in, but had yet to replace it. And that the plastic sheeting in the bathtub was for painting the walls. Never, not even in her worst nightmare could she have imagined the truth, that the man she had given everything to, before they married, regularly picked up women, brought them home, strangled them, then after cutting them to pieces in the bathtub, disposed of the bodies in the woods.

"Inconceivable stories for most people, are commonplace for detectives investigating serial killers. What never fails to shock them however, are the wives and mothers who refuse to relinquish their loved one's innocence. Another case, particularly disturbing, in Russia. Before beheading his victims, the killer carved out their hearts. When caught, literally, in the act, he confessed. Yet the man's wife refused to believe the charges. She dismissed evidence as "fairy tales," and even after sentencing, pledged undying loyalty. And so, you see, it's quite understandable that wives, mothers, neighbours, often describe these men as your average nice-neighbour-next-door types. I apologise for the graphic descriptions I use here, but these cases exemplify why this type of killer is so difficult to catch. Stella, I really am sorry if this analysis proves difficult. I should also add that very often, those nearest to them are overwhelmed with guilt. For what they consider a perceived ignorance, they, too, feel like victims. I believe these feelings misguided but, as I've outlined here, in most cases, it's simply impossible to imagine men they love as potential killers. So, Stella, whatever the outcome of this case, I think you should bear this in mind.

"From what I've gathered about Colin thus far, he fits such a profile. Of good character, kind. Many of you here have described him as *gentle*, with no violent or other destructive tendencies. Certainly not in his adult life. But I'd like to dig a little deeper. Into his background, more specifically his childhood. There may be signs of perhaps, deeper, untapped issues. If he is a killer, then clearly they are unresolved. Stella, I'll start with his old schoolbooks.

"Finally, one last trait common in serial killers. They tend to be pathological liars, skilled in manufacturing credible lies. Had Stella not run into Colin's colleague by chance, in all likelihood, we wouldn't be here now. She believed Colin about the UCAS conference taking place in Manchester. As is common in such cases, when she first suspected something, he had told her on a number of occasions the conference was in Manchester, not Norwich, she convinced herself that she had made a mistake. By second guessing herself, she compensated for his credible lies. Whether or not Colin is the killer, be assured, whoever is killing these women has psychopathic tendencies. Outwardly charming, inside - wicked. An extremely dangerous man. For this reason, I think we must be careful and proceed with extreme caution. Whatever risks we take, whatever we decide, I suggest we remain aware that Stella's welfare is paramount."

"Thank you, Allan," Stella interrupted, taking a drink of water. "I'd like to say something before we continue. I cannot deny I find this investigation disturbing. How could I not? If, potentially, I am putting myself in harm's way, I think I understand the risk level. But above all, whether Colin is responsible or not, as experienced professionals, to protect unsuspecting women, we have a duty to see this through. For this reason, as we move forward, please approach this case as if it were *not* personal to me. Let's say what needs to be said, no apologies. Women are at risk here. So please, no tiptoeing around me. Let's manage the facts, listen to expert opinion, investigate fully."

"Thank you Stella," Yvette continued. "Allan, if Colin is the killer, how has he been able to get away with this for so long?"

216

Dr. Waters cleared his throat.

"Good question. Well, on top of what I have just mentioned, the short answer is luck. If we look at some historical cases, probably the most famous, that of Ted Bundy in America in the 1970s and '80s, well, he had luck on his side. And I mention him as I believe his case has many similarities to our investigation."

"How so?" Stella asked.

"In interviews I've seen, and from transcripts I've read, those close to Bundy described him as bright, charming, with a kind, unemotional demeanour. I've not met Colin, but from what I gather, as I said, this is how many of you describe him. However, unlike Bundy, and most serial killers, Colin doesn't *appear* to lack empathy. However, is the Colin many of you know just acting? Is he simply concealing another side of his life?

"Bundy didn't care about the consequences of his crimes. Psychopath, very effective predator, he found torturing women sexually arousing. He gained most satisfaction by making the act itself a *fantasy*. For him, the sexual element was essential. By killing his victims slowly, it satisfied his hunger for power and control, it prolonged his own sadistic pleasure, it gave him a tremendous sense of empowerment. Like Bundy, whoever is committing these murders is incapable of feeling pity or remorse and, clearly, doesn't value human life. Of this, I'm sure.

"However, there is a striking difference too. Though our killer's behaviour is obsessive, compulsive, cyclical in nature, dominating his victim for sexual pleasure doesn't appear to be the primary objective. For him, the act of killing is paramount. And then, the signature. Is he provoking us? In interviews, Bundy said that at some point, he knew he would be caught. Perhaps this is the case with our killer? For now, however, this is as much as I have. I'll look through Colin's schoolbooks and let you know if I find anything of note."

"Thank you Allan. Thank you all. Perhaps that's enough for today," Celia said. "I'll be in touch about the next meeting. In the meantime, no matter how far-fetched, bring all ideas to the table."

***

At lunchtime, alone in a café, Stella's mind was racing. She had made the biggest mistake of her life. Colin couldn't possibly be a killer. He simply wasn't capable of such heinous brutality. Of this she was suddenly certain. But what about the evidence? Norwich. Corsica. Helen's visit. The pain in her eyes as she struggled to recount her sister's death. Her murder?

She pulled out her phone and tapped the screen.

"I'd like to make an appointment with Dr. Bergeron?"

***

Dr. Bergeron again saw sitting across from her the shy, nervous girl she had first met many years before.

"Stella, you've done the right thing in coming to see me. Firstly, tell me, what does your gut say here?"

"This is just it," she replied, sighing. "One moment

I'm cursing myself for even going there, involving colleagues, the firm. Even for believing Colin could think of such a thing. I just keep asking myself why? I have no concrete evidence, just a hunch, a feeling, but..."

"But what Stella? Say it."

"I don't know, it's hard to describe. But there's just *something*. Something telling me that, that, something's not quite right. Colin a killer? Of course it's ridiculous. Just saying it feels, I don't know - ludicrous. But the things I now know about him. About his childhood. Important things that he has never mentioned. Like what happened to Marjory. Why would he hide something so, so important in his past? I thought we shared everything. I told him about Emma. It's from what he hasn't told me, these suspicions, these shaky convictions, have emerged."

"Let's focus for a moment on these convictions," Dr. Bergeron replied. "Especially in times of doubt, such strong conviction and uncertainty often overlap. They can even feel the same thing. At times of high anxiety, feeling so sure yet so uncertain, at the same time, is not unusual. It's what's known as "artificial" certainty. The difference between what we actually *know* and what we really *experience*.

"Your work as a solicitor, your experiences in life have shaped deeply-held beliefs concerning morality, behaviour, especially with regards to men. In your mind, clear lines are drawn. When representing women, as you build a defence, you make sure there are no grey areas. Your convictions are guided by the evidence. However, in these early stages of a most complex, personal investigation, you should *expect* to feel confused. It doesn't feel like it right now, but you are already going in the right direction. The fact you called me is the evidence of this. You're already processing the problem, breaking it into pieces, stripping away the dross, weighing up the evidence. There *will* be a resolution. And whatever it is Stella, be prepared to manage a range of conflicting feelings - confusion, regret, guilt, feelings that will linger long after this is resolved, whatever the outcome. But you *will* get through this. You just have to know how to manage it. We talked about this in our early sessions. Remember?"

Stella nodded.

"On a cognitive level, ideas of which you *feel* certain are affecting, stirring your emotional state. With the gravity of what you're dealing with, this is normal. As you gather evidence, consciously and subconsciously, you'll be inching towards a solution. These are difficult moments, but part of a process. Even now, here, by talking to me, you're filtering ideas. There's no smooth ride, no shortcuts. In low moments, perhaps like now, when you're overwhelmed, trying to disentangle, order your feelings, remind yourself - that you're processing, dealing with each stage, that this is one more step towards a resolution. Towards clarity. Think of it, perhaps, as a series of small victories. Stella, you have what it takes to manage this. You've been here before.

"Think back to those early sessions. How scared and nervous you were. Like how you feel now. Remember how we spoke then about you reclaiming your happiness? Again, I want you to think about this. Then, I said, don't let others take your happiness."

Stella nodded.

"We talked about feelings of anxiety, frustration, guilt, betrayal. How they are magnified, amplified. As they are now. Well, together, we untangle them. As a wife, as a solicitor, you are swaying between feelings of which you are certain and yet - uncertain. This is to be expected. Push ahead, draw on the strength I saw in you as a girl. That I see in you as a woman. I've always seen strength in you Stella. Trust in that strength, trust in your convictions.

"You're already making the right choices. Confiding in Celia and Sara. Coming to see me. You're heading in the right direction. Remember that, this is important Stella. Your burden is our burden. No woman is an island. We help each other. Things right now feel, appear distorted. As you gather the evidence, as you move towards that resolution, as you trust in your convictions, keep reminding yourself why you *have* to pursue this line of investigation by, perhaps, considering the consequences of turning a blind eye. You must do what you believe is right."

Stella drew in a deep breath and closed her eyes.

"Stella, feeling vulnerable is part of the process, the journey. Give value to negative, confused feelings, to doubt. Each step you take, is a step closer to resolution."

"I know you're right," Stella acknowledged. "But it's just so hard - I feel so, just so, as if there's no escape from it all."

"Stella, most people would have just buried this,

got on with their lives. Or simply crumbled. Let it destroy their lives. But not you Stella. Like I say, it may not feel like it, but you are strong, you're tackling these unimaginable circumstances head on, you're reaching out. Stella, you're making all the right moves here, that is your strength. It really is. You're making the right decisions. You are now, you always have. But, tell me, at home - how are things with Colin? How are you coping?"

"At first, I thought facing him would be terrifying. But, but, I suppose, it's just a case of acting. Making sure things appear normal."

"Any tricky moments? How about … the bedroom?"

Stella drew in a deep breath.

"We rarely have sex. From the start, since we met, there has been this, I suppose, unspoken agreement that, that, what we have, our marriage, is not about sex. To be honest, I'm happy with this … arrangement. On the odd occasion, normally after too much wine, well … it's quite hard going, actually."

"In what way?"

"Well, I suppose it feels more of a burden, an obligation. For us both. Like I say, our marriage is not really about the bedroom, it's more, I wouldn't even say friendship, more about, *companionship* isn't the right word, maybe the *being there*. Someone to talk to, be around. But now, when I think about it, quite often when we are at home, we spend a lot of time separately. It suits us both. I think."

"This is not out of the ordinary Stella. I think more couples live like this than want to admit. As you move forward with the investigation, as you build the case, remember why you are doing this. It's *for* something. Something you believe strongly in. Something at your core. Protecting women and girls. This is why you're taking this risk Stella. I think you know this. It's the only path you can take. A difficult path, but one that will, ultimately, save lives.

"I remember when you first came to see me. Do you remember a question you asked me about how people should behave towards one another? You, a young girl, dealing with the most traumatic event in your life, instigated discussions around the morality of human behaviour. I was so very impressed. Well, you're still asking those questions. Personally, I think what you do for women is most magnificent. Yes, magnificent. Stella, keep reminding yourself of this."

***

Senior officers in Norwich were putting pressure on Yvette to move the investigation along. They suggested, recommended, the team considered "tracking." Aware of the legal and ethical complications involved, Yvette cautiously flagged this up as an option at the next meeting.

"How, exactly, would we do this?" Stella asked. "Using Colin's phone? What if he doesn't have it with him? Or it's not on? And do we need to discuss legal implications?" she added, glancing at Celia.

"Before I continue, I'd like to remind you of what Celia said," Yvette replied. "That nothing we say around this table leaves the room. OK. Well, the truth is, police forces already use all types of technology available in linking crimes and catching criminals. And, I should add, nowadays we're making more arrests a lot more quickly. I admit, using a tracker on Colin would be - a *grey* area. Certainly ethically," she continued, pausing, tapping her pen on the desk. "The press keeps an eye on us, they know we use it. We disclose no information and manage our use of covert surveillance technology with absolute stealth. Human rights groups track us as well. Likewise, we neither confirm nor deny its existence. To do so would completely hamstring us, prove most damaging to our operational capabilities, especially now criminals themselves are using technology for terror-related activities.

"As solicitors, I expected and understand your reluctance to use a tracking system. In some operations, I too feel like we're teetering a little close to the edge of, well, perhaps, *acceptable* policing. But, frankly, tracking is an asset that works. It helps catch dangerous criminals, it reduces crime, it's the reason most forces in the UK continue to use it.

"Occasionally, our use of technology crops up in news reports. Most recently, it's how, *hypothetically*, we use facial recognition cameras. Our opponents claim it breaches data protection and equality laws, but in almost all covert communications, the Met continues to use it. They have been since at least 2011. And many within the force argue we should use any means necessary to catch criminals. Why? Well, let's take this case. If Colin is our man, and if estimates about the frequency at which he might strike are right, he's thinking about his next victim right now. For this reason, I think we should consider tracking him."

"*Hypothetically* speaking," Sara asked, "if we were to use a tracking device, how would we do it?"

"Well, *hypothetically*," Yvette responded, "we have the hardware. We use what's called IMSI - international mobile subscriber identity. Very effective. It tracks mobile phone handsets, connecting with them by impersonating phone towers, pinpointing locations and intercepting calls and text messages."

Yvette's compelling argument rendered the room silent.

Quietly, as if speaking to himself, Dr. Waters broke the silence.

"I beseech you, wrest once the law to your authority. To do a great right, do a little wrong, and curb this cruel devil of his will."

"Shakespeare?" Celia asked.

"Indeed. *The Merchant of Venice*," he replied. "Bassanio's plea to Balthazar, his wife, well, Portia dressed as a man actually - it's complicated - but an example of our dilemma. Desperate for his good friend Antonio to be released from a bond with the despicable Shylock, in providing the bond, a pound of flesh, Antonio will undoubtedly die. Bassanio pleads with the Duke to, let's say, *circumvent* the law. Just a little. In effect, the same quandary in which we find ourselves. What I believe Yvette is getting at. Should we, can we allow ourselves to cut corners here? Bend the rules for the greater good? This is our moral conundrum."

Again the room fell silent.

"To be frank," Yvette continued, her patience strained, "I'm a detective, not a lawyer. As lawyers, this may be a black and white issue for you. You know exactly what lines you cannot cross, but, as detectives, sometimes, as with our use of technology, for us, the lines are often blurred. As Allan says, we often bend the rules, like he says, just a little, to do a *lot* of good. In my experience, yes, police occasionally 'do a little wrong' to catch criminals. And, like the man we're pursuing now, I think we should up the ante. I'm feeling the heat from my superiors.

"Look at this," she continued, holding up a tiny device between her finger and thumb. "This is a nano-tracker. The world's smallest tracker. By simply pairing it with an app on a smartphone, they pretty much track anything. They're used for all sorts of things, very popular when travelling, attached to luggage. Families use them to track older relatives with dementia who wander off. And as detectives, we use them. As you can see, they're so small, they fit easily in a shoe, a pocket. The target has no knowledge of being tracked."

"No. I'm not going to plant a tracker," Stella insisted, sighing. "For me, this *is* crossing that line. Besides, I think I swore to a code of conduct," she said, looking around the table.

Again, the room fell silent.

"But I have an idea," she continued. "I'd like to invite you all to dinner. At my house. Allan, Yvette, you can meet Colin."

"But aren't we just kicking the can down the road

a little bit?" Celia interrupted. "I'm not sure how Yvette and Allan meeting Colin can lead us anywhere?"

Stella looked directly at Yvette.

"On the side table just as you enter our house is a small ceramic bowl. It's where we keep our keys," Stella said, pausing. "Colin carries a very bulky wallet. Full of old receipts. He keeps it in the bowl when he's at home. It's always there. Even at dinner parties. Do nano-trackers fit in wallets?"

"I'll bring the wine," Yvette said, smiling, a mischievous look in her eyes.

"I'll bring dessert," quipped Dr. Waters. "Do you have a date in mind?"

"Colin loves to entertain. I'll set something up for this weekend," Stella replied.

"Well, it appears we have our next scheduled meeting," Celia said. "Stella, let me know if it's a go and I'll let the team know."

***

Celia, Sara and Yvette arrived together. Stella nodded towards the ceramic bowl on the side table as they entered. Alongside a number of keys, Colin's wallet. She led them through the house into the garden where Colin greeted them with aperitifs. Fifteen minutes later, Dr. Waters arrived. Colin shook his hand then disappeared inside to fetch another glass. When he didn't return, Stella found him in the kitchen, bent over the sink running hot water over a deep cut in his finger.

"What happened?" she asked.

"I was taking a glass out of the dishwasher, it just shattered," he replied. "There are more glasses in the freezer, take one of those and make Allan a drink. I'll be out in a minute, once the bleeding stops."

"Hold your hand in the air," Stella instructed.

Squeezing a paper towel around his finger, once the bleeding had stopped she wrapped it with a plaster.

"You're good to go. Here," she said, taking a glass from the freezer. "Make Allan a drink. I'll bring out the dips. Can you ask Yvette to give me a hand?"

As Yvette entered the kitchen, Stella handed her a plastic freezer bag inside of which, the blood-stained paper towel. Yvette slipped it into her coat pocket, picked up a tray of dips, and they joined the others in the garden.

Everyone agreed Colin's industry in the kitchen that afternoon had produced a most wonderful dinner. He thanked them for the unprovoked ripple of applause and shifted conversation, asking Yvette about her role at Thomas & Taylor. Sara calmly cut in, explaining that due to the sharp increase in cases of domestic abuse during lockdown, her experience in managing the firm's heavy caseloads was invaluable. Yvette countered, asking Colin about his role at UCL, his response pertaining to humdrum details of administrative responsibilities quickly dried up, at which point Dr. Waters shrewdly stepped in.

That afternoon he had begun looking through Colin's old schoolbooks, surprised to discover that, though a decade apart, and quite the coincidence, he and Colin had attended the same boarding school. For the next hour or so, they entertained the women with amusing stories of bizarre antics and rituals typical of an English boys' boarding school.

When Yvette asked for directions to the bathroom, Colin got to his feet.

"By the front door, next to the door that looks like a cupboard. By the side table. I'll show you."

"I got it," Stella said, springing up. "Besides, you need to rest that finger!" she added, smiling at him. "I'll fetch dessert while I'm at it."

Stella stood with her ear to the dining-room door as Yvette buried a nano-tracker deep into a corner fold of Colin's wallet. Moments later they entered with desserts, just as Colin was resurrecting memories of a Latin teacher, a notorious brute who for years had been getting away with beating boys, until one fateful night, caught up to no good in the boys' dormitory, he was never heard from again.

With the evening drawing to a close, Colin briefly excused himself, Yvette nodding to the others that the tracker was in place.

"A wedding present we haven't used yet," Colin announced, bouncing back into the room with a box of flutes and a bottle of champagne.

Stella popped the cork to a small cheer. They toasted Colin, thanking him for his efforts, the evening ending shortly after with Celia and Sara inviting everyone to dinner at theirs soon.

"Strange," Colin said, as Stella loaded the dishwasher.

He was holding the box containing the champagne

glasses.

"One of the flutes is missing."

"Oh, that's the one I broke," Stella lied, smiling, thinking of how Yvette had slipped Colin's glass into her bag shortly before leaving.

15

Yvette had been tracking Colin for two weeks. Never straying far from the UCL campus, the small blue icon on her phone indicated his movements. She knew where he had lunch, the pub he occasionally visited before going home, the location of his gym.

However, in week three, veering from normal patterns, the icon indicated Colin was in the city, at Fenchurch Street station. When suddenly it began moving at speed, Yvette thought he was running, perhaps on a bus, but when it slowed to a stop, at Limehouse station, she realised he was on a train.

The train raced eastward through the London suburbs, stopping at various stations along the way - Barking, Dagenham, Hornchurch, bypassing Basildon and Southend before finally slowing to a stop at Westcliff-on-Sea. Here, the icon nudging along at snail's pace indicated Colin was now on foot, a quick Google search locating him on a promenade, the Western Esplanade. When he suddenly stopped, Yvette waited patiently. She thought of calling Stella. But what if he was meeting someone? A lover?

For ten minutes the icon remained stationary, before moving again in the direction it had come, towards the station, where he boarded a train and returned to Fenchurch Street station.

Yvette alerted Celia who organised an urgent team meeting.

***

Gathered in the conference room the following morning, Yvette informed the team of his movements the previous day, adding that Simone had confirmed that the fingerprints on the rental car in Corsica were Colin's. The DNA on the handkerchief, found near the crime scene in Norwich, also a positive match.

"Did he mention anything about a trip," Yvette asked Stella.

"No."

"In his defence," Dr. Waters said, "on occasion, for a few hours, I too escape the city. Pop down to the coast, normally Brighton, take in some sea air. It can be most invigorating."

"Stella?" Yvette asked. "Any ideas?"

"Perhaps Allan is right, just a break from town?"

"If that's the case," Yvette replied, "why wouldn't he have mentioned it to you?"

"Perhaps the same reason he hasn't confessed to killing all those women!" Stella snapped back.

The room fell silent.

"Stella," Yvette began, "I'm . . ."

"No, no. Sorry Yvette. Sorry everyone, sorry. That was out of order. Sorry. No, Yvette, you're right. This, his movement, is unusual. We need to look into it. Where do we go from here?"

"Well, this sudden shift in Colin's routine may indicate, if he's responsible for these murders, that he may be in the early stages of a new plan, looking for a new target," Yvette replied.

"His next victim you mean?" Celia confirmed.

"Yes, I believe so. Unusual changes in patterns of behaviour often suggest people we tra... uh,

232

investigate, are restless, becoming impatient. I'll continue to monitor his movements for further irregularities. Frequency of trips, places he visits. I'll ask my Super if I can put a tail on him. A plainclothes officer."

"Why there? Westcliff?" Stella asked.

"We don't know," replied Yvette. "It appears to be random. Only he knows. But he has his reasons. Killers are calculated. Perhaps proximity to London. The frequency of trains to and from the city. We'll remain vigilant, I'll keep you updated,"

"If I may," Dr. Waters interjected. "As Yvette says, all we can do for now is keep him under surveillance. Our present dilemma is that we still know so little about how serial killers operate. Down to the unusual *nature* of each individual killer, identification and, ultimately, catching them is difficult. Science and technology help, but even so, predicting behaviour in a killer is at best a guess. The only person who really knows his next steps, his intentions, is the killer himself. We're up against it here I'm afraid."

Yvette nodded in agreement.

"One aspect of this investigation which continues to puzzle me," Dr. Waters continued, "is the absence of sexual gratification. It appears our killer is simply out for, well, the kill. For this reason, I believe that in all likelihood, his victims have no observable connection to him, he chooses women randomly, this absence of any perceptible relationship, again, making our task even more difficult. It suggests that Westcliff may simply be an arbitrary location. As Yvette says, if Colin is our man, we can only hope that monitoring his movements will provide insight into where the next attack may take place. Our preparation must be meticulous. But Yvette, I'm sure, is already thinking about this, and our next course of action."

"Allan is right," Yvette continued. "As of now, there appears to be little, if any relationship between him and his victims. Due to the random nature of his movements, with so little to go on, if a pattern emerges, we'll go from there."

"So, what now?" Celia asked.

"I'm not quite sure," Yvette replied. "From what we have, the DNA results, his movements, the evidence looks compelling. The problem is the risk of him striking again. And my boss is getting impatient. She says she may have to pull resources if we don't come up with something solid soon. But, I have an idea. Might help speed things up. First though, I want to make sure what I have in mind is above board, legally I mean. We know his defence team will bring in a long line of character witnesses to provide a glowing testimony of Colin's character. The charming, gentle, kind man - all of which he is, so I was thinking..."

Yvette paused.

"You were thinking?" Celia prodded, suspiciously.

"Let's confront him. Call him out," Yvette proposed.

"Such a move would just scare him off," Celia countered.

"That is a risk, certainly. But time is not on our side. Perhaps a risk we need to take. It could save lives."

"Confront him? How so?" Stella asked.

"We're not quite sure yet?" Yvette replied.

Again the room sank into a gloomy quiet.

"We seemed to have reached an impasse," Dr. Waters said. "We have no discernible evidence. Nothing of any use in court. The handkerchief in Norwich did indeed belong to Colin. The car in Corsica, parked by the cove around the time Amelie went missing, the one you rented, is covered in Colin's prints. All purely circumstantial evidence. So, still, we have nothing."

"Listen, I may have something," Stella said. "While Colin was in the shower this morning, I looked through his wallet for the train ticket. I only found a bunch of receipts. One is from a shop that sells . . . swords. I checked online and the shop sells," and reading from the shop's website, "a range of knives that cater to the needs of our customers. We do our best to supply the right product.' I think he was in Westcliff to buy a knife."

"Do you know where the knife is?" Yvette asked.

"No, no. I haven't had time to look. But I agree ... I think he's making plans. So, I have an idea," she said, looking at the expectant faces staring back at her. "As Allan says, we're at an impasse. If we continue as we are, so slowly, with such a hands-off approach, he'll strike again. We cannot allow that to happen. From the flimsy evidence we've gathered, and as it now appears he's bought a knife, as Yvette says, I think he may be preparing something."

"Stella, what do you propose?" Celia asked, curiously.

"I think Yvette is right. I think we should confront

him. Or rather I will. Call him out. Challenge him. I'll reveal what we know about him, about what we think he's done. I can wear a wire, get a confession."

"Absolutely not!" Celia said, suddenly on her feet. "No, no, no! We *cannot* put you in harm's way. No, not for anything."

"Celia," Stella replied hastily, "if Colin wanted to hurt me, he would have done so a long time ago. I know there's risk involved here, but if we plan carefully, choose a time, a place, somewhere public, I'll call him out. The worst that can happen is the investigation falls flat on its face and we won't be able to charge him with anything. My marriage will be over, but I'm willing to risk this. Women's lives are on the line here. And, if he is the killer, then at least he knows we're on to him. That will be deterrent enough for him not to strike again. In the meantime, we build a case, gather more credible evidence until we can bring substantial charges."

Shaking her head, Celia drew in a deep breath.

"Listen. We've reached a stalemate," Stella continued. "Think about how we'll feel if another woman dies while we're twiddling our thumbs. We *have* to get a confession. I know it's a bit of a stretch, but if he knows he's under suspicion, that he's an active target of investigation, then, well, you just never know, he might confess. Just maybe. Perhaps he's had enough - enough of whatever drives him to commit these murders. Like I say, at the very least, if he knows we're on to him, he won't strike again.

"You all know him as the rational, well-adjusted man. I'll try to convince him to do the right thing, give himself up. Confess. I'll empathise with him, suggest that keeping his secret hidden for so long must be exhausting. Since I first suspected something, I don't know, I've just been thinking - why all of a sudden does he get sloppy now? The Norwich/Manchester mix-up? Encouraging me to get closer to his mother? Perhaps he wants to be caught? If he senses it's the end of the road, he might let me in, he might just go for it. He may even feel relief. Perhaps it's what he's been waiting for."

"It might work," Yvette said, looking at the others.

Sara and Celia glanced at each other, then over at Stella.

"Stella," Celia said, "this is on you."

"Let's do it," she said.

"I'll have to run this by my Super," Yvette replied, enthusiastically. "And, I think it's time to bring in the Met too. Let's see what they say. But with the clock ticking, thank you Stella. I really do think this is our best bet."

***

Yvette invited the Chief Inspector from the Met. to the firm's offices.

As Stella entered the conference room, Yvette, smiling, shook her hand.

"Hi Stella. This is Chief Inspector Rogers from the Met. She'll be coordinating the operation. I've briefed her on the details of the case."

A short, slight woman, bright blue eyes, nice smile, rose and shook Stella's hand.

"Very pleased to meet you. May I call you Stella?" she asked politely, pulling a small notebook from her bag.

As they ran through a series of questions, Inspector Rogers' kind manner and diligence impressed, closing the interview by asking Stella if she had anything to add.

"Only that whether he's guilty or not, I'll just be glad when it's over and done with," she replied.

"Stella," Inspector Rogers continued, more informally. "With the DNA and fingerprints conclusive matches, we have very compelling evidence that these three crimes are connected, and Colin our main suspect. I'm familiar with the work you do here at Thomas & Taylor and, I must say, you are a credit to not only to your firm, but to your profession. What you are willing to risk to extract a confession, if successful, will not only make sentencing easier, but will certainly prevent more women from dying. Stella, not many women - wives - would take such a risk. We understand the delicate nature of this operation, we're still in the early stages of planning, but be assured we will do everything possible to expedite matters as quickly and effectively as possible."

"Thank you," Stella replied.

"Now, with regards to procedure. Our main concern, our priority, is your safety. We will minimise risk as best we can. I've briefed my team with details of the operation and, if possible, I'd like you to meet them this week. Along with the negotiator."

"Negotiator?" Stella asked, puzzled.

"A forensic psychologist and expert in crisis

negotiation. She's a highly-trained law enforcement agent who will be with you every step of the way. We must tread carefully, think about, anticipate, how Colin might respond. With her guidance, we'll draw up potential questions that, hopefully, may lead to a confession. We'll conduct a series of rehearsals, you'll be well prepared. Like I say, your safety is our main concern."

***

A week later, Inspector Rogers greeted Stella at the Metropolitan Police headquarters at New Scotland Yard. In a large conference room at the rear of the building, a dozen or so plain-clothes officers stood up when they entered. After brief introductions, Inspector Rogers outlined details of the operation. When informed who the killer was, and Stella's role in the operation, many of the officers glanced up from their notes at her.

"The operation will take place at Luigi's restaurant. Stella and her husband, Colin, are regulars there. We've been in touch, and though they understand the nature of the operation, they are unaware of the players involved. This includes Stella and her husband. There is a certain degree of urgency here, and so once we have a date, I'll let you know the specifics. But certainly within a week. All of you will be at the restaurant as diners, ready to intervene should things not go as planned. Sandro," she said, nodding at a lean, swarthy young man.

"Mam," he responded.

"You'll be a waiter. So bone up on your Italian wines. Stella will be wearing a wire and earpiece. Christine will provide instruction."

A woman at the front of the room flashed Stella a smile.

"OK. Let's get to work," Inspector Rogers concluded, dismissing the officers. "Stella, would you like to go with Christine to the interview room?"

Christine introduced herself then led Stella to a small room deep inside the building.

"Stella," she began, "I've read Yvette and Inspector Rogers' reports. Before we turn to the practicalities of the operation, I have a few questions. Is that OK?"

Stella nodded.

"Firstly, I'd like to know how you and Colin met."

Stella briefly considered the relevance of the question.

"I received an email from the UCL admissions office. They wanted me to give a talk. About my time at the university and my career path into the law profession. Quite standard procedure. It's not unusual for solicitors at the firm to give talks there, and at other institutions."

"How long had you been working at Thomas & Taylor at that point?"

"Oh, I'd say, well over a year."

"You say giving such talks is standard procedure? How so? Was the invitation sent to you personally, or was it a blanket email to all graduates at the firm?"

"I don't follow," Stella said, a little confused.

"Is there any reason to believe that the email wasn't random? That you may have been targeted?"

240

"No, no, that's quite impossible," she replied, pulling out her phone, scrolling through to the original email. "I can't imagine I was targeted. It was sent to me directly from Colin. As Head of Admissions. I suspect he got my name from the firm's website."

"I believe Thomas & Taylor took on three graduates from UCL the year you joined?"

"Yes. That's correct."

"Did they receive similar invites?"

Carol and Julie, friends and fellow graduates, made no mention of receiving invites.

"Are you saying that, that Colin might have in some way, orchestrated meeting me? Lured me in?"

"No, not exactly. However, I certainly wouldn't rule it out. Dr. Waters says in his report that serial killers often surround themselves with shields, safeguards if you like. Often planning months, years in advance, they are very calculating. Very skilful at fitting in. In good jobs, honest family men."

Stella suddenly drew in a short, sharp breath.

"Is there something else?" Christine asked, curiously.

"Yes. Yes," Stella replied.

Her mind wandered back to long hours she spent in the university library.

"Sorry. It's just that, now you mention it, I had met Colin before. Before he sent that email. Yes, before I gave the talk. He worked in the library when I was an undergraduate. But, other than a polite thank you when he checked out my books, we never spoke. He was the quiet type. He said little, just a shy smile and a nod. That was it. I actually thought he was gay."

"So he knew you as a law student?" Christine asked, intrigued.

"Yes, yes he did. I only ever checked out books to do with the law."

"And so he knew your name? Who you were?"

"Yes, I suppose he must have," she replied, her voice trailing off, a sudden, unexpected shiver rushing through her.

"OK. As Inspector Rogers mentioned in the briefing, you will wear an earpiece. I take it you've never worn one before."

Stella shook her head.

Christine pulled from her pocket what looked like a small plastic pebble. Holding it between her thumb and finger, she handed it to Stella.

"It's an earbud, wireless, perfectly safe. It's impossible to see, even from the side. Technically speaking, the Bluetooth dongle has what's called an induction neck loop that transmits the audio received wirelessly. There'll be a microphone hidden on the table and so I'll hear everything you say, as will the rest of the team. And you'll be able to hear me. I'll be with you throughout, guiding you, prompting you with questions. And I'll be watching. There'll also be a hidden camera, I'll see everything. Hearing my voice in your ear will be strange at first, but it's simply a matter of getting used to wearing the earbud. That will come with practice. Depending on how smoothly the conversation with Colin goes, how he behaves, I'll instruct you to change tact when and where necessary. When to slow down, when to keep the conversation going. It's important you stay on script. Pull back your hair."

Very gently, Christine placed the earbud in Stella's ear.

"We have different sizes, the one you'll be wearing will fit nicely. How does it feel?"

"I can hardly feel it at all," Stella replied.

"Exactly. Now, wait here," she said, and stepped out of the room.

Moments later, Stella felt the earbud vibrate and heard a low crackling buzz in her ear.

"Can you hear me?" Christine suddenly asked.

Before Stella had time to reply, she had returned to the room.

"You see? I was three rooms away. More or less the same distance I'll be from you in the restaurant. With plain clothes officers at every table, we've done all we can to minimise risk. Like I say, with practice, I think you can pull this off. How do you feel?"

"I just want to get it over and done with."

***

The following morning Stella received an email from Yvette. Sooner than expected, the operation would take place in three days. She was to contact Colin immediately and plan to meet him at Luigi's on Friday at seven-thirty. On Thursday at four-thirty, she should be at the restaurant for a rehearsal. A car would pick her up.

The speed at which the operation was unfolding unnerved her. When she finally called Colin, he didn't answer, and leaving a message came as a relief. Arriving home at seven-thirty, she still hadn't heard from him, so she called again. He didn't pick up, and sensing something not quite right, she called Yvette.

"Stella. I was expecting this call," she said. "He's not answering his phone, is he?"

"How did you know?"

"I've been monitoring his movements all day. He's currently at Paddington station."

"Paddington? What's he doing there?"

"He headed to Windsor at around one-thirty this afternoon."

"Windsor? What on earth has …?"

"He's been in Windsor Great Park. As far as we know, he hasn't met anyone. We have an officer tailing him. He's just been wandering in the woods. The team are looking into cases connected with that location. One has come up. Well over ten years ago. A woman, murdered, her body never found. There's probably no connection, not his MO. Stella, it's important you mention none of this when he gets home. Just remember, Luigi's, Friday night. Send me a message to confirm he'll be there."

***

At around eight-thirty, Colin arrived home. Stella found his lie, that he had to work late, strangely comforting. Further confirmation of his duplicitous nature.

She made him a sandwich, poured herself a glass of wine, and sat with him at the kitchen table.

"Did you get my message about Friday?" she asked.

"I saw it flash up on the screen but I've been in meetings all day. And then my phone died."

"Did you forget your charger - again?" she asked, playfully.

Colin smiled.

"You know me so well," he said.

"Better than you would ever care to imagine," she replied, immediately wishing she hadn't. "Anyway, dinner at Luigi's on Friday. We haven't been in a while."

"Sounds great. What time?"

"Shall we say seven-thirty? I'll call tomorrow and make the reservation. Hope we can get in, they're very busy on Fridays."

***

Officers were shuffling in and out of Luigi's with equipment when Stella arrived for the rehearsal. Inside, a technician on a ladder tinkering with a camera high up in the corner of the ceiling whispered into a small microphone. Moments later, Inspector Rogers and Christine appeared and led her to a small office at the back of the kitchen. Inside, on a large computer screen, various images of the restaurant's interior.

"We're almost ready," Christine said. "Sandro will stand in for Colin during the run-through. OK?"

"I think so," Stella whispered, hesitantly.

Christine picked up a walkie-talkie.

"Clive, how's the camera coming along?"

An image of a table flashed up on the screen.

"OK. That's great, we have a visual," she said. "Stella, let's test the earpiece. Then we'll begin."

Christine secured the device in Stella's ear and stepped outside.

"Can you hear me?" Christine whispered.

"Yes," Stella whispered back.

"Stella, can you hear me?" Christine repeated.

"Yes, yes. Perfectly," Stella replied, more loudly.

"Good," Christine said, stepping back into the office. "Let's go through and we'll get this going."

Sitting around tables talking in twos and threes, plain clothes officers. Leaning against the counter at the bar, Sandro nodded and smiled at Stella.

"OK everyone," Christine announced. "Let's get this going. Sandro, ready?" she asked, pushing him down onto the seat opposite Stella and returning to the kitchen.

Stella heard a sudden shuffling in her ear.

"Stella, can you hear me?" Christine asked.

"Yes," she replied.

"Good, good. OK. Sandro is Colin. Ask him the following questions."

Stella looked up at Sandro. He smiled.

"Good. That's good. The way you behave, what you say to him, make it as natural as possible. If you want to improvise, that's fine, but remember, natural. First question. Ask him where he trained as a police officer."

"Where did you train as a police officer?" Stella asked.

"Hendon," Sandro responded.

"The mic's too low. Clive, we need more sound on the table. Stella, ask Sandro to speak louder."

"She wants you to speak louder."

"Hendon," he repeated.

"OK, that's better. Clive, a tad more sound on the table. OK, Stella, just talk with Sandro about anything. Every now and then I'm going to interrupt with a question. Remember, keep it natural."

Stella and Sandro talked casually for about five minutes. She asked about his childhood, details of his career, then suddenly, Christine issued instruction.

"Ask him the family member he dislikes most and why."

Slightly unnerved, as instructed, Stella asked a series of awkward questions, relieved when Christine suddenly appeared at the table.

"Stella, that was great. You're a natural. I think we're almost ready. How do you feel?"

"Yes, OK. I think I can handle it. I just want to get it over and done with."

"Good. So, now, let's return to the station to tweak the script."

***

That evening, Stella called Celia and Sara. She assured them the operation was soundproof, the risk minimal, that she'd be surrounded by plainclothes officers.

"Whatever the outcome, you stay with us tomorrow," Celia insisted. "After the operation we'll be waiting for you in that pub on the corner, the one we've been to a couple of times. Near to Luigi's. Forget what it's called."

"The King's Arms," Stella said.

"Yes, that's the one. But we'll talk more about this in the morning at work. Plan to stay with us for as long as you need thereafter. This, my child, I'm afraid is non-negotiable."

"Thanks. I'd like that."

16

Sitting on the edge of the bath, Stella watched the water slowly rising. By the end of the day, it would be over. Like her marriage. Life was about to change beyond measure. If Colin confessed, he was going to prison. For life. If innocent . . . No! The evidence, now so compelling. The lies. And Marjory. Why had he never mentioned her? What happened on the cliffs? Why the train rides to the south coast? And Windsor?

She drew in a long, deep breath and slid below the water.

At work that morning she got little done. At midday, seeking solitude in Lincoln's Inn Fields, she sat on a bench, closed her eyes and listened to the calming swish of the trees as a warm breeze washed over her. Just one more day, she thought to herself. Tomorrow, it would all be over.

Celia and Sara were waiting in her office when she returned. Before leaving, they offered gentle words of encouragement, reminding her they would be waiting for her.

The phone rang. A car was on its way.

Alone in her office, Stella gazed up at the picture of Boudicca hanging on the office wall. Then, from the bottom drawer of her desk, she pulled out a notebook. In particularly low moments or when in need of inspiration, she always looked again at the timeline inside she had begun at university. Starting in the 19th century, dotted along the line, a list of farcical, ludicrous laws aimed at keeping women *in their place*.

Occasionally, when a new law somewhere in the world either served to advance or impede the lives of women and girls, she added a new entry.

The first law, enacted in 1857, always surprised her. To most speakers of English, the law has a familiar ring, an expression suggesting a "broadly accurate guide." But few are aware of its savage origins. With a woman monarch at the helm, and in a nation of renowned philosophers and scientists, the law known as the *Rule of Thumb* permitted a man to beat his wife on condition he used "a rod not thicker than his thumb." Three years later, in 1860, the Law of Coverture not only required women to transfer everything they owned to husbands after marriage, but encouraged physical and verbal abuse to keep errant wives under control.

For the next century, few notable legal advances came for women. In 1948 The Declaration of Human Rights proved a timely advancement. After two cataclysmic world wars, women were once more the target of devious, disgruntled men. As the numbers of women murdered during peacetime rocketed, this ray of light offered rudimentary protections by setting out rights and principles of equality, security, liberty, integrity and dignity for all people, including women. In 1956, for the first time, *rape* was legally defined. A decade later, with the arrival of the 1967 Abortion Act, women could finally decide for themselves what they did with their bodies. In the 1970s, the world's first refuge for victims of domestic abuse appeared in conjunction with campaigns strategically targeting boys, making it clear to them that violence against women or girls was unacceptable.

The phone suddenly rang. The car had arrived. Stella closed the notebook, returned it to the drawer, and as she put on her coat, before leaving, glanced again up at Boudicca.

***

Yvette was waiting outside Luigi's when Stella arrived. She took her through the noisy kitchen to the small office where Christine and Inspector Rogers were making final checks.

"How are you feeling?" Christine asked.

"I'm fine. Is there somewhere I can freshen up?" Stella replied, nervously.

Yvette led her to a tiny staff changing room in the rear of the kitchen.

"Did he say anything about the trip to Windsor?" she asked.

"No. Nothing. He just said he had to work late. God, Yvette, I hope I'm doing the right thing."

"Stella, we're nearly there. Just one more push."

Christine suddenly appeared.

"All OK Stella?" she asked, placing the earpiece carefully in her ear.

"Yes. I think so," she replied, sighing.

"Well, nearly there. Hold your nerve. You can do this."

A hush descended as Christine showed Stella to the table.

"Stella, let's have one more check of the mic. Any problems, let us know," she added, then disappeared into the kitchen.

"Stella, can you hear me?" Christine suddenly asked.

"Yes, yes. Can you hear me?" she replied.

"Stella, one moment. More sound on the mic Clive. Stella, can you hear me?"

"Yes, yes. Can you hear me?"

"Yes, yes, thanks Stella. Let's keep the sound at this level Clive. Stella, I can see you on camera. Give us a smile."

Stella looked up and forced a smile. Moments later, Christine reappeared at the table.

"Stella, remember that you're in no danger. Try and relax. Act as naturally as possible, like in the run-through. And remember, there's no rush here. Don't force things. For the first hour or so, you'll hear nothing from me. Talk about what you normally do when you meet here. Work. Weekend plans. Whatever's natural. And remember, if in the unlikely event he gets angry, just stay on script. That's important."

"Yes, I understand," Stella replied, nodding nervously.

"Good. We have officers at both ends of the street. They'll let us know when …"

Suddenly, she stopped, putting a finger to her ear and listening. An officer posted outside informed her Colin had just entered the street.

"OK everyone. It's time. He's nearly here. Sandro's at the door. He'll show Colin to the table. You've got this Stella. OK everyone. This is it. We're on."

"May I take a drink order?" asked a waiter

252

suddenly beside Stella.

"A large glass of Chablis, please."

Stella could feel her heart thumping. In her ear, Christine's soft, shallow breathing.

"OK everyone," she whispered. "He's nearly here. Two minutes. Stella, good luck. As natural as possible. It's just another Friday night. Stay calm. OK? Sandro. Get ready. One minute."

The sudden draught on her back, the restaurant door opening, signalled Colin's arrival.

"Hiya, you're early," he said, resting his hand on her shoulder as he leant down to kiss her cheek.

"I couldn't be bothered to go home and change, so I came straight here," Stella replied.

"You look nice."

"Thanks."

"Can I get you a drink, sir?" Sandro asked, suddenly at the table.

Looking up at him, Colin fixed him with dubious gaze.

"You're new here?"

"Yes, my first week," replied Sandro. "Perhaps a glass of Chablis. What the young lady is drinking?"

"Young lady," Colin said, smiling. "A real charmer! Why don't you bring us a bottle?"

Stella smiled politely at Sandro.

"Well done Stella, great start," Christine whispered.

"Are you OK?" he asked, "you look a little tired."

"Yes, yes, I'm fine. Been bit of a stressful week. You know how it is. How's your day been?"

"Slow. The highlight, seeing Maria. She brought

the baby in. Gorgeous little boy. He has Maria's eyes. Dark brown, Spanish."

"Oh, tell her I was asking for her next time you see her."

"I will."

"Good move," Christine said. "You're doing great."

"What shall we do this weekend?" Stella asked.

"Sir, your wine," Sandro interrupted, pouring an inch or so into the glass.

Colin sniffed then sipped it.

"Yes, that's fine," he said, nodding for Sandro to fill the glass.

"Are you ready to order, or do you need some more time?" he asked.

"Give us a couple of minutes," Stella suggested.

"Certainly madam."

"Cheers," Colin said, clinking Stella's glass. "Plans for the weekend? How about a drive in the country?"

"Stella, you're a star, keep it up," Christine whispered.

"Yes, that sounds good. Any place in mind?"

"I don't know. If we leave early, we can head down to see mum?"

"That's a bit of a drive. Unless we stay over. No, I think we should give her more notice. You know how she likes to cook something special when we come."

"Yes, you're right. Perhaps head north, into Cambridgeshire. There's some pretty villages up there."

Sandro arrived, flipped open his notebook and took their order.

As they ate, Christine intermittently remarked how well Stella was doing.

"Delicious," Colin exclaimed, dropping the fork onto an empty plate, and sitting back. "Easily the best Italian in London. By far. Do you fancy some dessert?"

"No, you go ahead. I might have some of yours," Stella replied.

Colin turned, looking for Sandro.

"Stella. Let's begin," Christine said, suddenly.

Stella topped up her glass with wine and drew in a long, deep breath.

"Colin," she said, taking a sip, looking directly at him. "There's something I want to talk to you about."

He noted the sudden change of tone, the sober look in her eyes.

"Colin," she added, pausing. "I can help you."

"You can what?" he replied, baffled.

"I can help you. Help you stop."

"Stop? Stop what?"

"I think you know. And I know. That's why I want to help you. We know what you've done. We know where you've been, where you go."

"Stella, what the hell are you talking about? What's this all about? What do you mean - we?" he said, shifting upright in his seat.

"Stella, slow down, don't rush things," Christine cautioned.

"Tell me what you do. Where you go. Why you go there?" she pressed.

"Stella. Please, what's happening here? Going places? What I do? Where is this all coming from?"

"Like I say, let me help you."

"Help me with what?"

"Colin, talk to me. Time's up."

"Time's up for what Stella?" he replied, nervously, his eyes darting from side to side.

"Stella, wait. Let him think," Christine said.

"What is this Stella? What are you playing at?" he asked, glancing around at other diners impervious to his raised voice.

Then, suddenly on his feet, he threw the napkin on the table and marched out.

"Stay put Stella," Christine instructed.

Outside, officers conveyed details of his movements.

"He's stopped," one said.

"What's he doing?" Christine asked.

"Well, he's clearly angry. Wait. He's coming back."
Stella trembled.

"OK Stella," said Christine. "Keep your nerve."

Moments later, Colin slumped back into his chair. Below a thin layer of perspiration on his brow, his forehead twitched.

"Stella," he said, in conciliatory tone, "I'm sorry. But I have no idea what you're trying to get at. Has someone said something to you I should know about? Don't leave me in the dark here."

"OK. He's ready to listen. Up the ante Stella," Christine urged.

"Like I say, I can help you. But Colin, you have to trust me. There's a way out of this. I can help you. But you *must* trust me. I know about you. What you do. What you've done. And I know how it all began. When you were eight. Up on the cliffs that summer. I know what you did to Marjory."

In the flickering candlelight, his face darkened. His gaze, ruthless. Again he was eight years old, up on the cliffs, Marjory laughing at him, humiliating him. His breathing heavy, a light film of sweat on his face made his skin glow.

"Tell me about Marjory," Stella added, glaring at him.

Placing his elbows on the table, he leaned forward.

"You want to know about that little bitch," he snapped. "I'll tell you. She made my life hell. Helen too. They always got everything they wanted. Marjory always running to my father, that fucker, telling him everything, making things up. Lies. All lies. But he believed her. Always. And he always came for me. Never touched her. Just beat me. She knew exactly what to say to set him against me, she knew what she was doing. Made my life hell. So, she got what she deserved that day. They all did."

"They?" Stella asked. "They?" she repeated.

He looked up. About to say something, he suddenly stopped.

"Let's just forget it," he said.

"You said *they*. Who are *they* Colin?" Stella demanded.

"Forget it Stella!" he snapped.

Again he glanced around, at other diners, talking and laughing, strangely oblivious to his raised voice.

"Push, Stella," Christine said.

"What did you do in Norwich Colin? What you did to Marjory on the cliffs that day? Who are *they*?"

Clearly exasperated, he released a muffled snort.

"And, and," Stella said, a quiver in her voice.

"Easy Stella, steady now," Christine whispered. "Calm yourself."

"And in Corsica! What did you do to Amelie? How could you? You went looking for an innocent girl that afternoon. And you found one. And you killed her. An innocent girl. You knew exactly what you were going to do to her. Didn't you? You killed Amelie, Colin. Why? Why did you kill her? Are you still punishing Marjory?"

He wiped sweat trickling down his forehead.

"It was Amelie, Colin. Just a girl. So sweet, so nice. Why did you kill Amelie, Colin?"

"Easy Stella," Christine said.

"Why her? Why Amelie? Why Colin? Why?" Stella demanded, now leaning towards him, glaring at him.

A mad panic rose in his eyes.

"I, I don't know, I don't know," he finally conceded. "I didn't mean to. She was just there. I didn't mean to. It just happened. I didn't think anything would happen. But Stella, listen, I, I . . ."

Suddenly, the restaurant fell silent. Overhead lights flickered on and he was surrounded by officers.

"Stella," he whimpered helplessly across the table at her. "What have you done?"

Looking directly at him, she swirled the last of her wine in the glass.

"A question you'll be asking yourself for the rest of your days," she casually replied.

As they led him away, she drew in a long, deep breath and knocked back the last of her wine.

17

Stella's testimony in court ensured Colin received a life sentence. Though Celia insisted she take time off, she returned to work a week later. Mid-afternoon on her first day, Sara summoned her to the conference room. Overwhelmed when greeted by the firm's solicitors on their feet applauding, this caring, unexpected gesture of solidarity brought tears to her eyes.

A month after sentencing, Stella received at the firm the first of many letters from Colin. Recognising his handwriting, she fed it unopened directly into the shredder, as she did with those that followed, about one a week.

One afternoon, Celia asked to see her.

"Stella. Come in, sit down. I need a quick word," she said, pulling an envelope from her tray. "I received this letter earlier in the week. It was addressed to me. It's from Colin. Now, you can tell me to back off, and I'll throw it in the trash. Or, if you'd like, I can inform you of its contents."

"I've received letters too. I don't read them. They go straight in the shredder."

"Apart from the letters, any other contact?"

"None."

"And you want to leave it like this?"

"Yes. Well, yes, I do," she said.

Celia noted her indecision.

"You're certain?"

"Not really," Stella conceded, collecting her

thoughts. "It's just that, sometimes, well, sometimes, I wonder. That's it. I just wonder. Why? Why he did it? What drove him to commit such monstrous crimes? What *really* happened to turn him into such a twisted psychopath? That's it really. Just why?"

Over dinner that evening, Celia, Sara and Stella discussed these lingering, unresolved issues.

"To wipe the slate clean, to *really* get on with your life," Celia suggested, "I think you should go and see him. Ask the questions, get the answers you need. But everything on your terms."

Over the next couple of weeks Stella drew up a shortlist of questions. After further, lengthy discussion with Celia and Sara she called HMP Belmarsh, a category *A* prison just south of the Thames in east London, and made an appointment to see Colin.

Arriving at the prison early, a warden patted Stella down and took her photograph, standard procedure for all visitors. With formalities complete, she was led to a large visiting hall. Inside, twenty or so tables spaced evenly throughout, and on the walls, signs reminding offenders and visitors of prison regulations.

As she waited, Stella reminded herself of Celia's advice. Remain calm. Stay in control. Walk at any time.

Suddenly the door through which she had entered swung open. A guard stepped into the room followed by Colin. His hair, just a year before, a solid, dark mop, now almost white. His face, considerably thinner, gaunt, pallid.

Head bowed, he slumped into the chair. Exhaling a whispered sigh, he looked up at her. Stella held his gaze.

"Thank you," he said, politely, a tremor in his voice.

"For what?" Stella replied, coldly.

"For coming."

An awkward silence followed. No rush, she thought. He was no longer a threat. She had seen to that.

"I think I'd like to explain," he began.

Stella continued to stare at him, a frigid, impenetrable gaze unnerving him.

"I have a, a *condition*. I'm not sure where it comes from, how it evolved, but, but I tried to manage it. I failed. I accept that. I've met with psychologists."

Unimpressed, Stella restrained herself. Was this a flicker of remorse? No. Men like Colin are incapable of such feelings. Another feeble, deranged murderer scratching about for an excuse.

"Stella, are you going to speak to me?" he said, a desperate quiver in his voice.

"I'll speak when I'm ready!" she snapped.

He drew in a long breath and glanced up at the ceiling.

"As I explained in my letters, the condition …"

"I never read your letters! I didn't even open them. I shredded every last one. Don't write to me again at the firm. Don't write to Celia, and don't send letters to the old address. I've moved. Just don't contact me. Anywhere. You're wasting your time."

"Moved? Sold the house?" Colin replied,

momentarily confused.

And his letters? So meticulous in explaining his condition. If she had read his letters, she might understand. His plan for how this first meeting would unfold now unexpectedly, spitefully thwarted, a sudden burst of resentment surged through him.

"Why didn't you read them?" he asked, the tone in his voice reflecting his disquiet.

Stella drew in an impatient breath.

"Because I chose not to. That simple. You have nothing to say to me."

"Well, why did you come"? he replied, curtly, now visibly upset.

She didn't respond.

"This condition," he continued, shakily. "Some also call it an addiction."

But he stopped. Why hadn't she read his letters?

"I've known about it, well, certainly since my late teens," he continued. "Even back then I knew there was something wrong. I had thoughts, strange desires, anxiety, I had to keep to myself, hidden. I didn't know what I wanted to do, where to turn. I suppose the condition, the addiction ..."

"Condition? Addiction? Did this condition, this addiction," Stella suddenly stormed, startling him, "make you throw Marjory off a cliff? Or kill all those other innocent women?"

But she stopped, abruptly. Maintain control. Show no vulnerability.

"How? How? How do you know, how did you find out about, her?" he asked, suddenly alarmed, his breathing heavy.

"Her? Your dead sister you mean? The one you killed? She has a name, Colin. Marjory. Say her name Colin! Marjory."

"I don't want to talk about her."

"Well, what shall we talk about? Your condition? Your addiction? Or any other fucking warped excuse you care to come up with!"

"Why are you being like this?"

"Like what Colin? Like what?"

"Cruel."

Her eyes widened, her heart thumped.

"Are you so fucking stupid, so dense, to call *me* cruel? Me? Cruel? It's you who's banged up in here for the most unimaginable acts of cruelty. Look at you. Just take a good look at yourself, poor old you. Born into privilege, into a comfy little world made just for *you*, Colin. A golden boy in a world made just for him. You had it all. You could have been anything Colin. There was literally nothing to stop you from getting what you wanted out of life. But what did you choose to do? Kill women. And why? Because you had a tough old time at your posh little boarding school? For not being mollycoddled at home? Because daddy reprimanded you for terrorising your sisters? And so, for having it tough as a kid, what did you choose to do to make things right in your shitty little life? Kill women. And you have the gall to say it's down to some condition, some addiction that made you commit these barbaric acts. Face the fuck up to it Colin, you're just a deranged and deluded serial killer. That's why you won't be getting out of here in any fit condition to pick up where you left off. And you call *me* cruel. I'm here purely out of curiosity. This is your opportunity, your only opportunity, to tell me what the fuck went on in your pathetic little world to make you kill women. Because believe me, this is the last time you will ever see me. And just be honest. I've not come here today to hear the *poor me* crap. I want the truth. You no longer have anything to lose. So, no more talk of *conditions* or *addictions*. You're a cold-blooded killer. Call it what it is!"

His face grew dark. He shuffled upright in his seat and gazed directly at her.

"OK Stella. You want me to talk? I'll talk. You want the truth. Well, here it is. Let's not start with my childhood, or what happened on the cliffs, but with when I first saw you. In the university library. Exactly what I was waiting for. Just what I needed. And I'm not talking about a girlfriend, a wife, sex. I needed a front. To keep going, to satisfy what I knew I would keep doing. So I *chose* you Stella. I wormed my way into your life and you didn't have a clue. I needed someone just like you. And then you appeared. And you took the bait. I thought when I sent that email inviting you to come and talk to students that you might suspect something when you discovered it was me. The boy from the library. I drew you in and you came willingly. Hook, line and sinker. I admit, when we married, at first, I enjoyed our life together. Only briefly, I even thought it might stifle this desire. Perhaps even cure my condition."

Mingled within Stella's fury, a shade of intrigue.

"This is sheer nonsense. *You* chose *me*?" she snapped.

"Yes. I chose you. I played a very long game to get you Stella. And it worked. Got there in the end. Didn't I? I got you."

"What the fuck are you talking about?"

"I had my eye on you from the moment I saw you. I even remember the first book you asked me to check out. *Women and Criminal Justice.* From then on, I watched you. The lonely one. Always on her own. And when, sometimes, I felt you looking at me, I knew you, or someone like you, would be ideal. I made notes of the books you borrowed, all to do with women and the law, and I grew excited. Someone like you, a standard bearer for women, offered the perfect cover. So I chose you."

Stella remained perfectly still.

"I'm a good judge of character. You fit the type I was looking for. Restrained, unsmiling, temperamental. Lonely. I didn't rush things. Snaring you required patience. You see, men like me, we understand patience. And so I waited."

He paused and studied his palms.

"About a year or so later, after you graduated, just by chance, I saw you. One lunchtime in Lincoln's Inn Fields. From a distance, I watched you ..."

"You did what?" she asked, suddenly incensed.

"I watched you Stella. Then I followed you, back to Thomas & Taylor. So I knew where you worked. Even then, I didn't rush in. Like I say, patience, the long game. I waited. For more than a year. During that time, I often wandered in Lincoln's Inn Fields secretly hoping you might be there. I didn't see you for the longest time. But just as I was thinking you might have moved firms, one afternoon, there you were. And, again, I followed you. And many times after that. And so I knew you still worked at Thomas & Taylor."

Stella considered walking out.

"And then I sent you the email. Asking you to come and talk to the undergraduates. I wasn't sure if you'd respond. If you hadn't, I might just have drawn a line under it. Sought another route. Another cover, another woman. You weren't the only one I had lined up. There were others. I had a list. Many others."

"You really thought that I, or another woman, might *cure* you of your, your sickness?" Stella asked in disbelief.

"Perhaps. You, or someone like you. Like I say, after choosing you, marrying you, I was confident, no, perhaps, hopeful, that our union would at the very least help control, or even rid me of this condition altogether. And for a while, it worked. But, only for a while. You should take some credit. You. You worked for a while. Until of course, you didn't."

Stella teetered on the edge of her seat.

"And then, not long after we married, well, I'll spare you the details. It happened again."

"It? You killed another woman, you mean?"

"Yes. You know the case. Lisa Miller. And then I knew that meeting and marrying you had done nothing to free me of my, my ..."

"...of the thrill of murdering women!"

"... my desire. And then it just continued. A way of not, of not getting caught, was - don't you see - it was you. I used you as a shield. A front."

"You think you used me?"

"Yes Stella. As a cover. Thomas & Taylor, doing its bit to create a utopia for womankind. Think about it. Who would ever suspect the husband of a solicitor working for this much-lauded firm to be a potential killer? Who, Stella? Think about it, not even your two pillars of strength, Celia and Sara. Or other women at the firm. No-one suspected a thing," he added, mockingly.

"The way you all let me in, trusted me. I remember the nights out, the drinking, the railing against men, the tirades, the whining and whingeing, in front of me, the token *woke* man, always nodding and smiling. None of you suspected the smiles and the laughter were for other reasons. Christ, I can still hear the crap you talked about. *Prescribed orders. Flawed hierarchy.* Or, a particular favourite, *addressing the balance.* Pointless, fucking whining. Gripe after fucking endless gripe. Just noise. More bullshit, nonsense, all of it sheer bullshit.

"You often said so yourself, Stella, that the world was made by men for men. How far have you got in changing that? How far has the world *really* moved on? The odd woman sliding up the greasy, political pole here and there. Tokenism. You know this. You're just too stubborn to admit it. And why? Well, I'll tell you why. You asked for the truth, so, wife, here it is. The truth.

"You see, most men perceive something lacking in women. A pervasive weakness. I've always known it. Felt it. And women try to smother men. Yes, smother. Rarely words of encouragement, just those that tear us down. Whinge, whinge, fucking whinge, making shit up. All that bollocks about *toxic masculinity*, and *getting in touch with your feminine side*. Absolute bullshit! Really? Is that the best on show? And the gripes about us not listening. But why should we listen? So we can all sink? So that you can drag us down with you? So we can all be damaged together?"

"I think it's clear you're damaged!" Stella interrupted.

"Perhaps. But who's responsible for that?

"Why don't you tell me Colin?"

"Well, for a start, a brutish father who only ever beat me, ignored me, then beat me again. And then, on top of that, surrounded by …"

"Your mother, Helen and Marjory?"

"That's right," he continued, the muscles in his face twitching. "Around them I might as well have been invisible. No enjoyment, nothing to stir in me a sense of ambition. I was never allowed to develop myself. Always alone. Nowhere to turn, no one to turn to. They were strangers to me."

"Your mother? A stranger?" Stella asked, perplexed.

"Yes. She could have persuaded him to keep me at home after …"

"After you pushed Marjory off the cliff?"

"She could have stopped him. From sending me to that prison of a boarding school. But she remained silent. She said nothing, did nothing, to protect me. That's what mothers are supposed to do. Protect. But she said nothing and I paid the price. I always felt *lesser*. That's how I felt."

He paused to draw in a breath.

"I felt it for the first time at boarding school. That desire. First, just a thought, then, then," he said, pausing to choose the words. "Then one day, alone in the village shop, I came out and a group of girls, older, maybe fifteen or sixteen, looked at me. I was only nine, maybe ten. They asked me my name. I told them and they laughed at me. I thought of Marjory up on the cliffs laughing at me and I felt a surge of anger. No, it was something more than that. More furious than rage, a deep loathing, and somehow, I just knew it had always been with me. Most boys at school felt unhappy, I just assumed they felt the same thing. What was in me, was in them too. Yes, stirring in them, a natural compulsion, yes, natural, which, once I left school, grew stronger.

"Like I say, I thought it stirred in all boys. And like them, I thought it was simply a case of controlling it. But after school, out on my own, out in the world, so many girls, with so much opportunity, I knew it was only a matter of time. And then one day, I don't know, it just felt so strong, irresistible, and, and I thought, just one …"

He stopped suddenly. Stella waited.

"After all, I'd done it before. Up on the cliffs," he continued, bowing his head. "And so, you see, it's as well I'm in here. I don't know, maybe a part of me wanted it to end? Perhaps, deep down, I always knew it would come to this. Because I knew I would never stop. You see, to me, and I guess to others like me, I suppose, what we do feels *logical*. I tried to explain this to the shrinks. They always ask if I'm sorry. But, and I don't mean it to sound cruel, well, I'm not sorry.

What's the point? I just don't feel it. I just feel … hollow. All the time. Always have. But regret? Remorse? No. I simply don't get it. What can it change? It won't bring them back. There's no healing to be done here. It's what it is.

"Men will always have what they want. No law will change that. In here, I watch, listen, to other men talk, openly, of what they really want. What they're capable of and what they'll risk to get it. It's not so different from the way boys at school talked about girls. We will never change. Why? Because we can't. We're unsalvageable. Irredeemable. We have no regrets.

"Sometimes, I think of you Stella. What you do, how hard you work to change things, tame us men. You must know by now you're fighting a losing battle. Trying to stem the tide, trying to prevent the, well, unpreventable. That's why you'll always be fighting a losing battle Stella. Just think of all the men like me still out there. Some will never be caught. They'll simply carry on. Like I did. So, you see Stella, perhaps I'm not so different from most men."

She sighed deeply.

"Is that it? Is that the best you could come up with? Something as shallow as this? Really? That men are imperfect? Is this really telling me, telling all women something we don't already know? And what? You suggest we just accept being murdered? Or constantly ignored, dismissed, mocked, vilified?

"Let me make this clear. I'm passionate, emotional even, about the senseless cruelty inflicted on women by men. On occasion, it comes close to breaking me.

Because I feel something. For people. For people like Emma, Amelie, all the women I represent."

She took a deep breath.

"And, believe me, I'll never break. Here, just look at you. The worst kind of evil. You. A pitiful, pathetic little scab trying to justify why you are the way you are. Self-pitying, opportunistic murderers like you searching deep within themselves for answers. Pointless, pure vanity. Don't bother asking the shrinks what you are. Don't overcomplicate things. You have *never* had anything to offer, you've always lacked purpose. But now, in here, you have purpose. To spend the rest of your days. Nothing more. Simply that.

"But my life has purpose. I know what I have to offer. No matter the setbacks, no matter how hard defending women is, it's a responsibility I bear every day with honour. I help others. I know what I do. But you? Look at you. Wretched, pathetic little scrap. Here, you'll spend the rest of your days. Long, slow days of simmering resentment. Every single day for the rest of your life. So much time for reflection, for those regrets you say men don't have to creep in, churn, fester inside you.

"Men try to belittle women. You have tried to make me feel ashamed, embarrassed. You have tried to belittle me. But you can't. You can't make me feel inferior. I make mistakes, but I'm in control of my life. You said you *chose* me. Well, it was *me* who caught *you*. Me. I put an end to your dirty little perversion. And who are you to talk about the real nature of men? Based on what? The warped stories you make up in your own vile little mind? To try and justify your actions? Or the trash you deal with in here? No. Most men are not like you. Most men don't do what you have done. They don't feel what you do. Remember that. And, remember, I put you in here. Me.

"Without you, and men like you, the world outside, albeit slowly, is changing. It's moving in the right direction. In the grand scheme of things, for women, the world is becoming a little brighter. Why? Because we know what we want. We always have. To be treated with dignity, respect, we want equality. It's really that simple. We've never wanted power over men, we've only ever just wanted to live freely. But in a world free of men like you. And now, I'm free of you. I put a stop to you, didn't I? Me. You couldn't slip through my net.

"And you talk about playing the long game. As if any man can teach a woman about the long game. We've been working at it for thousands of years. And for the sacrifices made by countless women, who have gone before, my generation is reaping the rewards. Things are getting better. Why? Because we, us women, we're making it happen. No matter where, or in what circumstances, women are brave, we grow stronger because we help each other. We take risks. We perform selfless acts. We make sacrifices for those we care about. This is what makes us brave, strong, and we're getting stronger. I'm a product of the hard work women have performed throughout the millennia. It's trickled down into me. And you're locked up in here because of me. I put you in here. Their work has paid off, it continues to pay off.

"You think what you have said to me today is the truth solely because you're a man. With your deranged, outdated views, you have talked down to me. And yet I put you in here. But I didn't do it alone. I had the help of other women, strong women. When I first had my suspicions that my husband might be a murderer, it was a huge risk for me to share what, initially, seemed impossible. I felt humiliated, but I was never alone. Every step of the way, other women, Celia, Sara, colleagues, helped and supported me. We women pull together, we build each other up, we mobilise. We make changes not just for ourselves, but for everyone's benefit. Women make amazing things happen.

"Vile and toxic misogyny will continue to fester. More perverse humans, like you, will crawl out of the sewers to do us harm. We know this. But what really matters is the here and now. A new generation of women, we know we're not alone. We have support. And not only from other women. But from men, many men, all of us together, working hard, helping to improve the lives of all women and girls who no longer feel as if they have to defer, or feel ashamed, or bow down to men in positions of power and influence simply because they are men. We no longer have to put up with demeaning comments generations of women have endured. Your delusions about the nature of women is unrecognisable to this new generation of young women and men, many now in positions of influence, ensuring equality and fairness are high on agendas. The future is bright.

"But you won't see these changes. It's a future you

could never understand. And so it's just as well you'll never be part of it. You'll be in here, locked up. Because you cannot be trusted to act like a civilised human being. It really is that simple. But no, even now, locked away in this shithole, in my presence, you want to assume a position of authority.

"I know it's never crossed your mind, but you should be ashamed. You say that you *chose* me. For cover. So you could murder women. You think I'm hurt, torn by this? That I should feel some sort of shame, guilt? On the contrary. Like I say, I'm surrounded by strength. Strong women do things worthwhile with our lives. We make a difference, we make life better for us all. And you? What have you done? Have you ever really made a contribution? To anyone or anything? Have you ever tried to make anyone happy? Me? Your mother? Anyone at all? No! You chose to murder women. You chose to deal in death and destruction. This is your legacy. This is the sum of your pitiful parts. The worst type of human being. When I leave here today, believe me, you will neither see nor hear from me again. If you remember anything about me, let it be that my life will never be about you. I don't feel shame about who I am or what I do. Despite a world with men like you still in it, I remain optimistic. The world is changing, we are evolving, movements are merging. We understand that what harms one, harms us all. Movements led by men and women. Together. But you'll not see any of this. Because you proved incapable. A Neanderthal. And, fortunately, no longer a threat. I made sure of that. That's what I came to say. And so, I must go.

Devon awaits."

"Devon?"

"Yes, to see your mother. We've grown very close."

"My mother? Why, why . . . Will you tell . . .?"

"I will tell your mother nothing. You are nothing to her. You have shamed and embarrassed her. You killed her daughter. And other women. How dare you expect anything of her! She has no desire to be reminded of you. No one does."

***

A cloudy afternoon had given way to an early evening of clear blue skies. In quiet contemplation, from a bench high on a cliff, two women look out at the wonder of a vast shimmering sea. Suddenly wrenched from their reveries, the piercing screams of two frantic little girls running up the cliff path towards them.

"Oh, it's Helen and the girls," Colin's mother said, her face suddenly brightening. "They've been so excited to meet you Stella. Helen told them you were coming. And she's so, well, we all are, so very, very grateful. She's so looking forward to getting to know you."

The girls raced into their grandmother's outstretched arms. Just behind them, out of breath, smiling as she approached, their mother.

"Stella, so lovely to see you again," she said. "It really is. The girls have been dying to meet you."

"And it's nice to see you Helen," Stella replied. "In, let's just say, more pleasant circumstances. And so these must be your girls," she said, turning towards them.

Disentangling themselves from within their grandmother's embrace, they looked up at her.

"Are you our auntie Stella?" the younger, perhaps six, asked. "Mummy said that you live in London and you do a really important job."

Stella smiled at Helen.

"Yes, I'm Stella. And yes, your auntie Stella. And yes, I live in London. What are your names?"

"I'm Felicity, I'm eight. This is Alice, she's five."

"Five and a half!" Alice corrected her, moodily.

"Mummy was talking with granny on the phone," Felicity continued. "She called you Superwoman. Do you have special powers?"

Helen, slightly embarrassed, laughed.

"I'll let you into a secret, girls," Stella said, beckoning them to come and sit beside her. "I do have one special power."

The girls looked at each other, their eyes widening as they clambered onto the bench next to her.

"I have the ability to know if little girls will grow up to be Superwomen," she said. "I know if they are, in fact, supergirls."

Breathlessly, the girls searched Stella's eyes, each eager to have her supergirl status confirmed.

"And when I saw you running up the path just now, at how fast you ran, I knew immediately that I was about to meet two supergirls."

The girls looked at each other and grinned.

"And do you know what you will be when you grow up?"

"Super Women!" they shouted, together, both

hopping off the bench, jumping up and down with excitement.

"And I have a question for you," Stella added. "Do you two supergirls like stories?"

"Yes, yes, we love stories," Alice said excitedly, leaning into Stella's lap.

"OK, why don't we take a little walk and I'll tell you a story. And then we can talk about what you girls should do with your superpowers," Stella said, getting to her feet and taking their hands.

As Stella led them up the path, Helen sat next to her mother and took her hand.

"Once upon a time," Stella began, "there was a warrior. She was the strongest human being in the whole world. She was invincible. Her name was Boudicca."

Printed in Great Britain
by Amazon